REVENGE
OF THE
WITCH

IMMORTAL RELICS BOOK THREE

STEPHANIE MIRRO

TANNHAUSER PRESS

ALSO BY STEPHANIE MIRRO

IMMORTAL RELICS

Curse of the Vampire

Fury of the Gods

COLLECTIONS

The Outsiders: An Hourlings Anthology

Dedication

For Tim.
You know what you did.

CHAPTER 1

Serafina

The library was on fire. Angry flames stretched toward the sky above Budapest while thick black smoke billowed out from within the building's depths. Part of the roof had already collapsed, much like Sera's hopes.

That motherf—

A loud boom from an explosion cut off Sera's thought. The ground rumbled, and the remainder of the building fell to the ground. Her jaw would have followed if it hadn't been attached to her face.

—ucker.

Just yesterday, she and Theo, the detective turned partner in saving the world, had been in that building researching Hungarian deities. The Library of the Hungarian

Academy of Sciences in Budapest had been one of the few places on the planet containing real, primary-source-level information from the cultures that worshipped the Ordog. The library was almost 200 years old.

And now, it was gone. Poof.

Sera closed her eyes against the pain and despair that crept into her heart, trying to drown out the keening wail of the sirens along with the image of the raging inferno. Not only was one of the most beautiful buildings and all its history gone, but her only lead to gaining any kind of useful knowledge against the Ordog had gone up in flames. Literally.

I have no words for once, Bacchus said, the ancient Roman god's voice filled with sorrow in her mind.

For the last two months, his voice had been with her, his thoughts mingling with hers at the most inappropriate times. Being lost for words was not something he experienced frequently. Like once in a century kind of frequent.

This was Danae's work, no doubt about it. And Sera had no idea how the immortal teenager, who was behind maximum-security prison walls and restrained with silver in France, had pulled this off. The only thing that made sense was that she had set it up as a contingency plan in the event of her capture. What. A. Bitch.

"Hey," Theo's calm voice sounded at her side.

She opened her eyes, though her gaze was still fixed on the crumbling building. The detective had told Sera to stay put when they first arrived and saw the fire that morning, while he went to ask questions. She wouldn't be much help in her near-catatonic state. The morning had started out so beautifully, too.

"They're still going to have to investigate," he continued, "but what little I could get out of the police, this sounded like a magical attack to me."

Magic meant witches had to be involved. Why in the gods' names would they still follow Danae after she had been imprisoned?

"They're going to be very confused and disappointed when they try and find the starting point and accelerant," he said.

"How could she do this?" Sera asked, her voice cracking. "It's… history."

"History doesn't mean much to some immortals," Theo explained quietly. "They lived through it."

All her life, Sera had been a book nerd, and it only got worse the older she got. Not that loving books was a bad thing, but being a bibliophile definitely interfered with forming a healthy social life. Studying history and then anthropology had been natural for her, especially since she followed in her mother's footsteps by pursuing archaeology as a career. Uncovering and preserving history ran in Sera's blood.

The flames turned blurry in her vision as tears finally welled up and slipped down her cheeks.

* * *

TWO DAYS LATER, SHE and Theo had flown back to Paris and driven straight to La Sante Prison. They needed to question Danae, the teenaged girl who had tried to take over the world with death magic and a horde of Bacchae, the vampire-like creatures who had ruined Sera's life. Yeah, that girl.

Sera sat across from Danae, wanting more than anything to smack that smirk right off the immortal witch's face. That, or rip her cruel blue eyes from their sockets. It wasn't as bad as it sounded; they would just grow right back.

Oh, it would also be lovely to decapitate her with the chains she wore, just like Sera had done to the girl's favorite bodyguard, Yumiko. Yes, that would be satisfying. Evil like this didn't deserve a merciful death.

So brutal, Bacchus said with a chuckle, though she sensed he felt the same way. He may have been Danae's creator, but the girl had gone and screwed everything up. For him and Sera both.

Alas, no such pleasure would come for them today. Instead, Sera was forced to stare at that smug Bacchae face across the cold, metal table of the interrogation room. She would simply enjoy the charcoal-like scent of burning flesh as the silver manacles etched their way down to the ancient girl's bones. Again and again.

Small victories.

The intense lights of the Bacchae's jail cell had nearly blinded Sera when she first entered the room, brighter still reflecting off the white walls and tiled floor. But, she knew the glare was intended for her protection. For all of the humans' protection. The Bacchae's senses were significantly stronger than a mortal's. The light would be quite painful to the witch, especially because she was only allowed enough liquid sustenance to keep her alive and nothing more.

Bacchae—the demi-god creatures made from Bacchus's blood and who spawned vampire lore with their glowing red eyes, need to consume blood, and superhuman strength—had turned out to be such a pain in Sera's ass.

"You do realize I'm going to kill you once we rescue my mom from the underworld, right?" She wasn't concerned with the French intelligence officers listening on the other side of the one-way glass window. They likely wouldn't mind the threat she made after the havoc Danae wreaked on their country.

Historical buildings had been damaged, and priceless treasures had been lost in the riots and panic following the outing of the Bacchae. Most people referred to them as vampires, and not in a darkly romantic sense. The pain of losing the library in Budapest still tugged at Sera's heart.

We, Bacchus corrected in Sera's mind. *We are going to kill her. Together.*

"I welcome the attempt," Danae said, her smirk unwavering. Her timing was almost as if she had heard the Roman god's thoughts.

The pinecone amulet encasing the god's essence grew warm against Sera's chest as Bacchus's anger swelled, but the answering crimson glow was well-hidden beneath her chunky sweater and scarf. Sera had always loved scarves, but now they were a necessity to hide the antique necklace the world thought stolen from a museum.

To be fair, Sera hadn't taken it, she had just ended up with the damn thing when Bacchus chose her as his next host. What the world didn't know wouldn't hurt them.

Except when it came to the Bacchae.

The world had seen unprecedented chaos when Danae outed them to the mortals.

Theo sighed and ran a hand through his mop of wavy

brown hair. Again. The poor guy had been dealing with the witch's sass and half-answers just as long as Sera had. If she was being honest with herself—which she really hated doing right now, couldn't she just get mad and stay mad?—the sigh was probably half for her, too. She hadn't exactly been handling the conversation well.

Could he really blame her, though?

Hell, only a month had passed since they had stopped the monster disguised as a teenage girl sitting across from them from taking over the world, and she had left a whole lot of destruction in her wake. Including dropping the nuclear bomb that Sera's mother was still alive. While her mother and eight other witches searched for the Bacchic amulet in a cave, Danae had trapped them all—in hell.

Twenty years spent as the devil's playthings.

As if that wasn't enough to rock her world, only a few weeks before that whole ordeal Sera had learned Theodore Pratt, a detective with the DCPD and the guy sitting next to her, wasn't human. That's right. He was a one-hundred-year-old immortal shapeshifter, courtesy of his merge with the Aztec god Xolotl.

To top it all off, Sera learned she could speak to other ancient gods thanks to a telepathic Gift passed on from her mother. You know, minor details.

The start of the new year had come and gone faster than Bacchus could finish a glass of wine—which is to say quite fast—and February was right around the corner. Sera's birth month, not that she had any intention of celebrating her twenty-fifth birthday this year.

Not after all that had happened.

Besides, admitting she was a quarter of a century-old

sounded so… old.

You're practically ancient, Bacchus quipped.

The joking never ended with him. Accepting an ancient god speaking in her thoughts thanks to the amulet she wore around her neck hadn't been easy. Especially a snarkier than average being like Bacchus.

"How are we supposed to believe what she says? That she's the only one who can bring the witches back?" Sera asked out loud though her questions were for both Theo and Bacchus.

"Magic follows its own system of rules, and death magic is one of the most strict," Theo said, his tone just barely withholding the annoyance she knew he felt. Not necessarily at her, but the entire situation. "She used the Ordog's magic to cast the spell banishing the coven to his underworld. It makes sense she must be the one to reverse it."

You've heard it about ten times now. Or maybe it was eleven? I lost count after one, Bacchus said before taking a sip of his ever-present glass of wine in the corner of her mind. *There is no falsehood in what she speaks. We need to move on to the how.*

The snark was strong with that one.

"How do we get to the underworld?" Sera asked.

Danae leaned back in her chair, not even wincing as fresh steam rose from the sizzling flesh around her wrists. The links of her chains clinked together with her adjustment. Her white straitjacket—loosened for now to allow at least a small measure of movement, though still secured to the floor—was a stark contrast to the long dark hair she wore pulled up into a ponytail.

"I love that you think I'll give you that information before you release me," she said.

"You know that decision isn't up to me." Balling her hands into fists, Sera clenched them in her lap until a sticky warmth oozed between her fingers. A soothing presence trickled like a stream through her veins until her fists unclenched, and the blood dried. One small perk to having her own personal divine parasite.

Sometimes I like to get mad, she told the god, though she secretly appreciated his help keeping her calm.

Not so secret to him, seeing how he could read her thoughts, but at least she didn't admit it outright to him. The last thing they needed was Sera thrown in jail next to Danae. Or maybe that's exactly what they needed. A tempting idea for after they rescued her mom and returned Danae to her silver-clad prison cell.

A deep chuckle rumbled through her mind. *Parasite, indeed.*

"I will give you one small piece of information," Danae said, her blue-grey eyes brightening with her rising excitement.

Dread crept its way up Sera's spine, and her shoulders tensed. Danae's pleasure at whatever she was about to say was most definitely not a good sign.

Xolotl growled his displeasure at the girl's game as well. Most of the time, Sera forgot the Aztec god merged with Theo was there, but Danae's presence brought him out fairly often. She had that effect on both people and gods.

"Anytime now," Theo said.

Storm-colored irises flicked to the detective then back to Sera, the only sign of Danae's internal annoyance. Aside from her near-constant smirk, that girl was basically a statue.

A smirking statue Sera wanted to shatter with a sledgehammer.

"To enter the underworld and return again requires one of two things," Danae began, holding up her fingers as if they couldn't count. The move also served to reveal the bones of her forearm and black, crispy skin.

Sera crinkled her nose in distaste at the remembered scent. After the first encounter in the interrogation room, Theo had the brilliant idea to coat the outside of their noses with scented Vicks. The ointment kept them from detecting the nauseating and sweet scent of charred human flesh. Well, technically Bacchae flesh. One of those smells that was almost good but shouldn't be.

"The first being a sacrifice," Danae continued. "A soul for a soul. You would need a mortal sacrifice for each mortal person who descends to hell with you, including yourself. You could just kill one of the witches, I suppose."

Her lips curled up into a smirk again.

Sera's nostrils flared outward with her hatred, and she itched to reach up and smack that smirk from the girl's face once again. They both knew that wasn't a possibility, which made her even madder.

Before Sera could retort, Danae continued, "Or, you must be immortal before entering the realm of the dead."

Closing her eyes against the torrent of emotions flooding through her mind and body, Sera took a deep breath in, ready to scream her frustration into the colorless room.

Immortality was the least of her desires in life. If it meant saving her mother, she would do anything. This just happened to be one hell of an anything.

A rough hand slipped into one of Sera's, clasping it gently. The gesture cooled her thoughts as effectively as Bacchus could.

She opened her eyes and let her gaze wander over the now-familiar features of Theo's face. His deep brown eyes nearly perfectly matched the hair that fell in soft waves around his face, and the darker tint to his skin spoke to his Latino ancestry. She still needed to ask Xolotl if his ethnicity played a role in choosing Theo, not that it mattered. It just helped to get her mind off things.

Dimples appeared in each of the detective's cheeks as he gave her a reassuring smile. It really wasn't fair that he was so ruggedly handsome when she had zero ability to focus on anything else except rescuing the witches and her mother.

"We'll figure it out," he said with a quick squeeze of his hand. "We always do."

* * *

ICE CRUNCHED BENEATH their boots as Sera and Theo followed the sidewalk back to the small car the French government had loaned them. A foot of snow covered the ground surrounding the maximum-security prison in the heart of Paris, and grey skies grumbled above them, threatening to unleash more at any moment.

Sera pulled her scarf up to cover her nose against the frigid air, though small puffs of warm breath still snuck out, visible through the fabric.

They had spent the entire day questioning Danae, trying to get more information out of her or trip her up somehow, but she had remained tight-lipped. Other than her snide comments, anyway.

She may have had several millennia of experience under her belt, but that girl was a teen through and through. Exhausting. The teeny tiny piece of Sera that considered having babies one day was slowly disappearing with each encounter. One less thing to worry about when contemplating immortality.

A whole month had passed since Sera discovered her mother was alive and held as a captive in the underworld. Not just any underworld. The realm of the Ordog, the creature who became synonymous with the devil when Christianity spread.

Yeah, that one.

Twenty years ago, her mother and a coven of witches had gone into a cave to track down the Bacchic amulet and had never returned. Sera had grown up thinking her mom had passed away in a freak caving accident, never questioning the lack of bodies. Everyone had assumed the group got lost within the dark depths of the earth.

She had spent almost every single day since learning otherwise searching for answers. Facing the devil wasn't something she took lightly, and she wanted to be prepared. But every day spent aboveground meant one more day of torture below. That thought fueled her during the day and kept her up most nights.

After waiting for traffic on the busy Parisian street to clear, Sera opened the passenger door of the blue coupe and slid onto the seat. Blowing air into her gloved palms close to her face, she warmed up her nose and cheeks.

A month meant the world was almost back to the way it was. Except now, everyone knew that Bacchae, the immortal vampire-like creatures, were real and becoming a part of society. Okay, so maybe the world wasn't quite back to the way it had been.

Humankind had become extremely suspicious of strangers because the Bacchae looked, sounded, and acted just like anyone else. Until the supernatural creatures got thirsty, of course. Then their fangs extended, and their eyes blazed red with their hunger.

And just what did they eat? Oh, that's right—humans.

They didn't even have to drink from humans. Sera had learned from the one Bacchae she had gotten to know that human blood just tasted better than other animals. It had the added benefit of making the Bacchae even more formidable than they already were as demi-gods.

The Eternals were part gods, anyway, created directly from Bacchus's own blood a couple of millennia ago. Now, the Bacchae were produced from another one of the Bacchae's blood, diluting the purity of the divine blood, but still, in essence, demi-gods.

Gazing out the window, Sera envied the bundled-up people walking by in the city, going about their normal, day-to-day activities, with only slightly furtive glances shot around them. They didn't have the weight of the world on their shoulders, knowing they needed to rescue some abducted witches from the devil's clutches.

The tendency to wallow in pity parties wasn't one of her best qualities, but sometimes wallowing made her feel better. Until wallowing made her forget to shake off the snow from outside first, of course. She shivered as ice caught on her scarf melted down her back, sneaking in through the top of her coat.

You know, if we merged, you wouldn't feel the cold at all anymore, Bacchus said with a nonchalant nudge in her mind. *Not like this, anyway.*

Merging. Immortal. One with a god.

All the same meaning, all freaking her right the fuck out. As it stood, she could simply remove the amulet and forget Bacchus whenever she wanted. She could go back to her previous life and pretend like this other world didn't exist. Well, except for the Bacchae, who just had to go and out themselves. The bastards.

But the point was she'd be ordinary again, which sounded glorious after everything she'd gone through. Her enhanced abilities came from Bacchus taking over her body, leaving exhaustion and blackouts in his wake. Take away the god from the equation, and she'd just be human. Probably a whole lot less tired, too.

Hey, I can always give you energy, Bacchus sniffed.

Unlike other people—and a lot of them judging by how many had jumped at the chance to become one of the Bacchae before the new moratorium was set—Sera had no desire to live forever. None. Zilch. Zip. Watching everyone she knew and loved get old and die again and again was not what she'd had in mind for her life.

Not like she was super close to anyone mortal, though, other than Nora, Renee, and her father. Studies had always come first for Sera, and that meant a small circle of friends. Mostly acquaintances. The more she thought about it, she didn't actually have many people she could actually lose to old age.

A tightness formed in her chest with the realization that her life had been so isolated. Maybe becoming immortal wouldn't be as bad as she thought.

Theo pushed the button to start the car and cranked up the heat.

At least she hadn't lost her father yet. Just like she thought would happen, his survivalist side had kicked in after the Bacchae had come out to the world, and he had helped keep his neighbors safe and fed when the power grids failed. Another small victory.

She was insanely proud of him and made sure to tell him that more than once when she visited three weeks ago. She had been able to visit shortly after Danae had been captured, before the failed excursion to Budapest. Because Sera and her friends had stopped Danae and convinced the Eternals to get the other Bacchae to stand down, the French president had made a deal with Air France. The airline had presented them with free flights, anywhere in the world for the rest of their lives. She had taken advantage of it right away, just in case they revoked the privilege.

She wasn't sure they knew about Theo's immortality yet. Oh well.

Her father still wasn't entirely sure the Bacchae were real because he hadn't seen them for himself. Their existence could be a government conspiracy in his mind. Sera assured him of the reality, but she hadn't told him about her mother just yet. She wasn't sure how he would take the news, and she couldn't be sure she could bring her mother back. Getting his hopes up only to fail would be devastating to them both. Plus, things were a bit confusing now that he was officially dating Susan.

Crap. Sera needed to call and tell him she'd be going incommunicado for a while once she and Theo figured out how to get to the underworld. Except she wouldn't tell him that last part.

Theo's voice interrupted her never-ending stream of thoughts, "I've got a merged friend in China who might—"

"I'm going to merge," Sera cut him off, meeting his confused eyes with her own steady gaze.

Are you entirely sure? Bacchus asked.

He'd remained quiet during her inner turmoil, but she knew he supported whatever decision she settled on.

It was either merge or become one of the Bacchae. If she just had to become immortal to free her mother and the other witches and make it back out again, she might as well be more powerful than the Bacchae witch who put them there.

When in doubt, be the best. Or something like that.

"There might be other options. We haven't…" Theo's voice trailed off as she gave him a small smile.

"It's possible. But I can't wait any longer. Every day that passes is another that my mom is enduring whatever torture the Ordog throws her way. And not just my mom, but the other witches, too. It could get worse for them if the Ordog finds out Danae's been captured. If he hasn't already."

A chill ran up her spine, shaking her shoulders. "Bacchus and I will merge, and then we go to hell."

Theo regarded her for another moment before nodding. He turned his focus to backing the car out of the tight parallel parking spot and into the steady flow of traffic.

"Only one minor detail."

"I know." Sera sighed. "We need Danae."

CHAPTER 2

Nora

After shutting her apartment door, Nora hung her purse and coat on the vintage iron coat stand beside it. Her feet and back ached from teaching in heels all day. The day had been even longer since the dean had given her some of Sera's classes to teach.

Her best friend was a saint. Nora didn't know how some of Sera's students had gotten into college in the first place.

She was ready to call it an early night, even though it meant she had become an old woman at the ripe old age of twenty-four. She wasn't even sure what day it was. The days all seemed to blur together ever since Solomon left for New Orleans.

After flipping on the bathroom light, Nora regarded her

tired eyes in the mirror. She let out a sigh. Her usually bright green irises dulled against the dark circles beneath.

She and Solomon had been inseparable since taking down Danae. They'd talked endlessly and long into the nights about their future together. The future they discussed was the whole reason he wasn't with her now. They wanted to have children together, and the Bacchae couldn't procreate. None of the immortal types could.

Some women were born to be teachers, or caregivers, or natural-born leaders. Nora had been born to be a mother. Nothing fueled her desire in life more than holding her own baby in her arms someday. Talking about wanting kids with other people always surprised them because Nora was known as a bit of a party girl, and she was just fine with that for now. Becoming a mom didn't have to be anytime soon. She enjoyed life far too much to settle down just yet, anyway.

But someday.

She opened a drawer and pulled out the toothpaste. After applying a pea-sized amount onto her electric toothbrush, Nora shut the tube back in the drawer. The two-minute timer clicked on, and she zoned out while letting the brush do all the work to keep her smile bright.

Solomon hadn't been quite so eager at the prospect of parenthood. He'd had two hundred years to become accustomed to the idea of *not* having children. Being together had become his desire in life, though, so she helped rekindle his desire to become a father, too. They may have been working on it still. If only he didn't need to be gone for so long.

Darling, it's only been two days, Freyja's musical voice chimed in her thoughts, hinting at a laugh.

"Two days too long," Nora said around her toothbrush, her blonde curls bobbing against her chin. "It's pretty clear he and I were made for each other."

Freyja's laugh tinkled in her mind, and the torc around her neck glowed pink with the goddess's mirth. Not that the goddess disagreed, Nora knew.

It had seemed a bit like destiny when Sera brought back the goddess's torc from Norway, especially since Sera and Theo had kicked Leif's ass while doing so. That witch had turned out to be such a menace and needed to be put down.

Hairs on the back of her neck rose as she remembered the terror of being alone in his basement, tied up and left in the dark. She shook herself, not wanting to traverse down that memory lane. She had come to terms with it and moved on. Karma would pay him back eventually.

After Nora agreed to become a temporary host for the Norse goddess, they had become fast friends thanks to their similar personalities. The goddess had also been more than happy to help Nora in her magical studies. Renee would be so proud when she returned from France.

Nora's phone rang just as she finished putting her toothbrush back in its holder. She pressed the green button on her phone, answering Sera's call on speaker so she could keep getting ready for bed.

"Hey, girl, how's France?" she asked her best friend, carrying her phone to her room and kicking off her heels onto the shoe rack sitting in her closet.

A sigh on the other end. "Trying to get information out of Danae must be my own form of torture from the Ordog."

Nora pulled her shirt over her head. "You're a better person than I am, being able to deal with that one."

"Hardly. It takes Bacchus *and* Theo to keep me restrained." Sera snorted. "But she did give us a breadcrumb this time."

After unclasping her bra, the most glorious feeling in the world, Nora flung it into the hamper. She raised an eyebrow at the thought of the witch being at all helpful. "Oh? A juicy breadcrumb, I hope."

"Only immortals can enter the underworld and return alive."

Nora's breath whooshed out as she pulled a silk nightgown over her head. "No way, babe. You can't trust what she says."

Not only had Sera made it clear, but Nora knew her probably better than Sera even knew herself. There was no way that the girl wanted to be immortal, just for different reasons than Nora. She would merge with Freyja in a heartbeat if it meant she could still have Solomon's babies.

Another sigh from Sera. "Bacchus does."

On this one, unfortunately, so do I, Freyja said.

"So then, you won't go. Theo can round up some of the other merged ones, and they can bring everyone back. Didn't he say there were like a dozen of them merged?"

Nora pushed her decorative pillows off the bed and climbed between the silk sheets. She shivered as the cold fabric touched her skin, missing Solomon's warmth even more.

"I can't ask others to risk their lives on my behalf," Sera said.

"Let them make up their own minds."

"It's my mom, Nor."

"I know, hon, but you don't want to be immortal. I

think your mom would understand," Nora said with as soothing a tone as she could muster.

She really wanted to throttle Bacchus for not talking her best friend out of a decision she knew Sera had already made. Unless he got something out of the arrangement, too. She wouldn't put it past him.

"You know I wouldn't be able to forgive myself, especially if they failed," Sera said.

"You sound like you've already made up your mind." After pumping out some of her nighttime lotion into her hand, Nora rubbed her two palms together to warm the liquid up.

"Only because debating it out with you solidified it for me."

"Ugh. Can we start over?" Nora asked, but she knew Sera was determined. She rubbed lotion over her arms. "Where did this whole merging thing even come from?"

"Jesus Christ."

"Everything okay?" Nora paused her movements to hear any small details coming through the phone.

"No, like the guy," Sera said, a laugh in her voice. "Before Jesus died, God—or Yahweh, Allah, whatever name he prefers—saw his worshippers massacred for their beliefs, and his essence was fading. He worried that it would only get worse. So he merged with Jesus before the crucifixion, which is how he rose from the dead."

"Well, this is the most fascinating history lesson I've ever heard," Nora said, rubbing the last of the lotion into her hands.

"Right?" Sera asked. "Only unlike the other merged gods today, this one took Jesus back to the divine realm with him. Bacchus was the next one to attempt merging."

"You say attempt like there's a chance of failure."

There is, Freyja's quiet voice chimed in, sending a chill up Nora's spine. She quickly pulled the blankets up over her like they could protect her.

"Anyway, I've already made up my mind about it all," Sera said. "But there's more."

Nora groaned, earning a chuckle from her friend. "Oh, goody."

"Once I've merged, we're going to ask the French to release Danae into our custody."

Anger flared up inside Nora as Sera explained what Theo had said about death magic and needing the girl to release the witches. "This just sucks."

"I know."

"You and Theo make any adult decisions yet?" Nora asked, twirling a blonde curl around her finger. Unlikely, but she wanted all the juicy details if they had.

A sigh on the other end. "I'm not ready yet, Nor. I want to be, trust me, but I'm too distracted."

"You'll always be too distracted," Nora said as kindly as she could, but that girl needed a distraction from her distractions. Just because she and Theo were trying to figure out a way into the underworld did not mean they couldn't form a relationship and…

Nora stopped her train of thought so fast the brakes would have squealed.

That was exactly why Sera wasn't moving forward. She was afraid to get attached to someone only to lose them again. Like Hiro. Nora's shoulders slumped in defeat. She would always fight for love first, but her best friend needed time, and Nora would do her best to respect that, no matter how difficult.

"Story of my life," Sera said with a somewhat sad chuckle.

Nora's phone beeped, and she looked down at the screen. Solomon was calling. "Hey girl, I'm going to let you go. Sol is calling, and then I need to get my beauty sleep."

Sera snorted. "Hardly. Love you."

"You, too." Nora clicked the button to switch calls. "Sol?"

"You sound more beautiful every time I call." The rich tenor of his voice sent tingles down her spine.

"And you sound sexier. I miss your face," she said, her body warming in response as she thought about more than just his face. She may have to spice things up over the phone.

Solomon chuckled. "I miss you, too. I'm afraid I have some bad news."

Nora's breath caught in her throat, and her inner flame extinguished. "What?"

"The latest lead was a bust. I'm attempting to track down my last option tonight, but if that falls through, I'll be heading home, empty-handed."

She let out her held breath. As much as she wanted him mortal again so they could move forward in their relationship, she needed him home safe with her even more so. He was already doing so much to make their dream a reality. The last thing she wanted was to lose him, and being one of the Bacchae wasn't exactly a safe thing to be in the world right now.

"I thought you said *bad* news."

He chuckled. "Of course, seeing you is wonderful, but

I'd love to come home with an answer to regaining my mortality."

"Just come home to me as soon as you can," she said, biting her lip as heat spread once again along with a vision of him. Naked. The very least she could do was start his night off right.

"In the meantime, what are you wearing right now, and how fast can we get it off?"

CHAPTER 3

Serafina

An hour outside of Paris, Theo parked the blue coupe in front of the stone cottage they had been staying in since just before they had taken down Danae. Several inches of snow covered the roof of the quaint two-storied home and hid the foliage growing wild around the old yet still sturdy foundation.

The cottage had been close enough to the self-proclaimed queen's estate to make it easy to raid. Or at least not as difficult as it could have been.

The house was also located a half mile down a dirt path, off a not-so-busy road. The closest town had a population under one thousand. The remoteness of the area kept nosy neighbors and members of the media from snooping around too much. Add in a touch of concealment magic, and they were well-hidden from the world.

When they walked up to the front stoop, the door stood open, and fresh snow coated the interior hallway. The entryway had clearly been left open for a while. An eerie chill raised the hairs on the back of Sera's neck, and she looked at Theo with a grimace.

"Not again," she said, a slight groan in her voice. The last time they had come back to a safe house with the door standing wide open, Danae had stolen the amulet. At least that wasn't a possibility this time. Unless she had more cronies working for her, which seemed likely after the library in Budapest.

Do people even use the word cronies anymore? Bacchus asked. *Or is this your quarter-century-old age talking?*

You're hilarious, Sera thought back as she reached toward her holster. When she couldn't find it with her hand, she grimaced. Still getting used to wearing a holster apparently meant she hadn't put the damn thing back on after the prison visit. It sat in the backseat of the car along with the silver bulleted handgun.

As she and Theo crept to the sides of the cottage door, both their eyes glowing gold with a god's presence, she could have smacked herself for the oversight. She should always know where her gun is, and that somewhere should be on her at all times. Bacchus's strength was pretty spectacular, but a well-aimed gun had proved to be far less messy than say, a chair leg or a car bumper or a ripped off limb.

His gun held ready, Theo tilted his nose up and sniffed but shook his head. Guess they were going in.

As she followed Theo inside, Sera glanced around the living room quickly, trying to assess the situation like she imagined a cop would. No one sat on the two couches facing each other. Low flames cracked and shifted wood in the fireplace large enough for someone to walk into, which meant someone was home or had been before the door was left open.

Nothing seemed to be out of place but foreboding continued to roil within her.

As she closed the front door behind them, a woman's unfamiliar laugh echoed out of the kitchen. Renee had been here alone when they left. Theo and Sera looked at each other, bewildered.

Still moving with caution, though Theo lowered his gun a little, they walked into the expansive kitchen. The back of Renee's head faced them, her silver and grey hair pulled back into a clip as she prepared a meal on the island. Above her hung a selection of copper pots and pans from a suspended cookware rack.

Beyond her, a black-skinned woman with equally dark close-cropped hair sat at the large dining table near the cottage's original brick oven. The woman locked her serpentine eyes on Sera.

Lasirenn.

Sera's back stiffened. She'd never heard the woman laugh before today. She also hadn't asked Theo if he had fulfilled his promise to the spirit yet, and she wasn't going to. It wasn't any of her business if he gave her the night together she had asked for in exchange for her help stopping Danae.

The water spirit had done her part and fought with them. Sera couldn't fault him for honoring his side of the bargain. Not to mention they had been lovers once before anyway. It's not like it would kindle a new spark or anything.

Besides, Sera didn't want to know if he slept with Lasirenn because she wasn't sure if it would change her feelings toward him. She didn't think it would, but she wouldn't know for sure until he uttered the words.

Therefore, she simply wouldn't ask.

Is this that self-talk thing I hear so much about? Bacchus asked from his chaise in the corner of her mind, lounging with a glass of red wine. His usual perch.

Whatever helps, she replied. Although she had to fight the urge to roll her eyes. If the two had slept together, then the deal was over, and they could all move on. Maybe she *should* ask.

Lasirenn's gaze drifted to Theo. "Bonjour, mon amour," she purred. "I spoke with Manny this morning."

Right after Danae's capture a month ago, the two of them had taken Manny, a twelve-year-old boy, and the Yoruban god Eshu to Haiti to live with Theo's friend Cassandra. The Haitian woman wasn't aligned with a god, but she did have the Sight.

The boy would do well in her house, and hopefully, Eshu would find another follower to connect with. Maybe even Cassandra herself.

Unlike the water spirit, the ancient gods who stored their essence in relics needed a human host to communicate and function. As a lesser deity and one with many followers—easier to achieve when sex is your altar of worship—Lasirenn maintained a physical body, much to Sera's annoyance from time to time.

The sly Yoruban god Eshu needed to let that boy grow up as normal as possible after his rough start at life. Sera wasn't so sure how normal his life could be after helping to bring down an Eternal trying to take over the world, all while living with a trickster god's essence stored in a key hung around his neck, but hey, it was worth a shot.

Renee turned around and gave them a smile, soft wrinkles forming at the corners of her eyes. "Grab a coffee and a seat. I'll have dinner prepared in another few minutes."

Theo set the safety and replaced his gun in its holster before facing the spirit again. "How is Manny?"

"Full of life. Joyful." Lasirenn paused. "Normal."

"That's good to hear," Theo said, moving through the kitchen toward the table. "What brings you back out to us?"

"Life has become predictable and boring since we parted. I would like to help in your quest to free the witches." Lasirenn plucked an orange from the basket of fruit sitting on the oblong table and dug her thumb into the top. The rind opened, and juice ran down her palm before hitting the wood.

Theo considered her for a moment as he sat in a chair across from her. "Thank you. We appreciate all the help we can get."

She brought her hand to her lips, licking the orange juice from her skin. Her eyes never left his. "You know how… helpful I can be."

For all that she hated what the innuendo implied, Sera couldn't help but enjoy watching the man shift in discomfort. He was so stoic and reserved most of the time, it was fun to see him squirm a bit.

Sera crossed the room and took the seat next to Lasirenn, grabbing another orange and testing it out with a squeeze. "Are these as good as you make them look?"

Triumph flared through Sera as the water spirit gaped at her. She probably expected an entirely different response from sensical Sera, but it had been a long, exhausting day with Danae. This game was too much fun. She could always blame it on Bacchus's sassy influence.

Pointing out one's faults is just rude, Bacchus said with a huff. *And, yes. I do know that's hypocritical of me.*

Smothering a smile so as not to be misconstrued, Sera worked on peeling the orange. She really had nothing against Lasirenn, except the fact the water spirit frequently seemed to want to get a rise out of Sera.

Her triumph dissolved into frustration at her own childish behavior, no better than the water spirit's. Not like either of them could claim Theo as their own, even if they both wanted otherwise. Sera wouldn't allow the distraction from rescuing her mother, and Theo wasn't interested in the other woman.

Or so he said.

Sera hoped someday the water spirit would see her as a friend instead of a foe, or at least a neutral party. But for now, it was kind of fun to play along, and fun wasn't something she had a lot of those days. Maybe Lasirenn needed to have some fun, too.

Renee chose that moment to deposit dinner on the table—pork chops with a honey-balsamic glaze and roasted Brussels sprouts that set Sera's mouth watering. While they ate, Theo and Sera took turns catching the two women up on their discussion with Danae. Even Theo couldn't resist this meal though immortals didn't need the sustenance any longer.

After Sera dropped the bomb that she would be

merging with Bacchus, Renee reached over to clasp her hand. "Are you sure?"

"Unfortunately, yes. I need to be there." Sera squeezed the woman's hand.

Renee had become a mother figure to Sera over the last few months as the woman helped Sera accept all of the supernatural changes she'd experienced. Renee had also been one of just three witches to escape the cave that had trapped Sera's mother and eight others when Danae had ambushed the group twenty years ago. It had been Renee's coven who had helped Sera's mother track down the amulet, never knowing one of the Bacchae also tracked them.

As much as she wanted her own mom to be there, Sera had found immense comfort in the other woman's company and words of wisdom. It helped that Renee had a Gift, in her case, a psychic ability that allowed her to *See* what wasn't always visible. She had first showcased her skills as a witch when she fought against Leif after he abducted Nora.

Just a typical day in the life for them now.

Renee had also been the one to talk Sera through her concerns about having feelings for the ruggedly handsome detective so soon after Sera's boyfriend Hiro died. She had suggested that Bacchus's lingering essence fueled the desire.

As usual, Renee had been right.

Don't get Sera wrong, Theo was a good-looking man and totally worth falling for. But the timing of it royally sucked. Her heart still ached as she thought of Hiro. He didn't deserve the death he had received at Danae's hands. Guilt rose with her sorrow, as it usually did when she thought of her boyfriend. He definitely deserved far better in love than Sera had been able to give him.

Thankfully the detective hadn't expected anything from her, even while snuggling her to sleep most nights. Gods, he was a good man. Maybe someday they could pursue that very tempting possibility, and she could do better this time around. Just not right now.

"Have you determined a way to enter the underworld?" Renee asked instead of pursuing an argument against merging. She removed her lavender-hued glasses and let them hang on the crystal chain around her neck.

"Not yet," Sera said. "The goal is to merge with Bacchus, then summon Hel again. We're hoping she can provide some insight."

"If she can't, I'm not sure who could," Renee said with a chuckle then hesitated briefly. "I know it's short notice, but I'll be heading back to the States in the morning. Even though Nora has Freyja now, I want to continue to pass on my magical studies."

The unsaid being before anything else could happen, of course.

Although Sera had known the time would come, her heart sank at the idea of not having Renee around. Especially now that Lasirenn had decided to "help." She would miss Renee's voice of reason amongst Sera's chaotic thoughts, not to mention the woman had become a free therapist of sorts.

What a time to not be more selfish.

Sera forced a smile. "I'm sure Nora is champing at the bit to get started again."

Renee leaned forward to clasp her hand across the table again. "You'll be fine."

It was like she could read Sera's mind. Who knew,

maybe she could *See* something with her magic more than the eyes could. Sera sure hoped so.

CHAPTER 4

Solomon

Years had passed since Solomon last visited New Orleans, but the city was remarkably similar, especially at night. Or perhaps more… unremarkably. The city that birthed the blues had flourished on its history for centuries. Changing wasn't something the city wanted to do much of, and Solomon certainly didn't blame them.

Tourism was alive and thriving in the Big Easy. Why change something that worked for them so well?

The only thing Solomon himself would change was the mud. His wing-tip shoes, while garnering plenty of compliments along with his knee-length herringbone coat, weren't ideal for traipsing across the patchwork paved streets and brick sidewalks. It wasn't unusually cold, nor did

Solomon feel the cold the way humans did, but he liked the way the coat looked with the shoes.

Nothing much the city officials could do about the mud, though.

He had been in the city for two days and already encountered more Immortals than he ever cared to. Even now, as he walked down Bourbon Street, though not the lively and raucous part the street was well known for, he passed others like him. As if their scent alone wasn't enough to tip him off of their existence—detected even through the puke and piss that lingered on the sidewalks and pavement—the newcomers looked up at him in the light of the streetlamps, startled as he passed.

They probably hadn't met many Immortals as old as he was.

After the High Council of Eternals had released Danae's hive-like mind control over the Immortal population, many had flocked to the city known for its magic and voodoo. They wanted to embrace their new longevity, as well as some of their more gothic tendencies. Immortality in the guise of vampirism had a particular type drawn to it.

Solomon, of course, had chosen Immortality to escape slavery—actual, plantation slavery in the pre-Civil War South. He hadn't yet realized what it meant when he had signed a lifelong contract with Lorenzo.

An *Immortal* lifetime.

His nostrils flared out as he thought of his maker and the last two hundred years Solomon had spent with him, doing the man's dirty work. With any luck, the ancient Italian had met his end in a scuffle when the military invaded his home in the District. It would have been challenging for any

Immortal to survive so many armed humans. Solomon didn't care much *who* killed the man, just that someone did.

Regardless, if Lorenzo had managed to escape like the cockroach he turned out to be, Solomon's time with him had come to an end.

After waiting for a car to pass, he crossed the street to another sidewalk glowing with the neon-colored signs above them. Not surprisingly, some of the locals of New Orleans had welcomed the influx of brand-new Immortals with open arms. The Immortals, however, were wisely staying to the shadows while the world adjusted.

New shops catering to those who enjoyed the taste of blood—as well as those who wanted to give it—had sprouted up within the historic French Quarter district and beyond. Although the general human population had been kept in the dark about the Immortals' arrival in the area and their subsequent need for nourishment, the High Council had approached the city government with an ultimatum disguised as a good deal: allow the shops to open and keep the humans safe.

City officials quickly realized the opportunity for additional taxes and tourist revenue once the Immortals became accepted into society and gave it the green light. Smart people. The rest of the country would soon follow suit. Solomon was sure it wouldn't be long after that before the underground blood bars became everyday shops and tourist traps.

But he wasn't there to play tourist.

Despite spending two days and nights scouring the streets, bars, and shops, as well as shaking off more than one drunken college girl looking to "meet a real live vampire,"

Solomon hadn't had any luck finding the woman he sought—a voodoo priestess who might have the answer he needed to become mortal again. Nothing would stop him from having children and growing old with Nora, and he grew increasingly impatient and frustrated at his failures.

Oh, but he did have too-many-to-count offers to turn eager men and women into Immortals. One woman even offered him a six-figure deal. Unfortunately for her, money wasn't something he needed—nor more new Immortals to deal with.

Immortals in their first few decades were wildly unpredictable and hard to control. Even more so since their full powers had been restored by Danae only a few months prior. Before that, their abilities had been waning for almost two decades after the Roman god and the coven of witches cast their reversal spell.

After weeks of research, he'd discovered that Bacchus had stripped Immortals' procreation ability as a punishment for Danae's lust for power, a fact which Danae had tried to hide from the rest of the Immortal population. The side effect of removing their special form of procreation included a slow diminishment of the rest of their enhanced skills.

Recently created Immortals had little self-control over their new instinct as predators, especially around excessive numbers of vulnerable prey. Five-course meals waltzing around in front of them all day every day.

Humans had no idea how fragile their lives really were. They better thank the gods that Bacchus had put in the protections that he had—an allergy to silver and the need to be invited into a human's place of residence. Without those, humans wouldn't have thrived at the top of the food chain.

A raucous laugh rang out of an open door as he passed, giving him pause. Speaking of new Immortals…

Three of them surrounded a young man in the low light of the doorway. Behind them, a poorly lit narrow alley led into what Solomon could only presume was a courtyard blood bar, hidden away from the streets of the Big Easy.

The Immortals' fangs extended, and they laughed as they herded the boy back into the alley's depths, the boy's gaze darting around like a frightened rabbit. Prey. Which is what he was to the Immortals.

Usually, Solomon wouldn't interfere—especially considering the kid had tried to enter a hidden bar populated with Immortals—but Solomon needed to let out some of his frustration after not finding what he sought.

Becoming Immortal had been easy. Discovering how to become mortal again was proving to be more difficult and aggravating than he ever imagined. The voodoo priestess was his last resort before it was back to the drawing board.

Solomon followed the group through the surprisingly long passage, grimacing as his shoes stuck to the stones the farther he went. As he reached the end, an Immortal who spent most of his mortal years lifting weights gave him a stiff nod at the next door, recognizing Solomon as one of his kind.

A guaranteed entry pass into the shark-infested waters.

The sweet scent of blood had assaulted his nose as soon as he stepped into the narrow alley, but here, it was overwhelming and highly intoxicating. Like any decent New Orleans bar, a bartender stood behind the pop-up counter with her tits pushed up high, somehow managing to stay confined in a tight black vinyl top. But instead of serving drinks, she collected names.

Between small groups of Immortals, the real draw to the place sat in a row of chairs along the back wall: human faces caught in moments of rapture as an Immortal drank their fill from the wrist.

Solomon's lip curled up. He understood the need for a business like this, where humans and Immortals alike would give their names to a bartender, either to be the next diner or the next meal. But understanding and enjoying something were two very different concepts. The allure of the hunt called to Solomon's beast, the one who had demanded blood for nearly two hundred years.

The tension in the small confines of the courtyard was tangible, a seductive flavor that danced across his tongue, urging his fangs to extend. Only the trickle of *influence* leaking from the older Immortal in the corner kept these predators at bay. She nodded at Solomon as he glanced her way, acknowledging their shared age. Or close enough to it. The city government had required all blood bars to keep on staff at all times a more mature Immortal who would be capable of controlling the younger ones' thirst.

Approaching the group he had followed in with a casual gait and a friendly smile, Solomon tucked his hands into his jacket pockets. As non-threatening as he could manage considering his six-foot-three height and black skin amid a sea of white. Yes, Immortality drew a specific type these days.

"I-I don't want to give you m-my blood," the kid stuttered, holding up a shaking arm in defense. "I've changed m-my mind."

"Excuse me, gentlemen and lady," Solomon said,

tipping his hat toward the pretty brunette. There were some old habits he preferred not to break.

The two Immortal men whipped around to face him, fangs bared, and pupils constricted like a cat's and burning red. All three of the new Immortals were young, presumably just old enough to legally be in a bar when created, and sported the current fashions. The '70s and '80s had certainly made a remarkable comeback in recent times.

Solomon would stick with his classic look.

"Well, now, is that any way to treat your elder?" Solomon asked, waiting for them to pick up his scent over the grime of the courtyard's floor. He tried not to think about how long it had been since thoroughly mopped, and rain didn't count.

But even new babes like these should be able to note the difference in his scent.

It was comical the way it happened like a domino effect, each one's nostrils flaring out as they realized who he was.

What he was.

"What do you want, old man?" the kid wearing the oversized blazer asked, sneering at Solomon after his initial wide-eyed reaction.

Old man? That was a first. Despite his years on Earth, Solomon hadn't even been thirty years old before Lorenzo changed him, barely older than these three. Yet he supposed he had looked at folks his age as much older when he was still a teen. Add in his two-hundred-year fragrance, and he guessed he *was* an old man.

"It seems to me that this young man is no longer enjoying your company," Solomon said, choosing to ignore the insult. "Per the Paris and Bacchae Treaty, you are to move along. Get in line to find a willing participant if you're hungry."

The Immortals looked at each other before laughing at Solomon. He had only partly hoped they would do as he said—he still needed to release some frustration, after all.

"You may not be aware of this, what with your dementia and all, but we ain't in Paris," the girl said, putting both hands on the hips of her high-waisted jeans. All she needed was some bubble gum to pop and some hairspray, and she'd fit right in a few decades ago.

Moving faster than the human would be able to comprehend, Solomon had both Immortal men sprawled on the stone floor and his extended fangs at the brunette's neck. Her skin indented where he pressed his teeth, but he didn't pierce through.

"It would be unwise to tempt me further with your disrespect," Solomon said, allowing the smallest amount of *influence* to wash over them, filling them with fear. "Be gone and obey the treaty."

Without another comment, the three bullies fled.

Conversations had ceased during the scuffle, replaced by whispers and the scent of fear drifting off the humans. No one would challenge him, not even the other *influencer.* And if the rest of the Immortals present were smart—which he highly doubted—they'd learn from these kids' mistakes. Young people caught in the excitement of Immortality weren't exactly known for making the smartest choices.

"Thanks," the kid muttered as he slipped around Solomon, casting a frightened glance up at Solomon's face before he ran for the alley.

"I didn't do it for you," Solomon said quietly, too quiet

for anyone to hear.

* * *

A HALF-HOUR LATER, and feeling somewhat less frustrated though still impatient, Solomon entered yet another bar, strictly for humans this time and darkened as much from the night outside as the poor lighting within.

When Solomon walked in, the bartender didn't bother to look up from his phone behind the counter. Solomon would have blamed it on the man's age, except his thinning grey hair and leathery skin spoke to more advanced years.

Modern technology had ensnared all ages.

The bar top itself stood along the left side of the long, narrow shop. Shadowy tables and booths filled the right side of the room. Gothic-style antique lamps adorned the walls above each table, but at least half the light bulbs had burned out or flickered as they got ready to do just that.

Once again, Solomon ignored the excessive stickiness squelching beneath his shoes and the smells drifting off the floor. He spied the man he was looking for slouched over in the farthest corner booth, away from the other clientele. The short man would have been lucky to say he was one hundred and ten pounds soaking wet and appeared to be drowning in his dark green army jacket. Every inch of him needed a bath. It had been at least a week since he had even changed clothes if Solomon's nose could be trusted, which it could.

Solomon dropped a thick envelope on the table before he slid into the bench opposite the dirt-stained man, also trying to ignore the stains on the seat. The stench of booze and old vomit wafted off the guy and the table, making

Solomon's lip curl in disgust.

"Thank you for meeting me," Solomon said, using a touch of his *influence* to sober the man up a little. "I've been told you know where to find Miss Laveau."

The Paris and Bacchae Treaty may have outlawed the use of the Bacchae's *influence* on the mortal population, but what they didn't know wouldn't kill them. A bit hypocritical after the previous encounter, maybe, but at least he wasn't trying to hurt anyone. Quite the opposite.

Stirring as if from a dream, the man blinked a few times at Solomon before recognition sunk in. His dazed gaze landed on the envelope, and he snatched it up greedily. "That I do, that I do. Follow me, sir."

The man stumbled out of the bench and nearly hit the floor before Solomon caught him. He mumbled something that might have been a thank you and waved for Solomon to follow him toward the back door of the bar. Solomon hadn't sobered him up entirely; he wanted to be forgotten after the encounter.

When they exited the bar into the alley, the sharp reek of rotting garbage and human feces hit Solomon nearly as hard as running into a brick wall. He had never done that, of course, but he could imagine it wasn't a pleasant experience, just like this one.

Before he could recover from the assault on his senses, his body went rigid, ceasing all motor functions. Pain lacerated every inch of his insides. Above the pain, the buzzing of electricity volts rang in his ears. A blunt object hit Solomon even harder on the back of his head, and he blacked out.

* * *

SOMEONE HUMMING A soft tune woke him. Solomon opened his eyes to find his world still in pitch-black. A thick blindfold covered the top half of his face allowing no gaps to let in light. He hissed in pain as he moved, chains burning their way through the flesh at his wrists.

Silver.

He hadn't a clue how long he had been out, but judging by how sluggish his limbs felt, he had been drugged as well as knocked out after the taser. He deserved the ill-treatment for his stupidity.

Bullfrogs croaked into the night. If it was still night. Hard to tell when he didn't know how much time had passed, but he was reasonably certain bullfrogs were nocturnal.

"Ah, der you are," said a woman's scratchy voice. A thick Creole dialect accented her words.

"And where might that be exactly?" he asked, letting irritation rise in his tone.

Why the hell had someone abducted him? Had one of his victim's families tracked him down now that his kind was known to the world? Solomon had killed hundreds of humans in his servitude to Lorenzo, any one of their families could have a vendetta.

He had been far too careless since Danae's capture.

"Tell me why you seek Miss Marie Laveau, and you may find out," the voice answered.

Ah. So not a vendetta, just a test.

"I seek mortality, and I'm told Miss Laveau may have the key." There was no point in hiding his reasoning from the woman he sought.

Silence filled the air. His nostrils flared as he tried to pick up any clues to indicate where he was or where Miss Laveau sat, but it was as if scents had been plucked from the air and hidden away. A brief whisper of fabric moved before the blindfold lifted from his face, and he blinked against the dim light.

He sat in a chair in the middle of a sparsely decorated cabin. A hunched over woman with dusky brown skin smiled at him, deep wrinkles lining the skin around her eyes and mouth. Clasping the lace shawl at her chest to keep it from falling, she hobbled back to her own chair, which creaked beneath her weight. Wisps of hair white as snow peeked out beneath the deep blue headwrap she wore. She had become Immortal much later in life than most.

"Marie Laveau, I presume," he said to her with a brief lowering of his chin. Unlike the Immortals he had faced earlier, he knew to respect his elders. Even ones who had him chained.

"Dat I am." After replacing the spectacles on her nose, she picked up a set of knitting needles and yarn next to her chair and resumed her task. "Mortality, hm? Why would one so young seek to return to da way of death?"

He smiled. To her, he must have seemed young, though in reality they had been born in the same century, most likely only a decade or two apart.

"Love."

The thread looped around her needle. "One can have love in immortality."

"I do not wish to live without her." The scent of still-burning flesh reached his nose. "Why am I still chained?"

Marie chuckled, looking at him over the rim of her thin wire-framed glasses as her hands moved. "Metaphorically or physically?"

Before he could respond, she uttered a command in Creole, and the chains dropped to the wooden floor. He inspected his wrists, which bore no sign of any harm. Immortality at its finest.

He'd miss some of these perks.

"Magic," he said with curiosity, no accusation behind his words.

"Voodoo," she corrected him. "I can only presume the woman you speak of does not want an immortal life."

He nodded. "She desires children, and I'd like to be the father."

Her needles stopped moving. "Gaining mortality is not as easy as casting a magic spell or using voodoo. You have to prove yourself worthy."

"I'm ready to do anything it takes," he said.

"Anyting?" She gazed into his eyes, her own dark with intent.

"Anything," he said firmly.

Marie sighed and set the knitting needles and threads in her lap. "Da key to mortality lies in only one place."

He waited, guessing she was drawing the answer out for theatrics.

"In death."

On second thought, perhaps it wasn't theatrics.

"Death," he repeated, hesitancy in his voice as his senses kicked into overdrive, readying for an attack.

He hadn't sensed any kind of malice behind her words, and he didn't think she was going to kill him herself. But that didn't imply he was right, and her advanced age didn't mean a damn thing as an Immortal.

"Mm, you must go to de underworld for your answer," she explained. "A woman dere has more answers. A friend of mine."

Ah. Of course he would.

After he and Miss Laveau discussed his trip to the underworld and who he would need to seek once there, Solomon headed straight to the airport. It was almost ironic that he'd be tagging along with Serafina. Why he had to go and fall in love with *that* girl's best friend was anyone's guess.

He had his answers, or part of them, now he just needed to go to hell. The joke of the phrase didn't sit well with him, but it also happened to be the truth.

* * *

WHEN SOLOMON ARRIVED back at Nora's apartment, he wasted no time sweeping the petite beauty up into his arms as if carrying her across a threshold. His heart swelled at the laugh it provoked from her.

"Maybe you should go away more often," Nora said after they broke off their drawn-out kiss.

He pushed back a stray blonde curl from her face, his elation quickly evaporating. "I may have to do just that."

Soft fingers entwined with his before pulling him over to the cream-colored sofa, where he explained what Marie Laveau had told him. His shoulders sagged as the glimmer in her eyes faded with the news. He hated being the bearer of bad news with the woman he loved.

"So both my soul mates have to go to the underworld?" Nora asked with an incredulous scoff. A pink glow appeared around her green irises, a new sign of her rising frustration. "Just my luck."

* * *

HOURS LATER, NORA LAY with her head tucked into the nook between Solomon's arm and chest, her cheek still flushed from their activities. He ran his hand up and down her bare back, her skin warm and slick to the touch, wishing for all the world that nothing would ever change.

That this right here could last forever.

She shifted against him, and he looked down to find her bright green eyes gazing up at him through thick eyelashes.

"I want you to drink from me," she said.

The predator within him rose faster than he expected. His breath hitched in his throat, and his gums ached with anticipated pleasure as his fangs extended. He had wanted to taste Nora's blood since the moment he saw her, even if his original intentions weren't honorable.

In just a few short months, he had grown to love this woman fiercely, and tasting her blood would deepen their already strong bond.

"Are you sure?" he asked, his voice strained. He wasn't sure she could even hear him.

"Yes," came her breathy reply. "I want to be yours in every sense of the word. I trust you."

That was all he needed. Resisting the urge to dominate and control with fear, he slid his arm out from under her and rolled onto his elbow, gazing into pear-hued eyes filled with nothing but love. He stroked her cheek, his heart beating faster from the warm, blood-infused skin simmering beneath his hand.

"You'll feel a sting, but it'll fade quickly," he said as he moved his hand to her neck, brushing her hair back. His fingers itched to pin his prey down, but this was not a hunt.

She was not prey; she gave herself willingly.

"You of all people should know I don't mind a little pain." She tilted her head to the side and reached a hand up behind his neck to draw him down.

Nearly groaning in anticipation, he opened his mouth and breathed in, loving the sweet scents of coconut and oatmeal that always accompanied her. But that was from her various soaps, and he wanted to know what flavors lay beneath—in her blood.

As he breathed out, the fine hairs along her skin fluttered. Her pulse thumped rapidly in tune with her heart. Not in fear, he could tell, but desire.

Gently, he kissed her neck, a place he had kissed many times before with the hope of tasting the river of life just beneath the surface. Never acting, never even *asking*, because he wanted it to be on her terms, and hers alone.

He licked along the line of her artery, allowing the anesthetic in his saliva to soak in for a moment before he bit. It wouldn't take all the pain away, pain that would only last mere moments, but it would help.

Then he struck.

She gasped, her body jumping slightly as his fangs pierced her flesh as easily as paper. His lips quivered as he waited, blood starting to seep out, wanting to be sure she wasn't going to change her mind. But she ran her hand up into his hair and pressed him to her again.

Laying his lips over her skin, he drank. Deep and hard.

His senses went wild as he took her in, tasting lavender and chocolate, even a hint of honey. Her blood was rich, full of vibrant energy, and filled him with an ecstasy unlike anything else.

She was his own personal brand of drug, and he was hooked for life.

CHAPTER 5

Serafina

Sera glanced at her watch yet again. Nine in the evening. As if it mattered. No matter what time the screen read, it was time.

Time to merge with a god.

What that truly meant, she could only imagine, but she tried not to. Sitting on the fluffy rug in front of the cottage's fireplace, she bounced her cross-legged knees with nervous energy.

Renee had left that morning, after a tear-filled goodbye at the airport. She'd offered to stay until after the merge, but there really wasn't any point other than pure selfishness on Sera's part. She really wanted to be selfish for once.

Instead, she'd put on a brave face and said she'd be just fine. Who knew she'd turned into such a good liar?

I did, Bacchus said. *Are you ready?*

Honestly? You tell me, you're able to see— Sera didn't get to finish her sentence before lightning struck her down. What she imagined being struck by lightning would feel like, anyway. For a split second, her body, her entire *being*, shattered into pieces, her vision engulfed in crimson. Every bone must have broken, every fiber melted. Her collarbones burned with fiery ice, and she couldn't breathe.

And then she was falling. Falling into a swirling vortex leading into a bottomless pit. She fell for what felt like minutes, then days, then years. She was Alice tumbling to Wonderland, only she wasn't chasing a cute, white bunny. Just a sassy ancient god.

Her descent eventually slowed, and she drifted in the nothingness, enjoying the lack of... everything. No thoughts, no feelings, no pain. Just peacefulness amongst a raging tornado keeping her afloat, weightless. She could stay here forever, let go of everything and everyone. Forget her entire life.

It was too good to last.

The vortex carried her up again, up and up. And as she rose, faces drifted close to hers in the swirling wind. Faces she didn't know, and yet *knew.* Places, times, gods, moments—centuries and millennia passed in the blink of an eye, and the pressure, oh gods, the pressure building inside her skull threatened to explode.

She pressed her hands against her head, thinking it might help keep her skull from splitting apart, as the pain of the new memories spread from her mind down her spine like dominoes. Every inch of her body remembered moments she had never known as her genetic code blended with Bacchus's.

Unable to hold it in anymore, a scream of anguish and rage ripped from her body, and she toppled over onto something soft, curling into a fetal position. Strong arms wrapped around her as she shook, holding her tight in a comforting way. A voice whispered soothing nonsense against her hair.

An eternity later, or maybe just moments, the pain started to subside.

It is done, Bacchus said. His divine essence, encased in the amulet for a millennium, had merged with her own.

Sera opened her eyes, not even knowing when she had closed them, and blinked a few times at the shag rug in front of her. Each strand, every fiber, and the microscopic pieces of dirt and ash from the nearby fireplace contained within moved before her vision as she exhaled. What she had once thought was just a white rug, now seemed to reflect and scatter all the colors of the rainbow. It was beautiful.

A deep snicker rolled through the room. *And that's just a rug.*

"I'm okay," she said to Theo, gently pushing out of his embrace and sitting up. She avoided lifting her gaze, not quite ready for what she'd see with her divinely enhanced eyes when she did.

She rubbed the sides of her forehead, which still buzzed with an electric current. Her entire body tingled, like a river of energy resided within her. Golden energy that flowed toward her center.

"I told you it hurts," Theo said with a slight chuckle.

"Understatement of the century." She snorted and accepted the hand mirror he passed to her, taking a deep breath. Biting her lip, she lifted the glass.

Her grey eyes stared back at her, only now they shimmered around the edges with a golden light. She pulled down the top of her sweater and tilted the mirror to get a look at the amulet. Well, her new tattoo of the amulet. The necklace itself was gone.

Delicate filigree grape leaves in silver ink trailed down the skin of her collarbone to the crimson pinecone-shaped pendant now forever a part of her. She reached up to run a finger across the image, no longer feeling the sharp edges of the pinecone. The lines of the tattoo tingled in response as she touched it.

At least now she wouldn't have to hide a stolen artifact from anyone.

She lowered the mirror and let go of her sweater, though her hand continued to trace the magical ink of the tattoo. She allowed her gaze to follow the pattern of Theo's socks, up his sweats, and nearly got lost in the details of his otherwise simple shirt. A variety of shades of blue made up every strand, each hue twined together to appear as one.

In reality, it was anything but simple.

When he reached an arm up, brushing his hair back from his face, the movement drew her gaze up to his chin. A dark brown fuzz tinted with reddish gold still covered his chin and cheeks, which didn't do much to hide the strong line of his jaw beneath. Not anymore.

The skin of his face was a russet brown, a tint similar to the terracotta amphorae of the Roman ages. Memories of the pottery she saw on dig sites blended seamlessly with Bacchus's memories from the actual making of those pieces of pottery several millennia ago.

Graduate classes were about to get a whole lot easier.

She could hear Theo breathing, the slight whistle in his inhale, the whoosh of his exhale. His heart drummed a steady beat beneath his chest. She let her gaze continue to wander up the soft lines of his face to his eyes.

Her breath caught in her throat.

His eyes were… otherworldly. Still the dark brown she had come to know and enjoyed losing herself in from time to time, but now laced with the crackle of lightning. The strikes came and went as fierce as a thunderstorm. She could easily drown in those eyes for days.

Movement out of her periphery drew her attention, and she snapped her head to the right. Was that who she thought it was? Bacchus?

Lounging on one of the couches in the cottage's living room, one leg thrown over the other, bouncing his barefoot lazily. He gazed at his glass of red wine as he swirled it before raising it to his lips. Curly brown hair hung down around his bearded face, and a crown of gleaming laurels sat on top of his head, a bit haphazardly for a deity. Sera wasn't sure she would have expected any different.

Everything about him shimmered in a golden haze, as if he weren't fully there, much like how Liviana had seen him in the temple when she became one of the Bacchae. Which meant this must really be him. Sera's mouth dropped open.

Is that you? For real? she asked in her mind.

Bacchus glanced over at her and sat up, drenching his white toga in red wine with the sudden movement. The wine stain and glass evaporated in a poof of swirling air.

Jupiter's balls! You can see me? He sounded as bewildered as she felt, and his gold-flecked green eyes opened wide.

Sera laughed, amazed she had caught the god by surprise. *Is this not part of the merge?* She had no idea what would be appropriate for greeting a god who had first become a close friend and now existed as a part of her own DNA.

Hardly, he said. *Your Gift must have something to do with it.*

A new figure added in a growling voice, *Your godspeak must have become more like a godsight.*

Almost afraid to look, Sera turned toward Theo and the shadowy being standing several feet behind him, leaning against the fireplace wall. She ignored Theo's furrowed brows for now as she stood and took tentative steps toward the creature she assumed was Xolotl. Unlike Bacchus, who retained a human look in Roman mythology, Xolotl was half man, half dog in Aztec stories.

And holy shit was he terrifying in person.

As he panted, saliva dripped from his tongue to the floor, where it sizzled and evaporated. His jaws jutted out like a snout and housed long canine teeth, fang-like in their ferocity. He closed his mouth and regarded her with pools of darkness in otherwise empty eye sockets. In one ear, a twisted and curved shell earring dangled from his lobe; in the other, a skull grinned back at her. She gulped, knowing deep down that it was real bone carved to appear like a human face.

Grey fuzz covered the length of his skin, and his hands were paw-like with sharp claws protruding from pads instead of nails from fingers. Ornamental jewelry hung around his neck, including the same spiraling conch shell breastplate that had become a tattoo on Theo's chest. He wore a skirt around his human-shaped hips and legs. A headdress stood tall from his head.

Like Bacchus, his entire being shimmered as if he wasn't really there, only his was a dark, shadowy haze.

"Wow," was all Sera could get out.

Greetings, Xolotl rumbled with an incline of his Doberman-shaped head.

"Is everything okay?" Theo asked, now standing beside her. He glanced to where Xolotl stood and back at her, his eyebrows pulled together.

"Yes, but I can *see* Bacchus and Xolotl," she said. "Like, actually in front of me."

Facts about Xolotl came to the forefront of her thoughts, courtesy of Bacchus's shared memories. The Aztec god would be a godsend in the underworld. "And best of all, he's traveled to hell before."

Theo's face went through a whirlwind of emotion in the blink of an eye, from confusion to amazement and awe. "I've never heard of this happening before."

As the surprise of seeing the gods in the flesh faded, Sera became aware of other changes to her senses once again. The scent of the fruit-scented soap Theo liked to use drifted off of him as it warmed in the heat of the fireplace. It was a scent she had come to enjoy in a new way, full of hope and temptation.

The light from the fire had once been just enough to light the darkened living room of the cottage, leaving dark shadows outside the flickering circle. But now the shadows lightened, and intricate details she had missed on the stone floor and wooden walls caught her attention. A spider the size of a pinhead wove its web in one corner of the ceiling, which didn't bother her nearly as much as the collection of dust mites on the floor in the same corner.

A crushing realization of living an immortal life hit her next, but instead of succumbing to the grief as she would have once done, even a few minutes ago, Sera felt calm. At peace. This merge meant she would be able to rescue her mother or die trying.

Whatever else happened because of it, the change was worth it.

Her eyes found Theo's once again, drawn to him as she found peace in her decision. He still gazed at her in awe and something else she couldn't quite place. She saw him as if for the first time, catching minute changes in his expression as his mind processed this experience.

Her breath hitched in her throat, and her body warmed as she remembered what he had said about not dating mortals and why. Now she was immortal. With him.

Were they ready to take that leap? Was *she*? Was she even what he wanted?

He reached up to brush her hair behind her ear, the roughness of his calloused palm scratching her cheek in a pleasant way. A fire ignited within her then, flaring out and through her entire body, pulsing between her legs. She craved his touch. At that moment, she didn't even care if part of her desire was fueled by Bacchus's frenzied nature and the merge.

To hell with waiting. She turned her cheek into his hand, kissing his palm.

His answering growl was all she needed to know that he felt the same. She reached out to draw him closer and—

"The fire sure warms this room up, doesn't it?" Lasirenn's unwelcome voice cut through the air, effectively ending the moment.

Her cheeks blazing from the interrupted moment, Sera turned to glare at the water spirit. Theo pulled back, coughing into his hand. No one would miss the woman if Sera killed her, right?

Bacchus chuckled from a shadowy corner of the room.

At least you were nice enough to stay quiet, Sera grumbled to him in their shared consciousness. *And out of my view.*

Ah, yes, Bacchus the Kind. He raised his wine glass into the air in a toast. *It has a nice ring to it, don't you think?*

"Impeccable timing," Sera said to Lasirenn instead of answering the god.

Lasirenn smirked. "So I see."

CHAPTER 6

Serafina

As the sun rose the day after the merge, Sera stood in the clearing behind the cottage, snow melting beneath her bare feet. Her red flannel pajama top and bottoms did little to stop the breeze from infiltrating to caress her skin. Still, the temperature of the snow and the breeze were just slight nuisances now.

She faced the east and greeted the sun like an old friend as it rose above the treetops. Maybe she should consider Helios a peer now.

The heat of the rays warmed her to the core, to her spirit. Her very soul.

Sera hadn't felt this alive since the summer dig. There was something about being outside, breathing in the clean rural air untainted by crowded city life, that just did it for her. Add in the god-like senses, and she felt like she had never experienced the world before. Perhaps she hadn't. Not like Bacchus had, anyway.

Although she didn't need rest like she did before the merge, half of her genetic code was still human. Her muscles had quivered with the exertion of the change shortly after Lasirenn's untimely interruption.

Only when Sera tried to rest, sleep had evaded her.

After she had laid down, she couldn't stop running the sheets through her hands, the texture soft and downy yet creating a zipper-like sound when her nails ran over the threads. Nocturnal animals had prowled outside the cottage window, their chitters and movements through the trees had been as loud as if they were in the room with her.

When Sera finally gave up on keeping her eyes closed, she had gone outside. She had stepped slowly toward the clearing, taking in all the new things she could see in the still dark of dawn as an immortal. As the morning light kissed the earth, she was all but mesmerized.

What had once been just a foot of snow covering the ground to her human senses, now became a crystallized blanket. Snowflakes melted into one another just enough to look solid, but their individual markings sparkled a greeting beneath her gaze. Each flake unique and distinct. Even against the bark of the surrounding trees and the leaves of the hardy shrubs beneath, the closest at least ten feet from where she stood, lay the delicate beauty of snow.

The sudden urge to run overtook her, and so she ran. Vaulting across the clearing and into the forest, her muscles no longer tired, her breath came easily, and her pulse continued to race. Twigs snapped beneath her feet, small snow flurries following in her wake as she disturbed the earth. She ran until her breath grew short and her lungs burned, not once tripping or slipping as her inner klutz previously demanded.

A shout of exhilaration burst from her lips.

Jumping over a fallen branch, she leaped onto a low-hanging limb of a nearby tree, landing in a squat as she held on with a hand. Leaped and landed as if it were the most natural thing in the world.

When Bacchus had taken over her body before their merge, the invasion of his essence had felt like a violation of the natural order of things. Her instinct had been to fight against it, and she had paid the price time and again for allowing a god to use her mortal limbs, succumbing to blackouts after each ordeal.

Now, her muscles were his muscles. His energy hers. They were one and the same. Well and genuinely merged. She panted, her warm breath creating visible puffs against the frigid air. When she sat down on the branch, the ice melted beneath her, soaking her pajama pants. Though the cold still didn't bother her, she reached for the divine magic now residing within her core like a gentle tingling feeling that never went away.

Sera hadn't realized what it was the night before right after the merge, but Bacchus's memory had come to her as she woke. She closed her eyes, visualizing the spiraling pool of golden magic that swirled in her center, flowing with the pulse of her blood.

It was pure energy, crackling with static, waiting to be used. As she called for the magic now and opened her eyes, a bolt of it shot out from her chest like electricity to pool into her awaiting palm.

The shape of the magic changed as she watched, sometimes forming a ball before melting into the pattern of her palm then onto something new. It was as if the thing were alive and excited to be used. For chaos, she was sure.

She smirked. Of course a god of chaos would choose a super logical, routine-oriented person like Sera.

"Dry," she whispered to the magic and placed her palm and the awaiting magic onto her pants, which were quickly turning into blocks of ice. The golden orb of magic spread through the fabric, warming and drying the material instantly. With one last flash, the magic dissolved from her view.

Enjoying the scenery? Bacchus sat beside her with his legs dangling beneath the branch. The end of his toga hung low, almost to the ground. For once, he didn't hold a glass of wine. Maybe the outside air and run did him some good, too.

"Why didn't you tell me about all of this?"

All of what?

"All the details, the beauty." Sera waved her hand around her, gesturing to everything before resting her hand on her chest with the last words. "The magic."

Bacchus looked around where her hand had indicated. *It's easy to lose sight of the beauty in the world when you stop looking.*

She closed her eyes and inhaled, relishing the new scents that invaded her senses. Pine, chestnut, beech, sap, earth— all things she had smelled before but only when up close and practically thrust in her face.

Now, using just her sense of smell, she knew a beech tree stood a few yards away. A variety of plants and dormant grasses gathered at the tree's base, and squirrels had visited the day before. Everything left a distinct scent behind.

The bark of the branch caught at the skin of her fingers and palms, minute edges digging their pattern into her skin. Wind whistled through the trees, loosening clumps of snow that fell to the ground. Sera's other senses filled in the gaps of her vision, and she knew she'd be able to run back to the cottage even with her eyes closed.

"I hope I never lose sight of it," she said at last.

Me, too.

* * *

SERA TOOK A DAY adjusting to life merged with a god and all the changes it brought to her senses and memories—which could be quite distracting. When she was convinced she could handle the change in environment, she and Theo headed back out to Paris. They had planned a meeting with Gabriel, their French intelligence contact at the American embassy.

He was one of two foreign agents who knew that there were more things out there than just the Bacchae. Things like Theo and Renee and now her, only he didn't know exactly *what* they were, despite his repeated attempts to find out.

Sera needed to convince the French to release Danae into her custody so she and Theo could take the girl to the underworld, except they wouldn't mention the underworld part. The world wasn't quite ready for that news. One bomb dropped at a time. In all likelihood, it was not going to go over well.

She hated being right.

"I'm not sure you understand how important it is that the Eternal come with us." Sera had wisely chosen to sit down so she wouldn't be tempted to use her new strength against the infuriating man. Chaos was now in her blood, too, after all. She was still tempted but wrapping her ankles around the base of the chair until it dug into her skin through her boots helped.

The secondhand on the man's watch ticked once, then twice.

Sera tried again, "We need her to free the prisoners."

The nostrils of Gabriel's sharply pointed nose flared out as he inhaled, and the French official held up his hand. The older man still retained a head of dark hair, no greys to be seen. His outfit—a pink, so pale it was almost white, button-down shirt with the sleeves crisply folded up to his elbows and navy-blue dress pants without a wrinkle in sight—was casual yet still fiercely fashionable.

So very French.

"Do not patronize me," he said in his thick accent. "I understand you *think* it is important, but we cannot afford to let her escape. With all due *respect*," he practically spat the word out, "you have no training of any kind that would reassure us of your capacity to do so, and you have yet to give us the answers we need concerning the location of said prisoners. If they even exist."

Bacchus stood behind Gabriel and poured the contents of his wine glass over the man's head. Such a shame it wasn't real enough to affect the guy.

The official pushed his chair back with an ear-splitting shriek as the metal feet ran across the linoleum floor of the man's office. "Many people lost loved ones when the

Bacchae ran free. You'll have to accept these deaths like the rest of us had to. Excuse me."

"But my mom's not dead—" Sera protested as he opened the door to leave.

Gabriel hesitated for a brief moment but didn't turn back around.

"I'm sorry for your loss," he said and left the room, pulling the door closed behind him. His dress shoes clacked down the hall, almost in time with her raging pulse.

It was only then that his words caught up to her—*like the rest of us.* The Bacchae had taken someone from him, too. And she was such a selfish ass she didn't even think to consider it or ask.

A battle raged inside of Sera. On the one hand, her heart hurt for the guy and whomever he had lost. She knew exactly how devastating it was to have someone she loved ripped away from her by the Bacchae, much too soon in life. She even saw it firsthand when she lost Hiro and had known it with every missed moment with her mother.

But on the other hand, Sera wanted to scream in frustration and throw the table across the office. Her fingers left dents in the arms of the metal chair as she restrained herself.

How hard was it to understand that her mother wasn't dead? Neither were the other witches who were with her in the cave when Danae attacked them twenty years ago. They could *save* nine lives if these people would just listen to her.

Even if her mother wasn't one of them, saving this group of forgotten witches would go a long way to heal her heart and soul. It would feel like they had truly beaten Danae once and for all. That alone was worth any risk.

Bacchus paced circles around the table in his agitation, his toga billowing out behind him as he walked.

We should just tell them about me, he said. *About all the gods.*

Absolutely not, Sera retorted as she rubbed her face with her hands.

Only a few select American officials knew the truth about the existence of the divine, and it hadn't been easy to keep it that way. *Haven't you ever seen* E.T.*? They'll lock us all up to study us.*

No, I haven't. Some of us were stuck in a cave when it came out. But you have me, and you're assuming they can catch us. He snapped his fingers and poofed from one corner of the room to another to prove his point.

I wasn't even born yet, and I still saw it, she scoffed. *It's a classic.*

"I guess we'll have to move on to plan B," Theo said before Bacchus could come back with more sass. Leaning back in his chair, Theo crossed one foot over the other knee.

She blinked at him. "I didn't know we had a plan B."

Grinning at her, dimples appeared in each of his cheeks. The flutter returned to her belly. She really couldn't wait for all of this to be behind them so she could see those dimples all day every day. The cuteness factor was off the charts.

"If they won't give us Danae, we'll just have to take her from them ourselves."

Sera gaped at him. "You're actually recommending we break the law? Who are you, and what have you done with Theodore?"

She thoroughly enjoyed this side to the man, but she wasn't going to tell him that. Not yet. She'd be too tempted to act on that enjoyment.

Xolotl chuckled from his place in the corner of the room, arms crossed. The canine god was so quiet and blended so well into the shadows that most of the time, Sera almost forgot he was there. Almost.

"Well, if you don't *want* to—"

"Oh, hell no, we're totally doing it," she said. "I just assumed Bacchus would have been the one with that idea."

She laughed as Bacchus stopped his pacing, his face drooping.

You're right, I'm losing my edge, the god said, sounding forlorn. *I blame you.*

CHAPTER 7

Serafina

Before heading back to the cottage, they decided to check in with Liviana, another Eternal on the High Council, and one who had played an intricate role in helping them stop Danae. Sera had found herself enjoying Liviana's cool-headed presence, but she thought it had more to do with the dreams.

To prepare Sera for the supernatural world, Bacchus had "gifted" her with flashbacks revealing the girl's journey to becoming one of the Bacchae.

His plan had royally backfired.

Sera cringed, staring out the car window as they pulled up to the government building housing the Eternals in Paris. She remembered her ill-treatment of the woman when Renee told Sera and Nora that vampires existed. But come on, who could have taken that seriously without seeing one in the flesh and fang?

I did try to help you, Bacchus said.

Who trusts dreams as reality? Sera asked as she pushed open the car door and climbed out.

She followed Theo through the revolving doors and into the security line. No guns or other weapons were allowed inside, so Sera didn't worry about forgetting hers on the car seat this time. She rolled her eyes at herself for the rookie mistake, and one she wouldn't make again.

After placing what little she carried on the conveyor belt, Sera stepped through the metal detector, letting out a small sigh of relief when it didn't beep. The guard waved her on. She'd never had a bad experience with one, but for some reason, the thought of setting off the alarm set her pulse racing.

An elevator ride and a few long halls later, Theo and Sera sat in a conference room across from Liviana. The Eternal wore half her hair up in an elaborately braided bun, while the rest of her long dark brown hair fell in soft curls around her shoulders. She hadn't been beautiful in her human life but becoming a demi-god had sharpened her features. Sera still wouldn't call her beautiful, but it was clear she was otherworldly. Divine.

Turned as a teenager like Danae, Liviana wore a crisp black suit with a crimson-colored blouse beneath. Sera couldn't quite tell whether she was making a fashion statement or a power statement. Either way, the ancient girl looked fantastic.

"It's nice to see you again," Liviana said with a smile.

"Likewise," Sera said.

When she had first spoken with the Eternal after taking down Danae, Sera had felt like a kid meeting a celebrity for the first time. On edge and jittery and saying all the wrong things.

Now, she met with an old friend.

The girl tilted her head as she gazed at Sera. Her eyes narrowed in concentration, not threat, before they opened wide again. "You've done it."

With a quick glance toward the two guards at the door, Sera nodded. She didn't want to be rude, but it wasn't something they could discuss with others present.

"We came to ask you about Danae."

Liviana must have expected it because she sighed and said, "I can't help you with that."

Theo and Sera exchanged a frustrated glance before Theo leaned forward, placing his arms on the table. "What *can* you help us with?"

"My hands are really tied," she said. "The French will be transporting Danae to the United States two days from now for her trial and presumed execution." Her gaze flicked to the guards who hadn't moved. "We will be accompanying the transport to keep Danae under control and quickly put down any… uprisings, should they occur."

Holy shit. The girl was feeding them information.

Sera wanted to reach over and hug her, but she couldn't risk alerting the guards. The two guards listening wouldn't care that Liviana spoke about the transfer; Theo and Sera were two of the goddamn heroes who took Danae down. But they also didn't know that these two heroes had the power of gods running through their veins.

"I'm sympathetic, really," Liviana continued. "But my

stance with the mortal community is iffy at best, and I'm not willing to rock the boat."

"We understand," Sera said, holding back her smile. "Thank you for meeting with us even though your hands are clearly tied."

* * *

BACK AT THE COTTAGE later that evening, Sera made a video call from her seat at the oblong dining room table. The wooden behemoth could comfortably seat twelve.

With its brick hearth oven in the corner of the back wall and the mint green wooden ceiling beams, the kitchen and dining room had become her favorite place in the house. She often found herself there just for comfort. The old-world charm lingered despite the modern updates to the cabinetry and appliances. She would miss it.

The room was also closest to the snack food and coffee. She may not need food the same way now, but she would never give up coffee. They could pry it from her cold, dead hands.

When Nora answered the call, she was in her apartment, sitting on her cream-colored couch. Solomon lurked next to her. Some might call it cuddling. He stayed put as Sera explained the plan she, Bacchus, and Theo had come up with.

"This is the worst plan B I've ever heard," Nora said, pursing her lips.

"I'd love to hear a better plan," Sera said, sipping from her mug. The floral notes of this particular brew swirled their way up with the steam.

"Literally anything else." Nora gave a flippant wave of her hand, the movement shaking the phone camera slightly.

Sera held back a smirk. "Well, when you come up with a better plan, let me know."

"Oh, I will." Nora glanced up at Solomon. "Should we tell her?"

Sera's heart sank. If they were getting married, she might blow a fuse. An actual fuse in the house with her newfound magic.

"Tell me what?"

"Sol is going to hell with you," Nora said.

Sera did her best not to let out a sigh of relief. Only a squeak of air made it through. His Bacchae strength would be useful, but she was moderately convinced they'd make it without him. Okay, his skills would probably be quite beneficial, but refusing out of spite didn't seem so bad. Also, she'd rather the Bacchae stay with Nora and keep her safe. The last thing Sera needed was to lose her best friend and soulmate.

At least Nora wasn't announcing their engagement.

"No thanks," Sera said.

"It wasn't an offer. He's going." Nora's eyebrow twitched as if she knew what Sera was thinking. She probably did; they had been best friends since elementary school. "He needs to speak to someone there about regaining his mortality."

Ugh. If Sera had to go to hell, she most certainly did not want to go with *him*. He may have claimed to have changed his ways, may have even proven it from time to time, but Sera still partly blamed him for Hiro's death. If Solomon had just chosen the right side to begin with, he might have been able to help them stop Danae before it escalated.

Then again, if Sera had just given the amulet back, she would never have involved him in any of this mess. Whose fault was it really?

Not like Bacchus would have let her give him up.

Regardless of what happened in the past, arguing with the blonde in the present would be futile. Nora always got her way, and she knew it.

* * *

BY THE TIME THEY were ready to break Danae out of military custody two days later, Nora hadn't come up with a better plan B. But Theo's plan B turned out to be easier than expected, which was nerve-wracking.

How could it be this easy to abduct an ancient Bacchae witch from the French and American militaries? Well, if a kid could rescue an alien in E.T…

Easy was subjective, of course.

The American vice president had assumed the presidency when the elected president, who had been abducted and tortured by Danae, could no longer serve. The poor man shook like a nervous Chihuahua. The American government had requested that the Bacchae witch return to the United States, where she had claimed her primary residence and where she had also done the most damage.

The whole deal had happened so quickly that Sera was pretty sure the French just wanted to be rid of her. Let her be someone else's problem.

Smart people, those French.

No one would expect an ambush by humans backed by

ancient gods. No one except the Eternals, of course, and luckily for Sera, the Eternals were willing to pretend they didn't know what the others planned to do. Sera always liked the girl who once haunted her dreams, even if she was one of the Bacchae.

So now Sera found herself hiding, alongside Theo and Lasirenn, in the nearly pitch-black belly of a massive cargo plane, listening to the deafening roar of the engines as they flew across the Atlantic Ocean. Theirs was one of two airplanes, the other of which held Danae, the Eternals, and a small contingent of marines.

Despite all the military and secret service presence, it hadn't been too difficult for them to sneak onto the plane. A little bit of divine misdirection went a long way with humans. And when the aircraft touched down on US soil in North Carolina, Nora, Renee, and Solomon would be waiting to help spirit them all away, Danae in tow. Easy peasy.

Magic had been super handy to have on their side.

There's that self-talk again, Bacchus quipped from somewhere above her.

Sera shifted her weight, trying to find a more comfortable spot as her leg went numb once again. The three humans, or at least the three beings with physical bodies, were crammed into a tiny pocket of space between two metal shipping containers. Even with a god's DNA, it was hard to get comfortable. The upside was that the freezing cold of the cargo hold didn't bother her.

"Your knee is digging into my side," Lasirenn complained in the dark.

Much to her displeasure, Sera had no trouble making

out the water spirit's figure with her god-enhanced vision.

"No one asked you to come on the plane," she snapped back.

Theo sighed. "This is going to be an even longer flight than it already is if you two don't stop squabbling."

He's right, you know, Bacchus said.

No one asked you, Sera grumbled to him as she pulled her knee away from the water spirit as much as she could. *Why didn't she just meet us there? She can turn into a freaking mermaid. She could have been there just as fast as this airplane.*

The Roman god chuckled. *You make it too easy to resist.*

Resist what?

Making you uncomfortable.

Maybe he was right, but it was more likely that Lasirenn didn't want Sera and Theo continuing the steamy moment they had started back at the cottage. Before the spirit had interrupted, that is. As if making out in an airplane's freezing cargo hold sounded appealing to anyone.

Although warming it up with some sexy naked time sounded nice in theory. Sera's gaze drifted to Theo, the start of a smile pulling at her cheek. Without the water spirit taking up space, Sera and Theo definitely would have had some room to get creative. Relieving some tension before the plan kicked into action sounded pretty damn good to Sera right about now.

Are you ever going to ask if he fulfilled his promise to her? Bacchus asked from his place on top of one of the shipping containers. He sat there like a kid with his feet dangling down and his hands gripping the sides. Xolotl stood regally beside him. The two gods were as different as yin and yang.

How dare you ruin my fantasy, she said, dropping her gaze

to avoid looking at the water spirit and Theo despite the pull to do just that. *And it's none of my business.*

Maybe not, but I'd really like to know, the god replied. *You know I love juicy gossip.*

I'm well aware of that. Why don't you just ask Xolotl? She glanced up at the canine god who hadn't moved an inch since they settled on board. His eyes always focused on the door, and his Doberman-like ears twitched and turned at the smallest sounds.

Bacchus glared up at the other god and huffed, causing one of his long curly brown strands of hair to flare out from his face. *I tried. He's refusing to say.*

Gods can be so infuriating, right? She grinned as Bacchus looked back at her, chastised.

CHAPTER 8

Serafina

The plane landed with a few bumpy jolts, causing Sera and Lasirenn to knock into each other again. This time neither of them complained. Tension rose thick in the air like a noticeable scent, as each of them prepared for the next part of the plan.

Freyja? Sera reached out with her mind.

Nothing would happen until the others were in place and ready. They needed the additional divine powers.

We're here, darling, the Norse goddess replied in her musical voice. Sera's heart warmed at the sound. It had been far too long since she had seen Nora.

When the airplane's massive cargo door lowered, interior lighting filled the hold with a soft glow. Nighttime still cloaked the outside due to crossing time zones, but any amount of light improved Sera's spirits after eight hours of sitting in darkness, even with her enhanced vision. They waited behind one of the metal shipping containers until the first boxes had been unloaded before sneaking out.

The two soldiers waiting at the bottom of the ramp never knew what hit them. Theo's plan was not to go in with force but rather deception, at least until they got to Danae. With the aid of the gods keeping lookout, Theo and Sera dragged the men's limp forms back into the plane, out of sight, and tugged the men's uniforms on over their own clothes.

After pulling her hair up into a bun and securing it under the soldier's cap, Sera looked back at the two still figures, nearly naked in the cold, and grimaced. She took a small amount of comfort in knowing someone would find them soon. Not much she could do about the headaches they would have when they came to, though.

Once they exited the plane, Sera glanced around, gaining her bearings. Despite the predawn hour, floodlights lit the tarmac almost as well as the sun. Lasirenn had dressed in all black, ready to melt into the shadows of the night, and she all but disappeared as she snuck away.

Several shouts drew Sera's attention to the right.

Inside the belly of the other cargo plane, a group of soldiers lifted a silver cage onto a rolling cart. Another handful of soldiers waited on the ground with guns raised and ready to fire. Danae stood inside the cage, bound with a silver embellished straitjacket, and chained to various poles to hold her upright and basically immobile.

Although Sera and Theo had taken every precaution to keep their plans hidden, the Eternal's sunken blue-grey eyes immediately found Sera's, and her dry, cracked lips quirked up.

"How the hell is she able to sense us?" Sera muttered under her breath to Theo.

"Doesn't matter as long as she keeps her mouth shut, which she will," he said.

"How can you be so sure?" she asked.

"She'll consider us the easier target to escape from."

The soldiers rolled the cart down the gangplank leading out of the plane and toward an awaiting truck.

Sera and Theo had no plans to shoot anyone as they walked toward the cage. Still, they held their guns ready like the other guards did, needing to play the part to avoid suspicion. A known supernatural terrorist was in the military's midst, and they were all ready to execute her should she sneeze the wrong way.

Sera didn't see any of the Eternals, and she hoped Liviana had chosen to aid their efforts by keeping herself and the others at a distance.

Bacchus walked right up to the cage holding Danae and through the bars as if they didn't exist. Silver didn't affect him in the least. The Bacchae's extreme allergic reaction to the metal was just some random limitation he came up with to keep the Bacchae under control. His inspiration came when the Roman goddess Diana cursed a lovesick man to burn at the touch of silver. The poor man's story then became a part of the vampire mythos, much to Bacchus's enjoyment.

The mythology theft had sure pissed off Diana, though.

The Roman god stared into the face of his now emaciated creation, sadness and anger vying for expression.

Steam rose from the girl's body whenever the silver chains met her skin.

Just say the word, love, Freyja said from the others' hiding place.

Sera glanced at Theo with a raised eyebrow, and he gave a quick nod. They were ready.

Now! Sera shouted in her mind, her Gift enabling her to speak to all the gods at once.

Lightning split across the night sky, and the accompanying thunderous rumbling shook the ground, feeling for all the world like a god's wrath come to life. The distraction worked like a charm. All mortal faces looked up in terror and surprise.

Then everything plunged into deep, impenetrable darkness. At least to the humans. The gods and their human hosts could see just fine.

Theo and Sera used the butts of their guns to knock out the soldiers surrounding the silver cage, and a fierce wind whipped around the landing strip, hiding the sounds. Shouts and curses were whisked away with the wind, effectively causing the chaos the gods hoped for.

Lasirenn materialized out of the shadows, swinging a set of keys on one of her fingers. Not that they needed them, but the theft would help hide their involvement and abilities. No harm in letting the government think the abductors required keys to flee the scene.

In the darkness, the three of them leaped into the cab of the truck pulling the cart, and Theo drove it toward the other end of the landing strip. The rest of their group waited in the trees, trusting in the pandemonium left behind to cover their tracks.

As they neared the tree line, Sera spotted Nora, surrounded by a pink aura, standing next to Solomon. On Nora's other side stood a wildly beautiful blonde woman with white as porcelain skin and piercing blue eyes.

Undoubtedly Freyja. Leather armor covered her body, including a horned helmet that may have been actual dragon horns for all Sera knew. While Theo stayed in the truck to keep it running, ready for them to leave as soon as possible, Sera jumped down to greet the others.

Nora ran over and gave Sera a tight squeeze, which she returned wholeheartedly. She could count on one hand the number of times she and her best friend had been apart for more than a week since grade school. It just didn't feel right to not see her every day.

Turning to Renee, Sera pulled the woman in for an equally warm hug.

"I told you you'd be fine," the woman said quietly into Sera's ear.

Drawing back to see Renee's face, Sera grinned. "As usual, you were right."

A tall, thin black man shimmering with blue stepped out from behind Renee. His chest was bare, adorned only by a beaded and bone torc. A loose reddish cloth covered his hips and legs, tied with a belt made of coins. The belt also held a collection of dried gourds of various sizes on one hip and an African tribal mask on the other hip. The god's hair had been pulled up into a topknot, which then flowed down his back in an elaborately braided arch.

Eshu? Sera asked the man beside Renee. Totally not what she had expected him to look like, but she didn't know who else it could be.

The one and only, sugar plum, he responded with a quick, flourishing bow.

His long hair fell over one shoulder with the movement, revealing another, though much smaller, grinning face at the end of the thick braid. One eye winked at Sera before he stood straight again and brushed his hair back.

Weird, she thought with a shudder, but she didn't have time to stop and question him about his second face. There would be time for that later if they succeeded in this first part of the plan.

Don't tell me you merged with Manny, she scolded, although a quick glance around didn't reveal the kid.

As the most recent host for Eshu's essence, the Dominican boy Manny had fought alongside Sera and the others as they stormed Danae's French estate. As a kid, everyone underestimated him, and with Eshu's help, he had been sneakier than a fox. While Sera appreciated his top-notch parkour and fighting skills, this was not the life she, or any of them, wanted for the boy.

Eshu grinned. *Nah, the kid's in a safe place with Cassandra. But this here witch makes a damn fine host for now. Maybe even forever if she's up for it.*

He leaned on Renee's shoulder even though the woman smiling at Sera couldn't see him. Just below her chin-length silver hair, a bronze key hung around her neck—the god's symbol. The two weren't merged, but while she wore the key, Eshu would be able to use her body as Bacchus did with Sera's before they became one.

Seeing Eshu had been a surprise, a good one, but after a quick glance behind her, Sera knew they needed to get on the road. At least the others had grown accustomed to her lengthy bouts of silence when she conversed with the gods.

"Oh joy," Danae's snide tone cut through the quiet. "The Scooby gang's back together again."

Nora glared at the caged girl, pink static sparking around the edges of her aura. "We need to gag her."

"We can take care of her later, let's get going," Renee said, ever the level-headed one, and ushered Nora and Solomon into the waiting car.

Sera climbed back into the truck next to Lasirenn. Renee had set up a safe house not too far away from the airport, entirely concealed with magic, and probably even stronger now that she worked with Eshu. A little bit of tension seeped out of Sera along with a deep sigh. This whole plan was going to work.

It had to—they were too deep into it to back out now.

As the group's small caravan set out toward the house, a blanket of dark blue shadows fell over the two vehicles, twinkling with pinpricks of silver light like stars in a rural night sky. Sera stuck her hand out the truck's window, trailing her fingers through the midnight mist that enveloped them. On the inside, her hand and arms had an almost blueish tint, but when her fingers pierced through the mist, her skin looked its regular pasty white.

"It's so pretty," she said, turning to look at Theo. His and Lasirenn's skin also held a bluish tint now.

"What is?" Theo asked from the driver's seat, his eyes scouring the dark road ahead of them.

"Eshu's concealment spell over the cars."

He glanced around them before looking back at her with a quick smile. "Must be more of your Gift. Nothing looks different to me."

What else am I going to see now? she asked Bacchus, who sprawled across the tiny back seat Lasirenn had refused to sit in. But then again, so had Sera.

I guess we'll have to wait and see, the god said, deadpan.

That was terrible. Sera snorted at his failed attempt at humor.

A slurping sound was his only reply.

* * *

JUST OVER AN HOUR LATER, they pulled up to the new safe house. Located in a rural part of North Carolina, the house was much farther away from any neighbors than they'd have been in more suburban neighborhoods.

The ranch-style home was on a few acres of land and set back from the road with a long gravel driveway. A field of wild grass stuck out through the light covering of snow and spread out behind the house, separated from a line of trees by a creek.

This was exactly the kind of home Sera would love to settle in someday. She'd have to keep it in mind when the time came. Because the time *would* come. For now, it was enough that they were well hidden, especially with the added magic.

After the group stepped out of their two vehicles and said real hellos, they gathered in a circle around the silver cell containing Danae, discussing what to do with her.

"Do you want to keep her inside the house or the garage?" Theo asked, almost like they were trying to decide where to keep an old piece of furniture. Sera bit her lip to keep from giggling. Thinking of Danae in that way sure helped take her mind off the journey to come.

The garage was detached, which made Sera a little more nervous about the witch's potential escape, no matter how unlikely. But the thought of keeping her in the house, even in her current skeletal state, made Sera want to punch a wall or vomit. Maybe both.

"The garage," she said.

Danae smirked. "Are you scared of what little old me might have to say?"

"Can we put a muzzle on her, at least?" Nora asked, glaring up at the teenaged Bacchae.

Sera grinned. "Absolutely."

After finding a thin blanket in the garage and tearing off a strip, Nora wasted no time hopping into the cage to gag the Eternal. Snow began to fall once again, coating the ground and vehicles in a fresh dusting.

"Let's get her in the garage and go warm-up," Renee said, pulling her scarf up higher.

After they pushed the silver cell into the garage, Sera glanced back at the Bacchae witch who had made Sera's life hell. Her entire family and her friends' lives, too. The girl gazed back calmly over the thick strip of fabric across her mouth, not once arguing against the treatment. Not that it would have done her any good, anyway.

Someday, Sera would welcome the sight of that Bacchae's body dissolving into sparkling dust. Someday *soon*.

CHAPTER 9

Serafina

When the sun finally made its debut over the eastern horizon, the group of gods, immortals, and mortals gathered outside once again, only this time they headed into the field with some supplies. Lasirenn stayed back to keep watch on Danae.

Solomon had offered, but the fear of Danae using her *influence* or hive mind on him meant he couldn't be much help at the moment. Her *influence* was useless against the godly types.

Sera still didn't like the Bacchae her friend dated, but she tried for Nora's sake to curb her attitude toward him. Tried being the keyword. It was a start.

Sleep had evaded most of them. Since neither Nora nor Renee had merged with a god and using any form of magic took its toll on their bodies, they had rested in the back bedroom of the home. The others took turns keeping watch on the bound Eternal. Except for Sera because Theo knew she probably would have "accidentally" stabbed the girl.

Fair.

In the light of the rising sun, patchy grass in the field proved long since dead or dormant and now covered in at least a foot of snow. This region of the country didn't always see a white winter, but Sera much preferred grey and snowy to grey and rainy. That was just miserable.

They trudged through the dusty white powder to the circle of standing sticks in the middle of the field. Renee had had the foresight to lay down the salt and coal and mark it with sticks before the snow came down too thick overnight.

Always thinking ahead, that woman.

The field's location provided enough space for a large circle, wide enough to keep the horse Hel rode in on safely inside the salt and coal.

Renee, Nora, and Freyja took their places in front of the circle, motioning the others to stay back. Not that they needed much encouragement to do so. From what the witches and Solomon had said, Hel and her horse were terrifying.

Sera would soon find out.

In the past, she would have been stamping her feet and blowing warm air into the palms of her gloves to keep her face warm, but merging with a god meant she didn't feel the elements as she once had. She knew it was cold, could feel the ice down to her bones, but it didn't bother her. The sensation was odd and one that would probably take some time to get used to. Definitely a neat perk to immortality, though, as long as she didn't get frostbite.

Reminding herself of the pleasant parts of her new life helped her avoid the devastating reality of living forever.

There could be worse outcomes than spending a lifetime with yours truly, Bacchus said, leaning on her shoulder.

Yeah? Like what? she teased him back.

He was right, of course. Things could always be worse. She could be someone like Danae, or Lorenzo, or *Chad.* She could be homeless or starving or dying of some terrible disease. With Bacchus's essence blended with hers, she would never be any of those things.

But playful banter with the god kept her mood afloat.

Nora and Renee raised their arms toward the circle and chanted a spell in some unknown language. The words sounded a little like the Norwegian Sera had heard on travels, but she was no linguist. Not outside Greek and Latin, anyway.

As the women continued to chant, the words began to make sense. The women called upon the elements to bring forth the goddess of death.

Do you know all languages? Sera asked Bacchus, excitement rising with her quickened breath.

Being able to communicate with anyone, in their own language, would open up so many doors in the academic world. She didn't even care at that moment that she didn't really need an academic career anymore.

Probably. His nonchalant reply earned an eye roll from Sera.

An eerie silence blanketed the field as the branches and remaining leaves ceased to rustle, pulling Sera's attention back to the matter at hand. The wind had vanished, and the snow muffled any other sounds. Her skin prickled as magic filled the air.

Flames burst from the ground like an explosion, sending small rocks and dirt flying into the air before filling the circle completely. The fire incinerated the snow and grass in an instant, and the heat from the blaze warmed Sera's cheeks even from where she stood, at least ten feet back.

Before she could do little more than raise an arm, the flames receded to the edges of the circle, and the middle collapsed into a black, tar-like hole.

Whinnying so ghastly it nearly made her eyebrows stand on end sounded from within the murky pit. A gigantic black stallion with only three legs leaped through and landed on the scorched earth. Nora hadn't exaggerated her description in the slightest.

As the stallion stamped his red-hot hooves, the sickly scent of sulfur wafted off of him, making Sera's stomach churn. A woman wearing a hooded black robe sat sidesaddle, blonde hair tumbling in soft curls down to her waist from beneath the hood. The woman tilted her head up slightly, and Sera had to suppress her gasp.

The face within the hood was both beautiful and horrific—one half retained its youthful glow, with a rosy cheek, bright blue eye, and red lips. A lovely contrast to her pale white skin. The other half had long since died, an empty eye socket gazing out at them while her teeth were bared in an eternal, lipless grin. What little flesh remained sagged from her bones.

Terrifying was an understatement.

All four of the gods bowed their heads to the woman atop the horse with respect.

"Freyja, goddess of the Vanir," the voice that came from the woman's mouth was close to what Sera imagined a banshee must sound like—shrieking like a hundred wailing souls. She gritted her teeth and resisted the urge to cover her ears, sensing Theo shift beside her. Now she knew why Renee had worn earplugs.

"Why have you called me to the mortal realm this time?" the goddess of death asked.

Sera pressed her lips together, holding back the inappropriately timed giggle that wanted to escape. The way Hel had just spoken reminded Sera very much of her father, who would let out a heaving sigh after she had done something she shouldn't have. Again.

"Hel, we beseech you to show us the way to your realm so that we may rescue the witches Danae doomed as gifts to the Ordog." Freyja's chiming voice came from both Nora's mouth and, to Sera's godsight Gift, her own as she stood confidently next to Nora.

Hel regarded the group, showing no sign of discomfort as the three-legged horse stamped his massive hooves and nickered beneath her. Her one blue eye and the empty socket focused on Sera.

"You speak of this girl's mother, though I can sense she is no longer just a human girl." Hel's head tilted to one side.

Sera stepped forward, Bacchus moving to stand beside her. "You're correct that Bacchus and I have become one. I intend to bring my mom home, no matter the cost. She's suffered enough."

Bacchus raised his glass of wine in a toast toward Hel.

"The way to the underworld is easy," said the goddess. "The way through it is long. The way back out is...

demanding. I sense you speak the truth when you say no matter the cost, but I am not so sure you understand what that may entail."

Sera stood tall under the goddess's scrutinizing gaze. She would go with or without the goddess's help. But help would definitely be great.

"Very well," Hel said at last and inclined her head in respect. "I will assist you on your journey. The Ordog could use a reminder of his place within the realms of the dead. Seek out the cave from which your mother disappeared. Summon me within, and I will lead you to Helheim."

The oversized horse whinnied and reared back on his two hind legs. Hel barely moved to stay atop the stallion's back as he turned and leaped back into the hole, which promptly closed behind them. The fire snuffed out, leaving no trace other than the lack of snow and fire-scorched earth.

Sera's heart clenched with anguish and fresh hatred. Of course it would be the cave where her mom had disappeared. Was that when Danae first encountered the Ordog? Is that how she escaped, through the underworld?

A vague memory from one of the texts housed within the Budapest library popped into her mind. The beginning of an idea formed in its wake.

Sera ignored the others calling her name as she turned and stomped her way back to the garage, which held the Bacchae witch she wanted to kill. Bacchus stood in the doorway with a hand up to stop her, but she walked right through his shimmering form to face the girl in silver.

Sera strode up to the bars of the cage and stood in front of Danae, simply staring at her. Danae gazed back, her face as still as a statue.

Mere moments passed before Sera heard the others rush into the room, probably thinking she was going to kill Danae. She couldn't blame them for the thought—it had definitely crossed her mind.

"Sera, wait…" Nora began, out of breath, but stopped when she saw Sera just standing there.

"Don't worry, guys. I'm not going to kill her," Sera said. A smile tugged at her cheeks. "I've got something planned for her."

A flicker of uncertainty crossed Danae's features before she smothered it.

CHAPTER 10

Serafina

Now that they had Danae in custody and had a general idea of where to enter the underworld, Sera itched to get going. More than itched. Time was slipping away from her, from her mother, and every second felt like an eternity passed.

Danae had claimed the witches were still alive, and Bacchus had believed her. But that was over a month ago. A month more of torture they'd had to endure at the hands of the Ordog. Would Sera arrive too late to save her mother? To save anyone?

The cave where Danae had ambushed the witches was located in Cloudland Canyon State Park in Georgia. From the safe house in North Carolina, the drive would take eight-hours with light traffic and no stops. So, more like half a day realistically, especially considering the new checkpoints when anyone crossed state lines on the interstates. Bacchae movements were being tracked and recorded by the government, which caused extensive delays.

After confirming the route they'd take, Solomon and Theo transferred the silver cage holding the gagged Eternal from the garage and into a small moving truck. Renee had been able to procure the vehicle for cash and without paperwork the day before the French loaded the Bacchae girl into the cargo plane.

The cab of the truck was only large enough to seat two, so Theo drove with Sera alongside, as she was unwilling to be separated from the Eternal. No room for Lasirenn this time. Oh darn.

"Are you doing okay?" Theo asked an hour into their trip. They had ridden mostly in silence up until then.

Sera didn't move her gaze from the window, although she wasn't really paying attention to anything outside, anyway. She had been lost in her thoughts.

"I just don't know what to expect, you know?" she said.

How did one even prepare for the underworld? Maybe it was going to be like the myths and stories she studied in school. Was Charon going to be waiting next to the river Styx, ready to ferry them across?

If anything, it would be something from Norse mythology waiting for them. Damn, Sera really wished she had expanded her studies outside of Roman and Greek mythology. Even Bacchus only knew so much; he had been more focused on wine and nymphs and irritating Jupiter. Maybe Freyja could educate them.

"Did you hear me?" Theo asked, startling her out of her

thoughts once again.

She turned to look at him guiltily. "Uh, nope, sorry."

He chuckled and took a hand off of the wheel to hold one of hers. He entwined his fingers with hers and gave them a squeeze. "I said you worry too much."

"Maybe you worry too little," she teased back as butterflies danced in her stomach.

Someday soon, she looked forward to getting lost in very different thoughts. Sexy thoughts. "I was thinking maybe Freyja could tell us what Helheim will be like. Bacchus and I don't know enough about Norse mythology to wager a guess."

Theo gave a grunt of approval. The heat from hand seeped into hers, and she longed to feel his touch on more of her skin.

Freyja, can you give us a quick rundown on what we can expect to encounter in the underworld? Sera reached out with her thoughts to the Norse goddess to distract her from her own heat-inducing thoughts.

Her Gift really came in handy for moments like this, moments when it was difficult not to think about how long it had been since she'd been intimate.

As much as I can, darling, the musical voice replied. *Once you enter the cave leading below, you'll continue in darkness until you reach a torrential river. There, you'll cross a bridge. After that, you'll pass fields much as you'd see in the mortal world. It will end abruptly at a wall where the dead enter Helheim through a gate.*

Then what? Sera asked.

Then you go in, Freyja said simply, as if it should have been obvious. *But I have a vague memory telling me that you should not go through the gate yourselves. Only the dead can. So, you'll need to find another way in.*

So, Helheim is like a city? Sera asked.

I haven't the foggiest, sweetie. During the Viking Age, I ruled over Fólkvangr, where half of the souls slain in battle came to rest. I had very little reason to wonder about Helheim's happenings. I'm sure it was dreadfully dull.

Can we enter through Fólkvangr instead? Sera asked.

Not unless you're a Viking who has died in battle. Freyja laughed before her tone took on a more melancholy tone. *Sadly, no new souls have entered my hall for centuries. Helheim is unique in this aspect, as the majority of mortals believe in some sort of afterlife. It will continue until… well, I suppose until no one believes in anything anymore.*

Sera had a hard time believing that would ever come to pass, especially if the gods ever made themselves known to the mortal world. However, from what she'd been told, actively worshipped gods with many followers existed on a separate plane from this one. They were content to carry on with their divine lives without worrying about the mortals who swore they did.

Would they come back if everyone stopped believing in them? Or would they simply fade into myth like some of the old gods?

* * *

A COUPLE OF HOURS LATER, they pulled into a gas station a few miles outside of Columbia to fill up the vehicles.

"I'm going to go in for some snacks and coffee," Sera said to Theo as she pushed open the truck's door.

"Only you would keep eating and drinking when you

don't need to." He grinned at her before stepping out of the truck.

Sera would drink coffee until the end of time. Not for the caffeine, of course. She no longer needed the stuff to keep her energized and focused, but that didn't stop her from enjoying the flavor and mouthfeel of the brew, even gas station brew.

Or maybe she was just desperate for some sort of normalcy.

Nora walked over, stretching her arms above her head and letting out a giant yawn. "I hope they have some good magazines. This drive is getting boring."

She looped her arm through Sera's and led her into the shop. Spying the coffee counter, Sera headed that direction while Nora perused the books and magazines. This far out from the chaos and ruin the District had seen meant life had fully returned to normal. Sera was sure some of the locals questioned the whole Bacchic uprising like her father did. A government conspiracy designed to cover something up.

As Sera filled up her cup, the hairs on the back of her neck bristled as the few other shoppers glanced her way. Eshu had covered their group with a camouflage spell, but she had no clue what identity he had given her. Maybe she had two heads or something.

She held back a snicker, not wanting to look too much like a crazy lady laughing to herself, but it came out as a snort. So much for that idea.

Bacchus floated over to the onlookers with the long end of his toga draped over one arm to avoid dragging on the dirty floor—as if it mattered to his immaterial self. He peered over their shoulders. Such a creeper.

Doing her best to ignore the uneasy feeling settling around her the longer they stayed, Sera grabbed a lid for her coffee and headed to the register. The clerk, who couldn't have been a day over the age of nineteen, didn't bother to look up from his tablet as she paid. His backward placed trucker's cap sat haphazardly over his long, stringy blond hair and had some weird band logo on the back of it. Kids these days.

Yes, she was getting old.

Serafina, they know who you are, Bacchus whispered at her side.

She stifled a gasp at his sudden appearance, but the movement caused the clerk to glance up at her. He returned his gaze to his phone for a moment before his head snapped up again.

How? Sera asked, her anxiety shooting through the roof.

The spell failed, he said.

Only then did she realize she no longer saw the bluish tint to everything like she had back in the truck. She had just thought the camouflage spell worked differently than cloaking the vehicles. Apparently not.

She dropped a few bills on the counter and aimed for the door.

"Hey, wait, aren't you—" the clerk stood up, holding up his phone as if he was comparing her to a picture. Or about to take one.

Sera wouldn't quite call themselves celebrities, but, against their wishes, their pictures had been broadcast on all the major media as the heroes against the Bacchae invasion. Going to the grocery store in France had turned into a royal pain in the ass. Every other shopper stopped to thank her and ask questions. Nora even briefly had a stalker in the District.

Grocery delivery service had become a godsend.

From what they had seen online over the last twenty-four hours—or rather what they had *not* seen—no one knew who had abducted Danae. Sera was sure there were a few educated American officials who would have a pretty good idea it was the gods, although they wouldn't have any proof to back their theory up. They had helped cover up the incident rescuing Manny on the District interstate, after all.

But Sera and the others didn't need to broadcast their location to the world and make it easy to track them down.

Freyja, tell Nora we need to go, Sera thought to the goddess using her godspeak Gift, ducking her head beneath her arm to hide from the potential photo. *Now. They know who we are.*

Eshu! What the hell happened? Sera called out in her mind as she pushed the door open.

The sudden wind whipped across her face, making her eyes water. Through the blur, she spotted the trickster god leaning against the hood of a bright white BMW full of snow bunnies, arms crossed and oblivious to her concern.

Not the four-legged kind of bunny, but the kind that tanned all year then dressed up in skin-tight clothing to show off their sleek physiques on the snowy slopes.

Three women sat inside the vehicle while one pumped gas in white pants so tight they must have been painted on. Eshu clearly admired the shapely view, not that Sera could blame him.

She had been mildly jealous of women who displayed their confidence for the world to see like a piece of artwork. Her pale skin would never hold a coffee and creamer color the way she wanted, only a lovely lobster hue. And working out at a gym long enough to form defined muscles was the least of her priorities while in school.

But that was before her world had been rocked with the introduction of the Roman god now forever a part of her. Now she just hoped those girls would continue to enjoy such leisurely activities in this new, supernatural world.

Eshu looked over at Sera as the clerk ran out behind her.

"Are vampires for real?" the clerk asked, his phone raised.

"Hey! Didn't anyone tell you it's rude to take someone's picture without asking?" Nora asked.

The clerk jumped from her ninja-like appearance by his side. She barely came up to the lanky kid's ribs, but still managed to grab the phone out of his outstretched hand.

"Give me back my phone," he snapped, reaching toward her.

Solomon chose that moment to make himself known, his eyes flashing red while his fangs extended from his mouth.

"I wouldn't if I were you."

CHAPTER 11

Serafina

The gas station attendant gulped as he snatched his hand back and gawked at Solomon. "Fuck, dude."

Guess he had never seen one of the Bacchae in the fang before. To be fair, Sera had had a similar reaction back when she first saw Solomon's extended canines when he ambushed her on the District streets. But back then, she had only learned about the Bacchae a few minutes prior, and the rest of the world was still in the dark. This kid had the upper hand.

Oh, shit, Eshu said as he pushed himself off the BMW and snapped his fingers. The coins collected along his belt clinked as he moved. *My bad.*

Everyone that had gathered to watch shook themselves as if waking from a dream, a bit confused before they shrugged and continued on with their day.

The clerk blinked a few times at Nora and Solomon, who had returned to his human features. "Uh, did you ask me a question?"

Nora's blonde curls bounced as she shook her head, her cheeks still pink with anger.

"You dropped your phone," she said as she handed the device back. She and Solomon followed Sera back to the car and truck.

"Let's hope no one actually took a photo or recorded anything," Renee said when they had all gathered beside the two vehicles.

"We need to leave," Theo said. "Eshu, we can't afford a slipup like that again."

Tell him not all of us have that man's… Eshu looked Sera up and down, appraising her. *Patience.*

She snorted. *Not like you could have done anything with those girls, anyway.*

Watching is half the fun, doll.

She ignored Eshu's ringing laughter as they all climbed back into the two vehicles and got back on the road. That had been far too close a call for comfort.

* * *

Solomon

IN THE BACKSEAT OF the used sedan Renee drove, Solomon pulled Nora to him, wrapping an arm around her petite shoulders. Kissing the top of her head, he breathed in the comforting oatmeal scent that held just a hint of coconut.

"You know, I can kind of take care of myself now. I don't need a knight in shining armor," Nora said as she snuggled closer. "I appreciate the gesture, though."

He chuckled. "You could always take care of yourself, but that doesn't mean I don't want to protect you."

Solomon could still feel his pulse racing. The kid had done little more than try to get his phone back, and Solomon had been ready to tear him limb from limb. What would he do to keep Nora safe when he became mortal again, when he didn't have his supernatural strength and speed? How would he protect their children?

The thought chilled him to the bone.

He would become mortal, for Nora. For them. There was no question about that. Nora wanted to have kids—a feat of which Immortals of all kinds were incapable—and he wanted to be a part of that journey with her. But he would need to ensure his mortal body was worthy of her and capable of keeping her safe, even if she did have a goddess's help.

With any luck, he would retain his skill and muscle memory with weapons when he became mortal again. If not, training would be among his top priorities.

It didn't help his mood that he knew firsthand just what type of atrocities humankind was capable of, what *he* was capable of. But after his change he would also have Immortals to fear, even more so now that they were out of the shadows. He wasn't as worried about the gods and witches—the gods didn't seem to care much unless something affected them, and Nora had turned out to be quite skilled with her magical abilities. Pride surged within him, and he laid his cheek on Nora's head, earning a contented purr.

Yes, she did have magic and Freyja for the time being. Perhaps she'd be the one protecting *him*. His mood darkened with the snow-filled clouds. But what if mortality changed him? What if she no longer loved him in a year, in ten years?

The hours flew by on their way to Cloudland Canyon State Park in Georgia. Solomon continued to brood on the truth and dangers of mortal life, stroking Nora's hair as she dozed across his lap.

* * *

THE DRIVE THROUGH THE state park was breathtaking at times. Or Solomon was sure it would have been if he could focus on anything other than his imminent separation from the woman he loved and wanted to protect at all costs. He knew he was protecting her heart by giving up his Immortal blood—if he succeeded—but he continued to clench his teeth anyway.

Second-guessing things was not his usual style, and the failure to predict the right path irked him to no end.

When they found the trail that would lead them toward the cave, they got out of the vehicles to travel the rest of the way on foot. Each of them carried a backpack or satchel filled with supplies, some magical and some tactical. No one was quite sure what would be needed in the underworld, and they could always remove unnecessary items after speaking with Hel.

Solomon had packed several bottles of blood as a safety precaution. Becoming too hungry amongst friends was far from wise. He also needed to be as powerful as possible for whatever journey lay ahead of him. Working for Lorenzo, bottling blood wasn't new to Solomon, but being able to waltz into a store and plunk down cash for it certainly was. Granted, he only knew of the one store so far, but it was a start.

Perhaps he'd be able to heat the blood with the fires of hell.

When everyone was ready, Theo opened the back of the truck holding Danae's cage, and Serafina hopped inside. Wisely, she approached the silver enclosure with caution. The Eternal had been able to work her gag free.

"I hope I don't need to remind you that you're in the presence of several gods and goddesses," Serafina said to the ancient Immortal.

"Several gods and goddesses with human hosts, you mean," Danae said with a tilt of her head to the side. "Not in their full glory anymore, are they?"

Serafina rolled her eyes as she unlocked the cell and opened the door. After snapping off the chain attaching Danae's ankle shackles together, Serafina grabbed the end of the chains securing the Eternal's straitjacket-style uniform and tugged at her to come out. When she was within arms' distance, Serafina pulled the gag back over the girl's mouth and tightened it.

No sign of pain crossed Danae's face, but the tightness would be uncomfortable at the very least.

Solomon didn't hate the woman who once called herself queen the way the others did, but he certainly understood why they did. She was capable of atrocities the others didn't know about and probably couldn't imagine.

Still, none of her wrath had been targeted at Solomon until the end, but he also understood her motives. As a rule of thumb, he typically reserved his hate for those who turned their attacks on him directly. Like Lorenzo.

When Serafina jumped down from the truck, he tensed. While Solomon didn't anticipate the Eternal making any attempts to flee, he also couldn't be sure.

His concern was in vain. The witch didn't even make an attempt to survey the area for an escape route after she followed Serafina. She remained calm and impassive, letting her gaze drift from person to person. The nonchalance of her behavior unsettled him.

The hairs on the back of his neck rose when her eyes settled on his, her power almost tangible in her gaze. She moved on without a sound when Serafina pulled at the chains, and they followed Renee into the forest.

Other than a few birds chirping overhead and the crunching of footsteps through the snow, the woods were quiet. Towering trees spread evergreen canopies over the ground below, and an occasional breeze came through, knocking fresh snow drifts down from some of the naked tree limbs beneath.

As they hiked up the steep slope of the canyon, deeper into the forest and closer to the rocky outcroppings where Renee said the cave would be, Solomon held Nora's gloved hand. He helped her step over fallen limbs and large rocks covered in ice barring their way. She and Renee were bundled up against the cold weather, experiencing it in a way the rest of the group didn't with their immortal blood.

He noticed the ever-clumsy Serafina seemed to be doing just fine on her own for once, even while keeping

Danae on a short leash. Merging with Bacchus had done the girl some good in that department. He held back a chuckle but made a mental note to tell Nora about his observation later.

He slowed his pace for the briefest of moments as he realized he didn't know when later might be. The underworld itself didn't frighten him; he had already lived in hell as a human child born into slavery. But he wasn't sure how long they would be gone and if he would even find the answer he needed to become mortal.

What would happen to Nora and him if he failed?

Watching her grow old and wither away while he maintained his eternal youth wasn't going to happen, nor was her merging with Freyja. She wanted children, and there was no chance he'd make her give up that dream. They hadn't discussed adoption, but it could be an option. If not, he would do the right thing and break it off with her, even if the very thought made his heart clench in agony.

The rest of the group made idle chit chat as they hiked, heightened nerves keeping everyone from having more in-depth conversations. Nora, like Solomon, remained silent, presumably just as lost in thought about what this descent to Helheim meant for them as he was.

"We're almost there," Renee said after an hour, her breath coming out hard and fast with the exertion from the steep climb.

They had been following, and in some cases hugging, a rock wall as it curved around the mountain. Not traversing a ledge, per se, but the ground leading back into the trees looked nearly vertical from this vantage point. No one wanted to experience *that* slip.

As they rounded the next outcropping, Renee led the group toward a sheer rock face, squinting against the howling wind. The angle of the rocks created a pretty fierce wind tunnel, making Solomon's eyes water.

He opened his mouth to suggest finding a better place to stop for a rest when Renee kept walking *into* the rock face as if it didn't exist. When her body passed through, Solomon's eyes widened as the rock wavered like it was made of jelly.

She came out again a moment later, a grin across her face. "Surprise."

The rest of the group shared Solomon's nervous laugh.

Renee held her scarf to her face against the biting wind. "We've all been so tense since the escape, I thought a little fun was to be had by not warning you."

"Well played," Theo said with a smile.

"It was that way when we arrived two decades ago. The cave has been hidden by magic," Renee explained. "I can only assume by the gods and goddesses of the underworld to keep the location secret."

"Should we summon Hel outside or in?" Serafina asked, pushing a strand of loose hair back behind her ear in a nervous habit, though the wind knocked it loose a moment later.

The girl hadn't shaken all her mortal ticks yet.

"Let's head inside in case anyone is hiking nearby," Renee said. "Don't want to cause alarm with a visit from a giant three-legged horse and a half-dead woman. Plus, it's freezing out here."

As if in reply, the wind howled through again, whipping her scarf out in front of her.

Theo hung back as the rest of the group ducked inside, almost all of them reaching a hand out to feel for the wall which didn't exist before trusting themselves to step through. The scene would have been comical to Solomon if it weren't such a tense situation.

The detective's nostrils flared, and he glanced around warily.

"You sense something?" Solomon asked when it was just the two of them remaining outside.

He didn't feel anything off, but he didn't have a god's help either. Not fully. His semi-divine blood had been diluted through the later Bacchae creations, and Lorenzo had never been a prized specimen.

"I'm not sure," Theo said, his eyebrows furrowed. "Something doesn't feel quite right, but it could just be the magic concealing the cave."

"Want me to hang back and keep an eye out?" Solomon asked. He didn't like the thought of not being by Nora's side, but he also knew it'd be best to have all the gods inside.

"Nah. I'm sure I'm just on edge. We all are." Theo gave a small smile.

With one last glance at the surrounding trees, still seeing and sensing nothing out of the ordinary, Solomon followed Theo inside.

CHAPTER 12

Serafina

After ducking through the faux rock wall entryway, Sera marveled at the sheer size of the cave, which was hidden from the mortal world's eyes. A little light filtered in from outside.

The chamber stretched wide and deep with a domed ceiling at least fifteen feet high, allowing all of them to move around comfortably. Puddles of muddy water filled small dips in the ground where the snow had blown in and melted in the warmer, almost sauna-like air.

If Sera ever found herself on the run from law enforcement or from another villain trying to fill Danae's soon-to-be-empty shoes, she would keep this cave in mind as the perfect hideout. She glanced at the Eternal's prison-issued sneakers, glad to be rid of the girl's stilettos. Those had been weapons all on their own with their silver-coated heels. Fashionable yet deadly.

Maybe Sera *should* have taken them as a memento.

About twenty yards in, the cave abruptly ended at a smooth rock face, similar to the fake one outside the cave. The only other exit was a much smaller tunnel, not even waist-high, that led into the pure darkness that existed deep underground. They would need to crawl through to keep going. Hopefully not for too long.

Sera's skin prickled at the idea of spiders lurking within the dark crevices, and there might even be bat guano coating the ground. While she was used to getting muddy on dig sites, the idea of crawling in literal poop made her wrinkle her nose. She had standards, damn it. She'd have to hope the magic concealing the cave also kept out the bats.

Who knew, maybe there was another secret entrance Renee didn't know about. She mentally crossed her fingers and toes.

You and me both, Bacchus said as he sniffed the air, his lip curling in distaste. *I do not enjoy sharing your sense of smell.*

Her god-enhanced vision adjusted to the darkness of the cave the farther back they went. Night may not have fallen, but gloomy wintry clouds had gathered overhead as they hiked, ready to let fresh snow fall upon the mountain. She was thankful she had Bacchus's eyes to guide her steps.

In fact, they all had immortal help of some kind to help them see in the cave without flammable or battery-operated assistance.

Glancing back over her shoulder toward the entrance of the cave, a waterfall of wavering glass shielded the way in—the magic hiding the cave from the world. The mood was contemplative as everyone took in their new surroundings.

Markings on the wall nearest to Sera caught her eye. No one said a word as she let the chain holding Danae slip from her hand and approached what turned out to be scorch marks on the smooth rocks. Magical flames had made these streaks and scores, here for eternity.

Sera trailed her fingers across one in particular, a smoky outline of a hand, delicate and small. Like her mother's had been. Her fingers tingled from the magical residue, and Bacchus's memories from twenty years ago flooded her mind.

The truth hit Sera hard.

This was where her mother had been and where her mother had been taken prisoner. Where she could have died. A chill spider-walked up Sera's spine. She stood where her mother had on her last day in the mortal world. Now, Sera was closer than she had ever been before to hugging her mother again.

And yet how much farther did she have to go to see her freed? She gritted her teeth against the fresh pain that washed through her.

The day would come when that pain would be gone, when it would be replaced by love and hope. It was close. Sera clenched her fists in front of her. So close.

When she turned back around to face the group, she knew tears wet her cheeks, but she held her head high, her shoulders back.

She was ready.

"What next?" Sera asked, ignoring the slight quiver in her voice.

"We summon Hel," Renee answered without hesitation.

She and Nora hurried to pour the salt and coal in a circle large enough to contain the giant horse the goddess rode while also allowing the rest of the group to hang back a few feet.

Sera may have seen the beast and its rider once before, but her heart still beat faster at the thought of facing it again, especially in such a confined space. That was one frightening creature, and the rider wasn't much better.

After reminding everyone else to stand back, the two mortal witches took their places next to the circle. They raised their arms and chanted the old Norse words that would summon the goddess.

As the spell took hold, the air was sucked from the cavern, constricting Sera's lungs. A breathless, panic-stricken moment later, the ground inside the salt and coal circle burst into flames. Reaching up, the fire licked the rock ceiling hungrily before it settled and withdrew to just the outer ring. Shadows danced along the walls as the simmering flames continued to burn. The middle of the circle collapsed into a black hole, deep and dark and endless.

The stallion's whinny echoed within the hole's depths before the black beast leaped forth, landing on his three legs before them but still within the circle. Sera shuddered. The last thing they needed was to set that creature loose on the world.

Hel sat atop the horse, sidesaddle, the bottom of her black robe nearly sweeping the ground as the beast stamped angrily beneath her, his hooves scorching the cavern ground. She laid a hand, the one that was still alive and covered with flesh, on the stallion's neck, and he settled with a final snort. The smell of rotten eggs wafting off the creature stung Sera's nostrils in the enclosed space.

The goddess turned toward them, the hood of her robe falling back. Seeing her half-dead face before in no way prepared Sera for seeing it again—a gasp slipped out anyway.

"Greetings once again, Freyja, goddess of the Vanir," Hel's wailing voice echoed in the cave, dust and small rocks shaking loose from the walls and ceiling. "And to Xolotl, Eshu, Mami Wata."

Each of the gods tilted their heads to the goddess in turn.

Her one eye settled on Sera before drifting to the Roman god standing next to Sera. "And to Bacchus, the one who has required us all to gather here in the first place."

Sera had no idea whether the pale goddess had made a joke or not, not with half her face being dead and all. Bacchus raised his wine glass in Hel's direction.

"Who will accompany you to the realm of the dead?" the goddess asked, directing her gaze toward Sera again.

"Only the immortals—Theodore, Solomon, and Lasirenn." Sera didn't feel the need to mention Danae. The less she had to speak of the girl or even acknowledge her existence, the better.

Hel nodded. "Then you shall be able to return here without sacrifice."

Sera's heart dropped into her stomach. The goddess confirmed what Danae had said. Part of her had still hoped the witch had been lying, even though Sera had already merged with Bacchus. Out of her periphery, she could see Danae's smirk. Sera clenched her fists by her sides, hating that the bitch hadn't been lying.

"Those of you who will stay behind, I wish you well," Hel said. "The rest of you, listen closely. The way to Helheim is fairly straight-forward, but you will need to take this with you."

She produced a ring with a twist of her wrist, from up her sleeve or out of thin air. Neat trick either way. From her distance, Sera couldn't make out any of the details except it was old and black, perhaps made of iron.

"When you reach a fork, the ring's presence will open the veil to the realms beneath, allowing you to access the road to Helheim. Without it, you would simply become lost within the depths of the earth."

Not a terrifying concept at all, Sera thought, her nostrils flaring out.

"You will come to the fork early on," Hel said. "Be sure to go left."

"What's to the right?" Theo asked.

Hel's living eye rolled to look at him. "The Ordog's lair. Every religion on this earth uses entrances to the underworld like this one. Once the Ordog became synonymous with Christ's devil, his realm was able to branch out and connect with all of the others, allowing mortals to stumble upon it even without an object like this ring to open the veil.

"Be forewarned, due to the number of humans who fear him as the devil, whether or not they know his true identity, he will not be easy to defeat. It is far easier to fear hell than worship the divine.

"Should he escape his realm, hell will rain down on Earth."

A chill ran down Sera's back as Hel's blue eye turned to

look at her again with this final warning. They were back to saving the world.

* * *

Solomon

NOTHING HAD SEEMED suspicious about the inside of the cave. Yet, Solomon couldn't shake the feeling they were being watched as Hel gave them directions to her hall. Perhaps Theo's wariness outside had unsettled Solomon as well.

Nothing smelled or looked out of the ordinary. He glanced at Danae out of habit, having spent weeks by her side before her downfall. She remained as impassive as ever.

And yet.

The goddess of death leaned down to hand Serafina the ring.

"I'm not sure if anyone else is picking up on anything," Solomon said, "but I'm getting a bad—" his sentence was interrupted by a fireball whooshing through the hidden entrance, landing inches away from his feet.

The blast threw him backward, heat blazing against his skin, and the smell of burning hair filling his nostrils. He quickly completed the tumble and leaped to his feet, his fangs extended. Dust and broken rocks fell around him.

Glancing toward Nora out of instinct, relief rushed through him. She stood with her hands out in front of her, encompassed and protected by a shimmering pink bubble.

The war goddess within her acted fast.

Outside the cave, the world erupted with Immortals, coming from all sides and angles, their fangs bared and claws readied for battle. Guns were virtually useless against the god-saddled humans, and these Immortals seemed to know enough not to bother.

That was a bad sign.

The Immortals moved into the cave in a coordinated attack as they streamed through the faux rock wall without hesitation, groups of five or more aiming for each of the gods and the water spirit. Ancient gods they might be, but invincible they were not. Not anymore, anyway.

A dreadful whinny echoed around the cavern, drawing Solomon's attention back to the goddess of the dead. A fist-sized rock had fallen into the coal and salt circle surrounding the helhest, breaking the binding. The beast reared back, fighting against the reins as Hel held him back. A wild stallion wanting its freedom.

From within the dark pit that had brought forth Hel, clawed hands gripped the sides, about to climb out.

Fear, unlike anything he had known before, gripped Solomon's insides as he smelled scorched skin and dried blood beneath the blackened claws. Flesh from some unfortunate victim hung off of more than one talon. He had no interest in becoming a victim, nor allowing anyone else to.

"Close the circle!" Solomon roared as he ran to the edge of the hole and stomped on the closest set of hands. A squeal came from the dark before the hands disappeared into the depths.

Another fireball blast whooshed through the cave,

smashing against the magical shield surrounding Nora and Renee. Their barrier exploded into shimmering pink sparks, sending Renee tumbling.

The helhest let out a high-pitched squeal before Hel wrestled it under control and directed it to dive back into the chasm. Hel tossed the ring toward Serafina before the hole sealed itself behind the goddess. After a brief fumble, Serafina closed her fist around the ring.

The scent of rotting garbage made its way to Solomon's nose, and he bared his teeth in disgust as he recognized the stench.

Leif.

That goddamn witch had been a thorn in Solomon's side for far too long. He should have killed the man the last time Solomon saw him in the District, before the crazed man had his meeting with Danae. Especially now that Solomon knew he had abducted Nora. Killing him then would have saved all of them a lot of trouble.

Was Leif trying to rescue Danae, or was he still after a god to call his very own?

"Go!" Nora yelled at Solomon, pushing him toward the smaller tunnel. "We'll hold them off with Freyja's help and seal the tunnel. I'll tell Sera and Theo." Her eyes glazed over for the briefest of moments.

Serafina's head snapped toward him, and she nodded. She yanked on the chain holding Danae and ran toward the small tunnel leading farther into the earth, practically dragging the laughing Eternal behind her.

A roar split the air, causing more rocks to crumble to the ground. Solomon dove out of the way of one large boulder about to fall on him. As Solomon coughed and waved away the dust, Theo shifted into his monstrous canine form and decapitated one of the Bacchae attackers in the process.

"Theo!" Solomon yelled in the dog's direction.

He didn't get to finish his warning. Another blast knocked him off his feet, causing him to tumble down the tunnel after Serafina, rocks falling all around him.

CHAPTER 13

Serafina

Coughing out the dust filling the air, Sera peeked an eye open, hoping she wasn't dead for real. At first, she saw only darkness—the eerie, all-consuming black existing inside the bowels of the earth. Her eyes adjusted as the divine part of her genetics took over, and a golden haze covered everything in the narrow tunnel.

She knew her eyesight had enhanced with her merge, but this was like god-powered night vision goggles. Another little perk of immortality she would cling to.

The passage into hell had been carved into a dome leading farther and farther down. Walls worn smooth over time held a glossy sheen, including the path she sat on, and Sera couldn't help but wonder if some kind of giant slug roamed these depths to keep the tunnels so clean. Or snakes.

She shuddered and let go of pursuing that train of thought.

A figure lay on the ground a few feet away, not moving. Solomon was getting back to his feet, wiping blood off his mouth with the back of his hand. Danae smirked at them both as if nothing had occurred. Thankfully, the witch's mouth was still gagged and her chains intact. How she had remained on her feet was beyond Sera.

The two Bacchae didn't seem to have any trouble seeing in the dim light their god-like vision provided. Bacchus himself was guzzling wine like it was going out of style.

How the hell had Leif known about their plan?

Sera opened her clenched fist, letting out a breath in relief. She still had the ring from Hel. The band sat heavy in her hand, and warm, as if the runes etched into the black iron let off heat. After slipping the ring onto a finger, surprised it was a snug fit, she glanced back the way they had come.

Apparently, the tunnel they had needed to crawl through to get where they were now was only a few feet long before it opened back up to standing height. The darkness had hidden this tunnel well. Boulders blocked the way back through toward the exit of the cave, sending goosebumps up Sera's arms as she realized the similarities to her mother's experience two decades prior. Trapped inside a cave leading to hell with a bloodthirsty immortal witch. At least this time, Danae was bound and gagged.

Silver linings. Literally.

Moving with caution, Sera crawled across the rock-strewn floor to the figure lying still. Was it one of their own or one of the Bacchae? If it was the latter, it would most likely be alive. If not...

Her enhanced vision didn't provide enough light to be able to see who the figure was yet, so she called forth a thread of magic from within herself to ignite a golden orb in her hand, illuminating the tunnel. Holding her breath in anticipation, Sera rolled the figure onto its back.

It was Renee, and she was still breathing.

Thank the gods, Sera thought, sitting back on her heels.

I'd say you're welcome, but..., Bacchus said, though his voice lacked its usual merriment.

Her relief at Renee being alive was short-lived as dread poured into Sera's heart like a thick sludge. According to both Danae and Hel, only an immortal could enter the underworld and get back out alive again. And despite her powerful magic, Renee was not immortal.

She stirred as Sera brushed dirt off the woman's clothes. Holding a hand to her scraped up forehead, Renee sat up with Sera's help. "Ouch."

"Seriously," Sera said. She waited for the other woman to realize where she was, not really wanting to be the bearer of bad news.

Renee glanced around, her eyes confused until she focused on the boulders blocking the way out.

"Well, this isn't good, is it?" Her small smile quivered at the corners.

Solomon offered his hands to help them both back up to their feet. Although she appreciated the gesture, Sera declined his offer and stood on her own. He was still the enemy as far as she was concerned. Well, more like an annoying acquaintance at this point. Regardless, she wasn't banged up like Renee was.

"No one else made it but us," he said.

Sera clenched her fists to keep herself from throttling or beheading Danae, sure the witch had something to do with the attack. Theo and Lasirenn should have been here, not Renee. It was going to be one difficult task to get her mother and the other witches free from the Ordog, but now they needed to figure out how to get Renee back out, too. Without the additional god power.

And just how deep would Lasirenn be able to sink her snake-like fangs into Theo by the time Sera returned?

Fuck!

I have wine if you need it, Bacchus said, conjuring another full glass of red wine and holding it out to her.

She waved his hand away and looked around. There was still another option. "Where's Eshu?"

Renee reached up to her neck, her face crestfallen as she felt beneath her scarf. "His key is gone."

A quick search of the narrow tunnel proved fruitless, and Eshu himself was nowhere to be seen or heard. Other than the large rocks blocking their way back out, there wasn't much else in the tunnel for a key to hide behind. The walls were smooth and had a glossy sheen to them.

"It must have fallen off outside before the opening collapsed," Solomon said.

Double fuck! There went Sera's great idea. If Renee made the decision to merge with Eshu before they entered the underworld, she'd be able to get back out again. But what if the key hadn't fallen off before the collapse? What if Eshu's relic was trapped beneath these boulders?

Sera placed a hand on the giant rocks, ready to force her way through if necessary. A forcefield of energy blocked her first attempt as if she were trying to bust through a cement wall as a mortal. Impossible.

It's been sealed by divine magic, Bacchus explained, leaning against a boulder.

The thought triggered an image of Nora... and Theo. She did her best not to think about the others and whether or not they had survived the attack. She couldn't let herself dwell on what she couldn't fix. Not yet, anyway. First, find her mother. Then, escape. And if necessary, come back and dig the key out.

But if anything *did* happen to the others, there would be hell to pay. She'd bring a damned demon back with her if she had to. Leif would get what was coming to him, one way or another.

"We'll figure it out, kiddo," Renee said as she patted Sera on the shoulder. "We've made it this far."

Sera nodded, drawing on the other woman's optimism for strength. "Alright. Let's get going."

She nudged Danae forward to lead the way farther into the tunnel. She didn't need to trust the Eternal not to run. There was only one way to go—down. Into the belly of the mountain. The very Earth itself. And if the ancient girl fell off the edge of a hidden ravine into never-ending darkness... oh well.

The air grew even damper as they walked, and the walls wept with the condensation. The golden orb of light Sera had created generated enough of a glow for everyone to see comfortably enough not to trip or step in any puddles.

When the tunnel forked a few minutes into their descent, just as Hel said it would, they went left as the goddess had directed. The runes etched into the otherwise simple iron band on her finger glowed as they entered the new tunnel.

Though she tried not to, Sera couldn't resist casting a glance down the right side as she passed. A warm breeze stirred cobwebs, their wispy strings reaching out like ghosts, but nothing else moved in the sinister-looking tunnel.

They could hurry this entire process up by going straight to the Ordog's lair. Going to Helheim first was only slowing them down. She didn't even know how long it would take them to get to the goddess's city, nor how much time they would lose getting to hell after that.

Why were they making such a long detour? They should just…

Despite the warm cave air, a deep chill passed through her body as she identified the unnatural pull calling to her from the other tunnel.

No. She would face the Ordog on her terms. Not his.

Time passed as they walked and squeezed past rock formations barring the path, but Sera had no clue how much time. The monotony of their journey drained her sense of progress until she was sure it had been several hours. Or maybe just one. It couldn't have been a day yet, she was sure. Almost sure. Maybe half of one?

She wondered where they might be beneath the world and where they might end up. They didn't need a map in this tunnel, thankfully, as there was only one path and one direction to go. Down.

While she, Solomon, and Danae didn't show any signs of slowing down, Renee started to lag before long. She didn't have the help of a god anymore, and she had refused Solomon's offer to carry her on his back, not wanting to be a burden to anyone.

But even with divine genetics, Sera was going a bit stir-crazy in the endless, monotonous passage to Helheim. Doubt plagued her with each step. How was she going to face the Ordog—and win—without Theo's help? They had become a team, and now she was headed straight into the devil's lair. The same devil who had been able to grant Danae use of his death magic while he remained trapped below ground. Goosebumps rushed over her arms and neck as she shivered.

How vast was his power to be able to do such a thing?

This is the wrong kind of self-talk to be having, Bacchus said gently.

Agreeing with him, Sera shook her head to clear her thoughts. As she opened her mouth to halt the group to take a rest, an odd rumbling caught her attention, vibrations felt underfoot. The sound vaguely reminded her of the wind chimes her mom used to collect on her travels, only this noise was harsher and becoming much louder the farther they walked.

"What in the gods' name is that?" Renee asked.

Pulling Danae along behind her this time, Sera rushed forward with renewed energy as something new finally broke up the tedium of their journey. The tunnel ended abruptly at the entrance of a large cavern. Stalactites hung from the jagged ceiling high above Sera's head, dripping moisture onto the ground at her feet.

"Whoa," Renee said as she stepped up next to Sera and adjusted her glasses.

Directly in front of them just a few yards away, the cave floor dropped out of sight. A stone bridge, wide enough that it would have allowed a car to cross, spanned the breadth of the chasm, its other end disappearing into mist and shadows.

Sera gritted her teeth as she approached the edge of the chasm. The noise below hurt her ears like nails on a chalkboard, only a hundred times worse. Keeping her feet firmly planted, Sera looked down over the pit, her eyes opening wide.

What she thought would be a black, bottomless abyss was actually a river. Except not so much a river as it was a metal-filled conveyer belt. Weapons of every size and type washed by in a deafening clatter as various metals and woods crashed against each other. What was moving them?

Sera couldn't get a glimpse below the surface to find out. There were just too many, all fighting for a spot on top.

"Over and onward, right?" Renee asked, a slight shake to her voice. Probably from equal parts fear and exhaustion.

Sera reached over and took the other woman's hand. "Right. We'll rest soon."

"We can rest here," Solomon said, gesturing to the flat ground around the bridge. It would have made a decent campsite.

"No," Renee said, "It's much too loud, even for my tired bones."

Sera squeezed her hand before letting it go. Her friend wasn't alone in that thought.

After prodding Danae ahead of her—just in case the stones crumbled—Sera started the ascent up the bridge. At least the structure looked sturdy considering what flowed beneath it. A shudder ran up Sera's spine. Falling into *that* river would surely be deadly.

She tried not to overthink what lay beneath them until they were midway over. At the highest point, Sera glanced over the edge, unable to resist. Her mouth ran dry as the weapons whooshed by until they disappeared under a rocky ledge into total darkness.

The real abyss.

As they started down the other side of the bridge, unable to see the end due to the fog, a hazy figure appeared before them, coming up through the mist. A *giant* hazy figure.

Sera reached to her side to casually rest her hand on her gun, although she really wasn't positive it would do her much good in the land of the dead, nor against a giant. She may just have to rely on Bacchus's skills instead.

Sera snuck a glance at Solomon who had narrowed his eyes, his jawline tight. Her own muscles tightened in readiness, her lips pressing together. For once, she was glad to have him by her side.

Nora would be gloating before long.

Bacchus glided up next to Sera on his floating chaise before he stepped down onto the stones of the bridge. The chaise poofed in a cloud of mist that drifted away over the river. The Roman god didn't look concerned, but his actions spoke for him.

The giant turned out to be a giantess. Long, pale blonde hair fell beside her shoulders in two intricate braids. She wore clothes and armor of the Viking Age—fur-lined boots, hide pants, and a large fur cloak draped over shoulders where it was clasped at her collarbone with a skull brooch. Leather vambraces and greaves hugged her limbs, and two battle axes that appeared almost as tall as Nora crossed over her back. Sera gulped.

The colossus of a woman regarded their group with

sharp, crystal blue eyes, a color that reminded Sera of a frozen lake. Though her demeanor was not one of anger, the newcomer made it clear she wasn't there just to greet them.

"You are not the color of the dead," her voice boomed through the cavern, shaking small rocks loose. "And yet, three of you are not mere mortals either. Explain yourselves."

Sera stepped forward. "I am Serafina Finch, merged with the god Bacchus of the Roman pantheon. With me are the immortal Bacchae Solomon and Danae, and the human witch Renee Colette."

The giantess assessed each of them as Sera spoke their names and bowed in Bacchus's direction beside Sera. The god tilted his head in return, a full wine glass swirling into being in his hand.

"Welcome to *Gjallarbrú*. I am Móðguðr." Pebbles landed at their feet as she spoke. "What is your purpose in the land of the dead?"

"This Bacchae," Sera said with a tug on the silver chains, making Danae stumble forward and earning herself a glare from the girl, "condemned a dozen witches to the Ordog, still alive. We're here to retrieve them."

And we seek the Holy Grail, Bacchus said with a giggle.

The giantess frowned at Bacchus, who had the wisdom to swallow his remaining laughter.

"Why did you come by way of Hel?" she asked.

"Hel herself was going to lead us to the gates and then to the realm of the Ordog," Sera explained, displaying the iron band on her finger, "but we were separated at the entrance."

Móðguðr nodded. "Very well. You have been deemed

worthy to pass." She stepped to the side, and Sera pushed Danae forward once again.

The woman put out a large hand to stop the Eternal, her forearm encased in a leather vambrace the length of Sera's leg and etched with Viking runes. "Except this one."

"With all due respect, we need her to show us the way to the Ordog," Sera said, her pulse quickening.

She did *not* want to fight this behemoth of a woman. Especially considering the giantess was in a full set of armor and probably had a few thousand years or more of experience using those axes.

"Then she must prove herself worthy," the giantess said as she locked eyes with Danae. "Remove her chains."

CHAPTER 14

Nora

Despite the supernatural wind sweeping dirt into her eyes in the cave, Nora kept her gaze focused on Leif and swallowed the acid rising in the back of her throat.

Wiry white hair stuck out from his head at all angles, matching the caterpillar bushes he must have called his eyebrows. Spectacles clung to his greasy nose, and his rotten brown teeth showed between thin lips as he grinned.

Gods, he's even more disgusting than the last time, Nora thought, which was saying a lot since the last time she had gotten much too close for anyone's good, what with his abducting her and all.

Her heart thudded hard within her chest as she remembered the terror he had put her through just a few months ago, all in the name of trying to get the amulet from Sera.

The nerve of him coming back.

His magic may have been stronger than before, but the deceitful witch still didn't have a god or goddess on his side. Oh how she was going to love putting this mutt down once and for all.

"Hey, aren't you that girl I kidnapped?" Leif asked with a sneer. He knew, the bastard.

"I should've known you were this dumb." Nora placed her hands on her hips. "You'll have to tell me how it feels to get your ass kicked for the… what is it now, third time?"

The caterpillars on his face nearly hid his eyes altogether as he narrowed them while reaching into one of his pockets at the same time.

May I, darling? Freyja asked politely as always, but the goddess's excited anger boiled within. Apparently Nora wasn't the only one ready for payback.

Absofuckinglutely, Nora said and allowed the goddess to take over.

A familiar tingling sensation spread through her limbs. Her head tilted back, and she laughed with Freyja, a chiming, musical sound that echoed across the area. Bacchae heads turned to look, their jaws dropping and eyes widening, as Nora's body lifted from the ground in a hazy pink vortex. Dust and rocks whipped through the air, while lightning zapped around her, striking the ground now several feet below her and leaving scorch marks.

She focused her attention on Leif, the maniacal witch who must have finally realized his mistake as he gaped at her. Whatever he sought in his pocket was now forgotten.

Lightning shot out from the vortex surrounding her and wrapped itself around his feet like an electrified chain, causing him to trip and fall. The sparking chain slithered up his body until he was fully bound.

The swirling pink cloud keeping her afloat drifted toward the other witch until Nora could see his fear-filled eyes staring up at her, a look she had longed to see for months. She gritted her teeth. He was terrible at playing the villain.

All sorts of witty remarks came to mind, but Nora's fury toward this man couldn't wait. She took back control of the magic from Freyja and held her hand out in front of her. As she slowly closed her fist in front of her, the chains squeezed around Leif as well. The more she closed her hand, the tighter the chains bound him.

His shrieks of pain tore across the cavern, causing some of the others who had come with him to flee in case they were next. Smart move because they would be.

The lightning binding him burned its way through his skin, electrocuting and charring him. His body sizzled and steamed as his skin and muscles melted toward the ground, leaving nothing but oozing bones and a nauseatingly sweet scent behind. The chain dissipated into the air.

He certainly wouldn't be bothering them again.

With their so-called leader vanquished—Nora almost laughed at the idea of Leif being a leader of anything—Lasirenn and Theo made quick work of the few Bacchae who remained.

When it was clear, Theo's shape shimmered and morphed back into his human form as he stalked toward his bag. The man was furious. And naked.

Oh my, Freyja said. *He looks like a delightful treat.*

Nora hadn't seen his tattoo since he first revealed it to her and Sera a couple of months ago, but it was just as beautiful as she remembered. It was like the Aztec god had cut a giant conch shell in half and laid the ridged top part on Theo's chest like armor, the spokes curling beneath his arms and over his shoulders. Pearlescent hues caught the light, sparkling as if the shell were real.

Unable to resist a peek, her eyes drifted downward. Oh my, indeed. Sera would be a very lucky girl if they ever decided to be more than just friends, or cuddle buddies. Whatever they were.

Nora turned her attention to brushing dirt off her arms and clothes. She didn't need to enjoy the view; she had her own hunk of an immortal man. Soon to be mortal. Butterflies tickled her insides at the thought.

"The tunnel is sealed, and Hel is gone," Theo said in a tight voice, pulling on new clothes he had packed, his previous outfit in shreds on the ground. The muscles along his jaw moved as he clenched his jaw.

"I *knew* something was off out there," he said, pulling at his shoelaces much too vigorously. "I can't believe I didn't trust my instincts."

As Nora's elation from defeating Leif wore off, she realized it was just the three of them. She turned in a circle, dismay clenching her heart like a vice. "Renee is gone, too."

Something glinted on the ground near Lasirenn's black boots. The water spirit bent to pick it up, showing them a bronze key. She turned the key around in her fingers and said, "And no Eshu to help her."

"Can we move the rocks?" Nora asked, her throat

constricting and her breath coming out short.

Theo placed a hand on the blocked tunnel before shaking his head. "Sealed with the same magic hiding this entire place."

Tears sprang to Nora's eyes, ready to leak down her cheeks. "She's never coming back."

"Hey," he said softly as he walked over and gave her shoulder a squeeze. "We don't know that. I wanted to be with them in her place, but at least she's still got Sol and Seracchus."

Freyja let out a tinkling laugh inside her mind.

Nora blinked at him, wiping tears off her face. "Did you just make an awful joke?"

He smiled, though it didn't reach his eyes. "Does Bacchera sound better?"

Despite the sorrow gripping her heart, she laughed, appreciating his attempt to get her mind off the worst-case scenario. He was right. Renee was in good hands with Sera and Sol. They'd figure out a way to bring her back. They had to.

"Neither sounds good. And besides," Nora scrunched up her nose, "you make it seem like they're dating."

Theo stuffed the containers filled with coal and salt used to summon Hel back into Nora's pack and handed it to her. "I'd ask if you have a problem with her dating older men, but I've already met your boyfriend."

She huffed and slung one of the backpack straps over her shoulder. "It's not the older man part. I'm all for her dating an older man." She gave Theo a meaningful look. "But Sera needs to get laid, and that's not happening with Bacchus. At least, I don't think it is."

Nora stopped midway to pulling the other backpack strap over her arm. "Wait, can they actually do that?"

"As much as I'd love to continue listening to this riveting conversation about Serafina's sex life or lack thereof," Lasirenn cut in, "there is no purpose in staying here any longer. The Bacchae may regroup and come back, and it would be wise to find a new host for Eshu."

Theo coughed and nodded. A slight blush tinged his cheeks, but Nora guessed it was more likely from her comments about Sera getting laid than Lasirenn's interruption.

"You're right," he said. "Let's get going."

"Theo, darling, I'll need a place to stay." Lasirenn sauntered over to him, trailing her fingers down his arm to clasp his hand. "You have a home in the District, yes?"

Anger surged inside Nora. Was this woman seriously hitting on her best friend's man while Sera was in *hell* trying to rescue her mom and a bunch of other witches?

Absolutely not.

Nora didn't even care that Theo and Sera weren't technically dating. They would be soon if Nora had any say in the matter. That girl needed a happy ending in her life.

"You can stay with me," Nora said before she realized what had come out of her mouth.

Fuck. She flashed a smile through clenched teeth.

Lasirenn turned her eyes on Nora, her irises lightening to amber while her pupils constricted like a snake's.

Was that a threat?

"As much as I appreciate the offer," the serpent said, "Theo has contacts in the immortal world that we can use to help Eshu."

The man looked helpless caught between the two women, his mouth hanging slightly open.

"Well, it's a good thing cell phones and the internet were invented then, isn't it?" Nora asked before turning her back and heading for the cave entrance. She scrunched up her face when she was sure they wouldn't see her.

Seriously, what was wrong with this woman? There was zero percent chance she'd let that python sink her venomous fangs into Theo. She had Sera's back for life. The distraction from thinking about Solomon twenty-four-seven would be nice, too.

Such thoughts from you when you're angry, darling, Freyja said, humor in her tone despite the chastisement.

It makes me feel better.

I can tell.

As she stepped through the veil of magic, a wave of warmth from the goddess washed over Nora to counteract the frigid air outside the cave. At least an inch of fluffy white snow covered their footprints on the ground, courtesy of the storm that had finally broken during the short time they had been inside. Thick flakes continued to fall, making it both difficult to see as well as shimmy along the edge of the mountain back toward the trail they had followed up from the vehicles.

The three of them made their way back in silence. Even the woods remained quiet thanks to the dense covering of snow. Although they had killed Leif and scattered the Bacchae, Nora couldn't stop the feeling of dread settling heavily in her stomach, as if they were about to be attacked at any moment. Every few feet, she glanced behind her. Nothing besides the shadows moved, but goosebumps continued to rise.

You're safe with me, Freyja said, laying a soothing blanket over her anxious thoughts.

Nora trusted the goddess, but the feeling didn't go away.

When they arrived back at the trail's parking lot, the car and truck had been covered in white powder. The snow was coming down even harder now, obscuring the view just a few feet in front of her.

"Let's leave the truck here, just in case—" Theo started to say.

Four vehicles squealed into view, red and blue lights flashing against the flurries, and figures dressed in police uniforms surged out of the surrounding forest, guns raised. The snow had hidden them well.

"Don't move!"

CHAPTER 15

Serafina

Sera couldn't believe what she had just heard. Remove Danae's chains? Was this giantess really a deranged demon, or was this some sort of a test? If it wasn't a test, things were about to get *real* ugly, real fast.

Solomon let out a sound of protest and stepped forward. "Without the silver, it will be difficult to keep her from fleeing."

Exactly what Sera was thinking. At least they could agree on this being a terrible idea.

"Yes," the giantess nodded, not taking her gaze from the Bacchae witch. "She must vow to remain by your side and loyal to her promise to see you to the Ordog, safe from all harm."

Despite the gag in her mouth, Danae's lips pulled up

into a grin.

"What happens if she breaks her vow?" Solomon asked.

"She will meet her end in the river *Gjöll*." The giantess swept her hand toward the flowing metal conveyor belt below them.

Okay, that actually didn't sound like too bad of a deal to Sera. She almost hoped Danae would break her vow. Too bad they needed the witch, for a little while longer, anyway. She looked to Solomon and Renee.

"We don't have another option at this point," Renee said.

Solomon eyed the Eternal a moment longer before nodding. They all agreed then. A terrible option but the only one.

Sera approached Danae, loosening and pulling down the gag.

"Do you agree to Móðguðr's terms?" She gazed into the laughing blue eyes staring back at her, fighting the desire to grab the girl by the throat, crushing it until she disintegrated into amber flurries.

Danae stretched her mouth open and closed a few times and licked her lips. Red marks left behind from the gag streaked across her cheeks. A small consolation prize.

"Follow you idiots to my friend the Ordog or be thrown into a pile of old swords," Danae said. "Got it."

"That's not an agreement," Sera said, pausing as she reached toward the girl's straitjacket of chains.

"I'm hurt," Danae said, her lips pouting. "It's like you don't trust me."

Sera waited, not willing to get into a verbal fight with this girl. The fighting would come later, and it would be quite physical and very satisfying. The excitement for that fight must have shown on Sera's face.

Danae narrowed her eyes. "I accept the terms."

I'm sure she thinks she'll escape somehow, Bacchus said as he raised a hand to caress the girl's face. His shimmering skin left a trail of golden sparks as it passed. *The Ordog isn't "friends" with anyone.*

Can we count on her staying with us until we get there, at the very least? she asked.

Yes.

Sera loosened the chains that bound the Bacchae and watched the girl shrug off the jacket before handing the whole thing to Móðguðr. The giantess tossed it casually into the river below, where the fabric and chains mixed with the other metals and disappeared. Sera winced at the grating sound.

"You may pass," the woman said and stepped back once again.

"Thank you," Sera said to the giantess.

Keeping an eye on Danae despite her vow to remain loyal, Sera continued down the bridge toward the other, mist-covered side. Not much could be seen ahead of them due to the cloudiness, but Sera continued to follow the path with as much confidence as she could muster. Droplets of warm water accumulated on her skin and clothes.

When she stepped off the bridge onto solid ground, the fog cleared before her, pulled back like a curtain. Fields of tall grasses dotted with tiny yellow flowers lay around them, stretching as far as the eye could see beneath blue skies which couldn't possibly be real.

In fact, none of it could be real as it existed in the middle of the earth. Even the warm breeze that swept through and toyed with Sera's hair made her almost forget the fact that they were underground.

Putting her logic to the side and embracing the fantasy, a dark line stretched from east to west in the distant horizon. Or was it north to south? Did direction even make a difference in the underworld?

Sera pulled out the pocket-sized compass to check, but the arrow just spun in lazy circles and never settled. She tucked it back into her jeans. So much for bringing that.

"Is that the wall?" Renee asked, shielding her eyes from the sun.

Except there was no sun, not really. Not even in the fake blue sky. The light was just bright enough to feel otherwise.

"I hope so," Sera said, also hoping it wasn't as far away as it appeared.

Maybe the distance was an illusion, kind of like side mirrors on a car. She mentally crossed her fingers, earning a chuckle from Bacchus.

"Looks like it will take at least a day to get there," Danae said as she made a show of stretching her arms. "Maybe more."

Sera resisted the urge to roll her eyes. "Don't act like you don't know."

The Bacchae witch shrugged before bending down to scoop up a handful of wildflowers. "Time moves differently when you're Immortal."

She brought the pretty flowers to her nose and inhaled, a smile pulling at her lips. Then she crushed the yellow flowers in her hand and let the remains drift into the wind.

Such a dramatic teenaged Eternal.

Once not too long ago, Sera had thought Danae was quite regal, albeit terrifying. But that queen-like image had evaporated as her snarky remarks became more frequent. Definitely one of Bacchus's creations.

The Roman god huffed but didn't disagree.

"She's unfortunately not wrong on either point," Solomon said. "Let's go as far as we can before resting." He caught Sera's eye before tilting his head meaningfully at Renee, who gazed glassy-eyed into the distance.

So off they went.

The fields were beautiful, full of colorful flowers and waving grass. From time to time, small herds of horses would drift close enough that a brown and white speckled foal would come to check them out as they walked. Sera tried holding her hand up to one of the more daring foals, the grass coming up high enough to tickle his belly, but he nickered and leaped away out of reach.

The light never changed, so she had no idea whether night would ever come or how long they had even been walking. She only had the wall to judge distance, a wall which grew taller and longer and more foreboding the farther they journeyed. Sera had no idea whether it was meant to keep people out... or in. Her skin crawled at the thought.

As Renee continued to droop, her gait slowing to a shuffle, Sera called a halt to their walk.

They settled down beside the greenery, using their packs as pillows. Renee's breathing deepened only a moment after her head hit the ground.

While Sera sat next to the older woman, Solomon closed his eyes as well, but she was reasonably certain he didn't need to sleep the way humans did. She hadn't cared enough to ask any of the Bacchae yet. If she did ever care, she'd ask Liviana. Why couldn't all the Bacchae have ended up like that level-headed Eternal?

You do realize I live for and create chaos, right? Bacchus asked, earning a quiet chuckle from her.

Oh, she knew it very well. She wrapped her arms around her pulled up legs, resting her chin on a knee and stared at the distant wall.

Life had been nothing but chaos ever since she dug up the pinecone-shaped amulet last summer. Not even a year had passed yet, and she hadn't started really thinking about what she would do with her life once this was all over. Once she rescued her mom and embraced her immortality. Would she go back to school after all this? She wasn't sure that made much sense. But then, what was time now that she had an infinite number of years? Might as well get an advanced degree or two or three to go along with it.

A tiny thrill of excitement coursed through her veins as she thought about the future. She could study all the things. Everything she ever wanted to learn, and then some. She could travel to all the exotic places her teaching salary would never be able to pay for. And maybe, just maybe, she'd have a handsome, kind, patient, also immortal man to accompany her. As long as Lasirenn…

No, she wouldn't go there.

A gentle breeze swept through, causing the grass to sway. Despite the abundance of plants, no smells reached Sera's nose. The place was full of life and color but strangely devoid of scent.

"I used to run through fields like this," Danae said.

Sera cocked an eyebrow as she glanced at the girl. Sitting with her legs crossed, Danae had her eyes shut, her face turned up toward the sky. Still fake, but sky nonetheless. If it wasn't for the prison uniform, she could be meditating or doing a yoga sequence for all anyone knew.

"Huh." Sera wasn't sure what else to say. Engaging in conversation with the girl wasn't exactly a priority. Quite the opposite.

"Nothing makes you feel so alive," Danae continued. "The feeling of dirt beneath your feet, grasses tickling your limbs and face as you pass. Your blood pumping through every inch of your body to caress your very soul."

Sera let her gaze drift out over the sea of yellows and greens, knowing the feeling Danae described. Knew it well. Although, she'd never tell that to the girl she hated with every fiber of her being. But being on a dig in the Italian countryside—hell, even in rural Virginia—felt like healing for her soul. She hoped she'd have a chance to experience that again someday.

Maybe she'd also be able to save up enough in her immortal life to buy a little villa in Umbria or Tuscany. The tiny hilltop town of Orvieto would be the perfect place to settle.

"The only thing that comes close is draining a human of its life force."

As Bacchus burst out laughing, Sera snapped her gaze back to Danae, who now stared at Renee with hunger in her eyes. A predator hunting its prey. What a way to ruin a moment.

Even Solomon sat up at the girl's comment, eyeing her with caution.

"Don't even think about it," Sera snapped.

The mood effectively ruined, she glared at Bacchus for his reaction.

Wiping tears from his eyes as he continued to chortle, he said, *Oh, that girl. What a hoot.*

After what felt like another hour or two, though she honestly wasn't sure of the time, Sera woke Renee with a gentle shake. The woman groaned and turned bloodshot eyes on Sera.

"I'm too old to be gallivanting around the underworld," Renee said with a half-hearted chuckle. She pushed up to a sitting position.

"We'll see if we can rest more in Helheim." Sera patted the woman's shoulder and helped her to her feet before handing her the bag she had laid on. "Do you have anything in your magical supplies that might help with the exhaustion?"

"Nothing other than some protein bars." Renee smiled at Sera, though it didn't quite reach her eyes as it usually did. "I hadn't planned on going with you."

"I have a spell that would give her energy," Danae said as she picked dirt out from under a nail.

Sera slung her own bag over her shoulder. "As if we'd trust you and your magic."

The Eternal examined her nails. "Suit yourself."

"Why would you even offer?" Sera asked.

The girl met Renee's tired gaze. "A witch with that much power deserves respect, don't you agree?"

Rolling her eyes, Sera knew it was a jab at her for not respecting Danae. As if anyone in their right mind would show appreciation to that monster.

We can give Renee some energy, Bacchus said. *Just pull from our magic.*

Sera's jaw dropped as she turned to look at the god. *Why didn't you say so before?*

He considered her for a moment, as if genuinely puzzled. *Why didn't you just ask?*

I didn't know it was a possibility. She could just throttle him.

I'm not accustomed to thinking of others' well-being. Bacchus shrugged and took a sip of wine. *It's hard enough keeping you alive.*

Grumbling at the god, Sera turned to Renee. "Apparently, we can help."

Closing her eyes for a brief moment to focus, Sera found the embers within her, writhing and spinning around the center of her being, waiting to be used. She pulled out a golden strand and let it travel down her arm and pool into her hand, changing shape every few seconds like it couldn't settle on what it wanted to be.

She looked at Renee. "Ready?"

Renee's eyelids remained half shut as she nodded, exhaustion clearly weighing her down.

"Energy," Sera whispered to the orb of magic before placing it on the woman's shoulder and stepping back.

The orb oozed into her skin and disappeared. A moment later, Renee's body glowed a yellowish hue and her eyes snapped open wide, a golden tinge briefly illuminating her brown irises.

"Woo! What a ride," Renee said, sounding more awake than someone who'd had a few cups of coffee. She rubbed her arms. "I haven't felt like this since the '70s."

Sera grinned, happy she was able to help. She'd have to

explore this magical well within her after they got back to the mortal world, find out what else she could do with it.

But for now, she said, "Alright, let's get moving."

* * *

SERA TILTED HER HEAD BACK, trying to gauge how high the top of the stone wall was. Three stories, at least. Their long walk next to their fields had ended at last. Only now they had to figure out how to scale a wall with a mortal. A really tall wall, with each stone reaching to her waist.

When they had been far enough away from it to make out the gate, they had strayed from the path into the high grasses. Some sort of massively oversized dog or wolf stood beside the equally large arching gate, allowing a line of people to enter one by one. Every few entrees, the creature would growl, a rumble so deep and loud she could hear it from a distance. The hairs on Sera's arms rose in response.

Yet another giant being she didn't want to have to fight.

She hadn't seen another soul on their walk, but somehow a line had formed to enter through the gate and never seemed to stop. Whenever someone walked into Helheim, a new person would shimmer into being at the end of the line.

Freyja's vague memory of not going through the gate must have referred to whatever guarded it. How the goddess had forgotten *that* detail was anyone's guess. But then again, the Norse goddess had probably seen far scarier things than this creature.

A shudder ran across Sera's shoulders at the idea of facing something scarier. She would probably be doing just that with the Ordog.

They had kept to the beast's back, finding a place to scale the wall without being spotted.

"I can jump high, but not quite that high," Solomon said with a quick smile.

"Climb it is then." Sera removed her backpack and pulled out the rope.

Thanks to Freyja's limited description of the journey to Hel, they had at least been prepared to scale a wall. Sera just hadn't expected one three stories high. She glanced down the length of stones toward the gate. If their rope wasn't long enough, they might have to face that beast after all.

Solomon tied the three-prong hook to one end of the rope, gave it a few swings, then launched it up the wall. The hooks bit into the other edge of the top of the wall and stuck. Success on the first try.

Sera still didn't like the guy, hadn't forgiven him for dragging her more into the mess she found herself in, but having a supposedly friendly Bacchae around was coming in handy. Although she was confident she could have secured the rope herself if she had to. Just maybe not on the first try.

"Alright, Solomon you go up first," Sera said. "Then we'll send up Renee, then Danae, then me. Got it?"

Solomon frowned. "Are you sure you trust yourself with her?"

"More so than you," Sera said. "We don't know how much her *influence* could work down here. If any."

After giving a sharp nod, Solomon eyed the wall. He took Renee's backpack and looped it over his own pack—a gentlemanly gesture that made a corner of Sera's lips turn up. Even with the extra weight, he still scaled the wall with ease. His feet found minute cracks in the stone as his hands nimbly pulled his body up the rope.

Once he reached the top, Sera helped tie a sling under Renee's arms, and Solomon pulled the rope as she walked up the wall.

"Your turn next," Sera said to the Eternal.

Danae stood gazing off into the distance until Renee cleared the top. The Bacchae turned her blue-grey eyes on Sera but didn't budge, even when the end of the rope dropped back down.

"Have you forgotten your vow already?" Sera asked, almost hoping that was the case. One less problem to worry about. She was sure they could figure out a way to rescue the witches with Hel's help.

"I can see the wish on your face," Danae said, "but you won't make it to the Ordog without me. Not in one piece, anyway."

"Then get a move on." Sera jerked her thumb at the rope.

With one last glance at the far horizon, Danae scaled the wall without using the rope, her fingers and toes finding small crevices in the wall. Sera's skin crawled, both from the witch's ease of climbing as well as her distant gaze.

Was she simply reliving another memory? Sera didn't think so. The girl's gaze seemed more like she was waiting for someone, or some*thing*, to arrive. Either way, Sera didn't like it one bit, and she wasn't going to wait around to find out.

As Sera grabbed her backpack off the ground, a sudden, fast wind whipped by, bringing with it the stench of sulfur and decay. She scrunched up her nose as she looked to her left, the direction the wind came from.

Vice-like fear froze her in place as three blurred shapes raced across the fields toward the wall. Toward her. Even from a distance, she could sense the *offness* of the creatures. The unnatural movements of their four legs only added to the terror rising within her.

Sera, quick! Bacchus said as he pushed her toward the wall and the awaiting rope. But even with the god's help, she couldn't move. It was as if a spell had been cast over her as she watched the shapes approach.

She was stuck, and she was going to die.

The creatures stopped a dozen feet away, lowering their heads and snarling at her. Saliva dripped out of canine-shaped mouths, but the teeth within were more like rows of shark teeth than dogs'. From where she stood, Sera couldn't tell if their tar-like skin was fur or not, but the inky blackness of whatever covered them oozed to the ground beneath their feet where it sizzled and burned the grass.

When the rotten egg scent reached her again, Sera would have gagged if she could move. Acid burned the back of her throat.

A surge of energy rushed through her as Bacchus forced his divine essence to break their hold. Shaking free of the terror-induced freeze, Sera stared down the hounds of hell, her heart pounding within her chest. She only had a split second to act before they did.

Pushing with all her god-assisted might, Sera leaped from the ground toward the wall, hoping to grab high enough that the beasts couldn't reach her. She grabbed hold of the rope with one hand just as screeching howls sounded below her. Kicking against the wall, she reached higher up with the other hand.

A sharp fiery pain tore through her calf as one of the creatures caught her. She slipped down the rope, her palm burning in protest before she could grab hold again, the beast's weight pulling against her.

Unable to hold it back, she cried out as her calf muscles and tendons ripped under the animal's razor-sharp teeth. The feeling of her bone being crushed almost made her pass out before her godly powers finally took over and eased the pain even though the creature still held on.

Her body shuddered while she clung to the rope, but she continued to move up the wall as Solomon pulled from the top. Raising her other foot, Sera slammed her boot down on the hound's snout, a satisfying crunch and whimper filling the air. The creature released her and fell to the ground below.

The three demons prowled beneath her, glaring up with glowing green eyes as Solomon pulled Sera all the way to the top.

After flopping down on top of the wall, which was much broader than she expected, Sera closed her eyes and panted. Her mouth had run dry, and her heart continued to beat wildly within her chest from the close encounter. From her knee down, the shredded fabric of her jeans flapped in the breeze. Now she'd have to traipse through the underworld with only half a pant leg. Just fabulous.

"I see you've met some of the Ordog's minions," Danae's child-like voice held a laugh in it.

"You knew they were coming," Solomon accused her, his eyebrows pulled tight together. A flash of red pierced through his irises.

"Of course not," the girl said. "But what a delightful

performance by our very own heroine, wasn't it?"

Sera sat up and glared at Danae, the girl clapping her hands together in fake delight.

And then the sight behind the Bacchae caught Sera's eye, and she let out a gasp.

CHAPTER 16

Nora

"**D**on't move!" shouted a voice into the megaphone again, as if anyone could have missed it the first time.

Although Nora had zero reasons to worry, she put her hands up in a gesture of surrender to ease the tension. Theo and Lasirenn did the same beside her. At least the spirit had that much common sense. The last thing they needed was a shootout with the police.

"My name is Theodore Pratt," he called out. "I'm with the DC Police Department."

"We know who you are," the man with the megaphone said into it. "Keep your hands where we can see them."

Officers surged forward with guns raised and surrounded them. Three stepped close to yank the two immortals' and Nora's hands down and cuff their wrists behind their backs.

"Ouch!" Nora glared up at the officer who held her arm too tight. He was at least a foot taller than she was. "If you're afraid of someone *my* size, then you're in the wrong line of work."

"What are we being arrested for?" Theo asked, his jaw clenched tight as an officer dragged him toward the vehicles.

"You'll be told when you get back to Quantico for questioning," the officer answered in a gruff voice.

"That's not how this process works." Theo dug his feet into the ground, and they stopped walking.

The officer tugged at Theo's arm with little success.

The man with the megaphone strode over, though he lowered the device. Unlike the others, he was dressed in a crisp black suit. He faced Theo directly, his eyes stern.

"It is now that we have vamps to deal with."

Ugh. Nora hated that term. It wasn't even an accurate description. Not fully. Before she could protest out loud, she and the others were shoved into the back seats of police cars, one for each of them. To keep them separated and unable to talk, she was sure.

Nora fumed, and she was certain Theo would be even angrier with this complete lack of regard for the law.

That's slightly hypocritical, isn't it darling? Freyja's voice chimed.

Nora started to retort before she realized the goddess was right. They had broken a few major laws by abducting Danae, a supernatural terrorist. She let a rueful smile tug at her lips, ignoring the officer narrowing his eyes at her in the rearview mirror.

I suppose you're right, she said.

Of course I am, the goddess said. *Now, you just get some rest.*

A tingling sensation spread through Nora's arms down to her hands, and a moment later the cuffs fell to the seat behind her. She rubbed her wrists.

At least she would rest in comfort.

* * *

NORA LET OUT A GIANT YAWN, not even caring if it would be considered rude or not. She had been in the interrogation room for hours, and she was beyond over it.

"Listen, I know you guys want answers, but I simply don't have them," Nora said, probably for the fifteenth time. Maybe only the seventh. She had lost count. Also, she didn't really care. They were doing their jobs, and she was doing hers.

When one of the officers—Matt or Mark or something with an M, but she just called him the Short One in her head—opened his mouth to speak again, the door opened, and Theo strode in.

"Come on," Theo said. "We're done here."

"Finally," Nora said with a huff before she stood and followed him out, disregarding the protests from the two officers. "I need a bath and my bed."

Theo chuckled as he led her down the hall. Lasirenn waited for them in the foyer. When Nora opened her mouth to speak, Theo shook his head.

"Not here," he said.

A few minutes later, they were back in a sedan borrowed from the FBI, driving north on I-95 toward the District from Quantico. Driving wasn't really the right word when crawling forward less than fifteen miles per hour. Maybe coasting was a better word. As usual for the area, traffic sucked.

"How'd you get us out?" Nora asked from the front passenger seat. She hadn't allowed Lasirenn the opportunity to sit next to Theo.

"I have a contact in the bureau. High up. She knows who I am, *what* I am."

"Fancy. What now?"

"You go home and bathe," Theo said, turning his head to grin at her huff. "And Lasirenn and I will try to find Eshu a host."

Nora didn't like the sound of that. "Why don't Freyja and I help you? Lasirenn, you can go back to… wherever it is you're from." She flicked her wrist like she was shooing a fly.

"I think I'll stay," Lasirenn said from the back seat. "I am enjoying this little adventure."

"It shouldn't be that difficult," Theo said before giving a quick honk to a car trying to cut them off. "Don't you have classes to get back to?"

Nora groaned. She had honestly forgotten, which wasn't super surprising. "You just *had* to remind me, didn't you?"

But the man was right. It made far more sense for the water spirit to accompany him than it did her. She may not like the way Lasirenn looked at him with desire for days— Nora knew that look well, she had the same one for Solomon too often to count—but she'd have to trust Theo.

The others better hurry up and get out of hell soon or else she might have to go in after them.

* * *

I BELIEVE I'VE FINALLY figured it out, Freyja's excited voice stirred Nora from her doze.

Her couch was one of her favorite places to catch a quick nap, and it certainly hadn't disappointed that time after her last class of the day.

"Hm?"

You're a Muse.

"That's nice," Nora said with a giant yawn as she stretched.

She had only missed one day of classes, but for the rest of the week, she'd had to deal with a line of never-ending students during her office hours. Only some of them asked about actual school-related topics. The rest wanted to know what happened to Danae after a news story had finally come out announcing the Eternal's disappearance.

Why did everyone assume Nora knew what happened? They were right, of course, but the assumption was infuriating. Or maybe she should be pleased they thought she had that kind of skill, to abduct a supernatural terrorist so easily.

That's right, kids. Now do your homework or else.

No, darling, you're descended from one of the Muses.

Nora stood and walked to her kitchen where she set a tea kettle on to boil. "Okay."

She wasn't sure how the story had leaked, but clearly the CIA or Interpol—or whoever the hell was involved— weren't as great at keeping secrets as they thought they were. Or maybe Theo leaked it to keep them too busy to sniff around his comings and goings. Yeah, that's probably what happened. Smart man.

I don't think you're following, dear. Freyja sighed.

"Probably not." Nora rubbed the sleep from her eyes.

She'd have to ask Theo if he leaked the news to the press. She made a mental note to herself to ask him next time they checked in with each other, which should be soon.

Let's start over, shall we? Freyja chuckled. *I have noticed that everything seems to happen effortlessly for you. Magically, at any rate. I thought perhaps it had been due to my influence, but I've never seen anyone take to my magic quite like you.*

"Aw, thank you."

The tea kettle let out a piercing whistle as it finished, and Nora poured the steaming water over her tea bag in the cup. She hoped he had found out *something* about the others in the underworld. Every day that passed without knowing their fate killed her a little bit inside. Had she made the wrong decision letting Solomon go with them?

He was the perfect man. *Her* perfect man. Why was she trying to change him? Sure, she wanted to have kids and to be a mom more than almost anything, but maybe adoption should have been the way they went. She had chosen an immortal as her life partner, for the gods' sake. Had she embraced that more openly, maybe he wouldn't have been so eager to find mortality.

She pressed her fingers to the bridge of her nose. No sense going down that path right now. If he came back still immortal, then adoption would be their answer. End of story. She picked up her teacup.

Of course, my darling, but my point is, it's not just that you're magically inclined, it's that you're part god.

As she raised the cup to her mouth, Nora paused, the

goddess's words finally sinking in. "Wait. I'm what?"

There we go, Freyja said, relief evident in her voice. *Yes, my love, you have divine blood running through you. Erato's, if I'm not mistaken.*

Nora took a slow sip of her tea, allowing the words to digest. The news should surprise her more, but with all that had happened lately, it almost seemed par for the course. Vampires, witches, werewolves—er, weredogs?—and gods. Not to mention the demons the others were facing in hell.

Why not throw in some Muses?

"Erato? Is she the erotic love poetry one?" Mythology had always been Sera's strong suit, not Nora's, but the name was pretty easy to decipher.

That's the one.

"How fitting," Nora smirked.

She was more than adventurous than some when it came to sex, having embraced her nature as a teen. Not that being bisexual made her promiscuous, but she found it opened up so many more exciting experiences than being a boring old hetero. Quite the invigorating workout, too, especially with Solomon.

Her body warmed at the memories, scorching until she throbbed. The goddess's association with love was starting to rub off on her, or maybe it was the muse blood.

"What does that mean for me?" she asked, getting her mind back on the subject at hand, though her body continued to thrum. Solomon was her person, through and through. "Being a descendant of a muse?"

It means you'll do quite well without my help, Freyja said quietly.

They hadn't discussed the topic of saying goodbye just

yet, and Nora wasn't sure she was ready to do so without Solomon by her side. She chewed on her bottom lip, hoping and wishing he would be back soon. Praying that Solomon would come back to her with an answer. The uncertainty of it all drove her mad. Mortal or immortal, they would be together forever.

She set down her cup. But for now, she needed to take care of this delicious ache between her legs.

CHAPTER 17

Serafina

Helheim was indeed a city, and much, much bigger than Sera thought it would be. When she first caught sight of the buildings below, a gasp had slipped out, not quite expecting the size of it all.

Then again, it held the souls of the dead for gods knows how many thousands of years. Maybe she should be surprised it wasn't even more extensive.

The dark and foreboding city was littered with Viking era buildings and long halls with pointed roofs that glistened as if wet from the light fog that settled over everything. No sky could be seen through the low-hanging grey clouds, and no color but grey seemed to be present in the entire city.

Atop a hill in the middle of it all—the highest point that could be seen through the misty air from their vantage point—the largest and most elaborate of the halls loomed. Smoke billowed from its chimney.

Chances were that was where they'd find Hel.

"Wow," Renee said beside her. "We made it."

"Let's just hope there are no more obstacles in the city itself," Solomon said, lowering their rope on the other side of the wall. With a quick nod in her direction, he gripped the line and dropped out of sight.

Reaching a hand up, Sera rubbed at her collarbone where the image of the pinecone amulet rested. Fiddling with the necklace had become a habit while mortal, and she longed for the sense of comfort it brought as her anxiety spiked. They had made it to Helheim, which meant they were almost to her mother… and the Ordog.

They knew nothing about the Hungarian deity except for heresy and fantastical drawings from someone's imagination. No historical records, not even primary sources from hundreds of years ago, held the truth. At least, Sera assumed they didn't. But knowing what she knew now, maybe that was naive of her to think.

Were they really ready to face the being that had become synonymous with the devil?

Her stomach churned as she considered the possible outcomes. If they somehow defeated him—even killed him—that would mean the devil was gone. What would happen to the evil souls that believed in him then? Did good and evil even exist, or were they simply a construct of humankind?

And if they didn't defeat him, if he was able to kill them or take them prisoner, what would happen to the world?

Was Hel right? Would he be able to create a literal hell on earth?

Giving her head a quick shake, hoping the act would repress her pinball-like thoughts, Sera helped Renee loop the rope around her waist to lower her down the stones.

Danae gave Sera a quick wink before stepping off the edge. Sera gasped and ran to look down. The girl stood from a crouch on the ground and waved up at her, earning an eye roll from Sera. Renee wasn't even halfway down the wall. At least the Eternal had sped up their descent.

After Sera climbed down the inside wall, they headed into the gloom-filled home of the dead. Cobblestone streets wound through the circular city like a maze, leading them ever upward toward the center.

For the most part, the colorless souls inhabiting Helheim ignored them, continuing on with their afterlives without concern. Sera and the others didn't exactly blend in with their vibrant colors in comparison, but only a few of the souls shot furtive glances in their direction.

Most of the souls seemed to be performing the same daily activities that they did when they were alive, a fact that fascinated the archaeologist in Sera. They passed wood-framed shops and inns with thatched roofs, smithies with smoke billowing out the tops, and even a few whorehouses. The buildings had been made with stacking logs like cabins or in the woven lattice method of wattle and daub.

Apparently, life didn't always end when one died. The question was whether they chose to be here or had to be. Freyja hadn't given them any kind of etiquette rules to follow, but Bacchus's memories made it clear that striking up a conversation with the dead wouldn't be polite. Kind of like a slap in the face talking with a whole group of living beings.

She pressed her lips together and focused on the stones of the street to keep herself from stopping and asking the inhabitants questions. They weren't there for history, but man was it tempting.

Oh my… Bacchus murmured.

Get out of there, Sera scolded the god, catching him peeking inside a madam's door. The wicked gleam in his eye meant nothing good. Making a face at him, she pushed his dirty thoughts out of hers. No time for *that* of all things.

The longhouse they approached at the top of the otherwise barren hill was even more immense in person than Sera had imagined it would be, towering several stories high—higher even than the wall. The building had to have been made by giants, which Sera now knew was a real possibility. What she could see of the roof was reminiscent of a Viking ship with a dragon head prow jutting over the entryway to the hall.

The dragon itself glared down at those approaching as if daring anyone to defy the goddess within. The beast's amber-colored eyes seemed to follow Sera wherever she moved, like those creepy as sin paintings in haunted houses. Her pulse quickened beneath its gaze, wondering if it saw her as a meal. There was a reason she avoided haunted houses as a general rule in life.

They entered the colossal wooden building, finding themselves in a temple-like hall lined with thick log columns and filled with congregating Vikings from all eras. A few souls from more modern times mingled, as well. A line of people formed in the middle, leading up to a dais where a throne was placed.

And on that throne sat Hel.

Only here in her own realm, she was three times as large as she had been in the mortal world. Bigger even than Móðguðr. Courtesy of her giant ancestry, Sera guessed. No wonder she had constructed such a large building.

Behind the black-robed goddess, a massive tree root extended down from a hole in the roof, twisting and reaching but not quite touching the ground far beneath it. Realizing her mouth was hanging open from the sheer size of everything here, Sera snapped it shut.

She and the others joined the souls waiting their turn to approach the goddess, not wanting to be disrespectful in Hel's house of worship by jumping to the front of the procession. Sera ground her teeth against her growing impatience. Waiting in lines in the underworld seemed even more unappealing than aboveground.

Did all the world's religions result in waiting in a line when one died? That would just be cruel and unusual punishment.

Sera tried to listen as each soul pleaded his or her case to the goddess, but the words came out garbled somehow, as if magic prevented her from hearing what they said. Chances were, that's exactly what happened. Even Bacchus's knowledge of languages couldn't decipher the words.

As each person finished speaking, Hel would either nod and open her palm to a light-filled doorway to the side of the hall. The soul would thank her profusely before rising and moving toward the light. Or Hel would shake her head and point back toward the city. Those souls would hang their heads, some even sobbing or wailing before departing.

Do you know what they have to do to pass on? she asked Bacchus in a hushed voice even in her mind. Centuries or more must have passed for some of these souls.

The souls here are in a sort of limbo, Bacchus replied, stroking his thick beard. *They must prove they have earned a right to be in a better place.*

Before she could ask any other questions, it was their turn. Sera didn't believe the goddess's decaying face could look any worse than it did the last time she saw her, but seeing it three times larger challenged that belief. Her mouth ran dry as image after image flashed through her imagination of what the Ordog might look like in his own realm.

A hand rested on her shoulder, flooding her frayed nerves with calm and halting her chaotic thoughts.

I would've thought you'd love my mind right now, she thought to the Roman god.

He chuckled beside her.

Hel's one good eye focused on Danae. "I was not sure you would accept Móðguðr's terms."

Unlike on the mortal plane, Hel's voice didn't sound like hundreds of wailing souls. It was vaguely reminiscent of Freyja's, with a musical quality, though much deeper in tone. Almost sultry.

The thought of the other Norse goddess tugged at Sera's heart, and she hoped for the umpteenth time that Nora had made it out of the cave safe. Rescuing her mom only to lose her best friend and soulmate would be unfathomable.

"This wouldn't be the first time a god has underestimated me," Danae said, a casual smirk on her lips.

Hel continued to stare at the girl in silence, no emotions

or thoughts on her half-decayed face. Just when Sera began to wonder if the goddess had somehow fallen asleep with her eye open, she turned her gaze on the rest of the group.

"Welcome to my home, travelers," Hel said. "Here, those who have died of disease and old age find refuge for a time before they move on. I have prepared food and rooms for you to rest in before your final journey."

"Thank you for your hospitality," Sera said, lowering her head in respect. She wasn't sure what was appropriate, but she was part god now, and bowing seemed too much.

Besides, Bacchus didn't bow next to her.

"You fear for the lives of your friends," Hel said. "Fear not. I can tell you they have not joined the realm of the dead, though I do not know how they fare otherwise."

Relief filled Sera's soul, and tears pricked the corners of her eyes. She would hold on to the hope that they had been able to fight off Leif and returned to normal life. As normal as it could be, anyway. "Thank you."

Hel turned her gaze on Solomon. "You seek something else."

The Bacchae stepped forward. "Greetings once again, Lady of Helheim. I seek one who can remove my Immortal blood."

Hel regarded him in silence for several moments. "What you seek will not be easy."

Solomon smiled. "Nothing worthwhile ever is."

For the briefest of moments, Sera could have sworn the goddess's lip turned up into a returning smile. But it was gone before she could be sure.

"You will find a woman who can help you in the market. Ask for Ragna."

He bowed and stepped back. "Thank you."

"Go. Eat and rest. Your quest becomes most difficult when you leave here."

Sera held back a groan. As if it had been easy to get this far. Her pant leg was still shredded where that diabolical creature tried to rip off her calf, though her wound had been healed before she even reached the top of the wall. And poor Renee looked like she was about to drop where she stood, the magical energy having faded. No wonder she had been so quiet.

They thanked the goddess as a hunched over soul shuffled over to them and led them out of the hall through a door that opened into a much smaller room. As promised, a table laden with food took up the entirety of the back wall. A glass jug filled with a deep red liquid sat at one end, but it was too thick to be wine.

Sera caught Solomon's flared nostrils as he also picked up the metallic scent of blood. She hadn't noticed before how his skin had turned a bit chalky, the skin beneath his eyes darkening. Like Renee, he wasn't a god. He needed to refuel.

Even though Sera no longer needed food as often as she had previously—not even close—her stomach rumbled at the sight of the meal ahead of them. Hopefully Hel wasn't using food to bind them to the underworld like Hades did to Persephone. They'd have to risk it. The temptation to eat was too hard to resist when it was steaming right in front of them.

They filled their bellies full to the point of discomfort, except for Danae. Sera wouldn't permit the girl to drink any of the blood, even if it put Renee slightly at risk should the hunger become too much for the Eternal. There was no way Sera would let anything happen to her friend, just like there was no way she'd allow the immortal girl to regain any strength. She could suffer and wither away for all Sera cared, and the glares cast her way did little to change her mind.

When they finished eating—or drinking in Solomon's case—they were led into yet another room, this one holding several cots lined against the walls. Renee practically collapsed onto the one nearest the door, removing her lavender glasses in the process.

"I don't think I've ever been so exhausted before," she managed to get out before she promptly fell asleep, her glasses dangling from her limp hand.

Sera's heart clenched as she watched her friend, her mentor really, breath the deep breathing of sleep. Renee was here because of the careless slip up at the gas station. That was the only explanation. There was no other way Leif could have discovered their plan. Sera had been too trusting that the others would feel the same sense of urgency she did, not that she blamed them.

How could they feel what she did? Their mothers weren't being held captive by a demonic creature of the underworld. It didn't matter now, though. She wouldn't make that mistake twice.

Solomon appeared at her side. "I'm going to head out. I don't need rest and there's no point in delaying any longer. If I can, I'll join you again as soon as possible."

Sera hesitated for a moment before saying, "As much as I'd appreciate your strength against the Ordog, I hope I only see you again at Nora's side."

That was as nice as she was going to get, but she had an

inkling that her feelings would change if she survived the fight against the Ordog. They kind of already had changed.

Ugh. Nora was going to rub it in Sera's face so hard.

He chuckled before ducking out of the room, leaving Sera with Danae.

Double ugh.

"Look at you, befriending the enemy," the Eternal said as she sat down on one of the cots. She pulled her legs up to sit cross-legged, leaning her back against the wall. "Are we going to brush each other's hair and gossip now?"

Sera rolled her eyes and ignored the girl, not rising to the bait. Thousands of years of experience under her belt and her maturity level had stayed the same. In Sera's eyes, the inability to mature was one of the significant drawbacks to becoming immortal. At least she was starting out an eternal life a decade older and wiser than Danae.

After lying down on an empty cot, Sera closed her eyes. What she really wanted to do was watch Danae like a hawk, but she had to trust the witch would stay put. That river of metal had been pretty intense and would be an ugly way to die. Besides, it wasn't like Hel was going to let the girl just prance all through her realm.

Placing her hands over her belly, Sera found peace in focusing on the rising and falling of her stomach as she breathed.

I'll keep an eye out, Bacchus said close by before making a slurping sound.

Not if you keep drinking that way.

He chuckled. *I've been drinking this way since the dawn of man. Trust me, I can handle my wine.*

CHAPTER 18

Serafina

Muscles ached and bones cracked as Sera stretched out her limbs on the cot.

I thought merging with you was supposed to help this? she thought irritably as she sat up and rubbed the sleep from her eyes.

You're still part human, he snitted back at her. He lay on the other side of her cot with his eyes closed and an empty glass dangling from one hand.

When Sera realized they were alone in the room with Renee who was still fast asleep, panic seized her heart. Danae was gone. Gasping for breath, Sera leaped to her feet and practically flew out the door.

Great muscles of Mars! Bacchus yelped behind her as he tumbled off the bed, landing on his back with a thud.

The Eternal sat at the table, which was once again covered in freshly prepared food, casually sipping on a glass of red liquid. Color had returned to the girl's face, and Sera's nostrils flared as she caught the familiar metallic scent.

Danae raised an eyebrow in her direction, amusement flickering across her face. "I got thirsty, but Mommy didn't leave me a cup by my bed."

"You agreed to remain loyal," Sera said through clenched teeth.

"And I am," the girl said, her tone dripping with ice, "but that doesn't mean I have to obey your every command."

"No, but don't think I won't kill you in a heartbeat if you try anything."

"What's that phrase you modern humans like to say?" She pretended to look thoughtful, tapping a finger against her chin. "No funny business?"

Rolling her eyes, Sera left the girl to wake Renee.

* * *

AFTER SERA AND RENEE had eaten to regain as much energy and strength as possible, they found Hel waiting for them in her throne room once again. Unlike before, no souls stood in line to beseech the goddess of death. There were no other souls at all, and their footsteps echoed across the empty hall.

The goddess herself stood next to the ornate wooden door some of the souls had passed through earlier. Only now the doorway was shut tight.

"I trust you rested well?" Hel asked.

"Yes, thank you for your hospitality." Sera removed the iron band from her finger and held it out toward the goddess. "And for your assistance getting us this far."

As Hel moved closer to Sera to take the ring, the conflicting scents of rosewater and rotten meat wafted beneath her nose. Catching a glimpse of white bone showing beneath the goddess's blackened cheek, Sera swallowed hard and focused on the blue eye, trying hard not to notice any details from the dead side of Hel's face.

Taking the ring in her healthy hand, Hel held it up before her. With the ring grasped between her finger and thumb, she drew a vertical line down in the air, and the iron band stretched into a dagger.

"Through this door is the path leading to the Ordog," she said. "While I cannot interfere in the lives of mortal men and women, I am not prohibited from assisting when it concerns the gods. The Ordog's overreach most assuredly affects us all."

The goddess placed the dagger in Sera's hands. "Take this with you and consider it a gift. The runes make it capable of slaying a god, should the aim be true. It must pierce the heart directly."

The blade was at least a foot long and jagged, almost more of a short sword than a dagger, and made of black iron with ancient Norse runes etched into the metal. Bone made up the handle, with grooves worn into the grip for her fingers. Despite the heavy metal used to forge the blade, the dagger felt light in Sera's hands—almost lighter than the ring had been.

She didn't know what to say. Hel may have just given her the key to stopping the Ordog, even without Theo by her side. Maybe, just maybe, she was strong enough to do this. She did have Bacchus, after all.

Humans didn't invent chaos theory for nothing, the Roman god said from his chaise.

Or maybe she'd end up tripping over a rock and impaling herself on the dagger thanks to her lifelong clumsiness. At least then she wouldn't be around to see the end of the world. "Thank you."

Hel took a step back. "I would like a word with the witch before you go."

Sera paused as she tucked the dagger into her pack. "With all due respect, Danae isn't super accommodating with chats."

"Not the Bacchae," Hel said. Her gaze moved to Renee. "The mortal."

Without waiting for a reply, the goddess turned and took a few steps away from the group.

Renee looked at Sera and Danae uneasily before following Hel. The two women spoke too quietly for Sera to hear from where she stood.

Can you hear what she's saying to Renee? Sera asked Bacchus, who had drifted a bit closer on his floating chaise.

It is unwise to eavesdrop on the divine, he replied with a sniff, floating back toward her.

Oh please. That's rich coming from you. She snorted in her mind.

Even if I wanted to, I couldn't, Bacchus said. *Her magic cloaks their words.*

Ha! So you tried, Sera said triumphantly. She knew the god too well.

Before either of them could say anything more, Renee

and Hel returned. Renee's face was thoughtful, but not unhappy with whatever they discussed. As much as Sera wanted to ask what Hel had said, she knew Renee would tell her if she felt right about doing so.

"One last word of warning," Hel said. "Time moves differently in the underworld. When you resurface to the land of the living, you may find days, if not weeks have passed."

Sera nodded, hoping the others wouldn't worry too much at the unknown length of time. Xolotl should be able to inform them of this nuance with his experience in the underworld.

"I wish you success in your endeavor. May we meet again in the far distant future," Hel said, raising her skeletal hand toward the door.

The portal swung open with a groan. Unlike before, no light spilled forth.

Instead, impenetrable darkness loomed before them.

* * *

AN HOUR INTO THEIR journey through the caves, Sera realized how much she had come to depend on Solomon's presence, not to mention his strength and control over Danae. But now he was gone. Sera may have had a god's powers, but Solomon had a calming presence she had relied upon without even realizing it, much like she did with Theo.

No wonder Nora had fallen so hard.

Coming full circle, I see, Bacchus chose that moment to chime in.

Yeah, yeah, Sera said with an eye roll in the god's direction. *Maybe he's not so bad.*

Bacchus drifted along beside her on his chaise. She'd be lying if she said she wasn't a little bit jealous of his mode of transportation. Although, technically, it was her feet carrying them both on this journey. To be fair to him—if she wanted to be, that is, which wasn't always the case—she didn't feel any real exhaustion from their excursion so far, not even after the demon attack outside the wall.

The path they followed was dark, an eerie dark that her glowing magical orb struggled to light up and her godsight had trouble piercing. Unlike the first tunnel they had entered, this one was not a smooth, narrow dome with walls and a ceiling within reach. The path they walked on now was made of loose dirt, wide enough to allow three to walk side by side if they chose.

No walls surrounded them to keep them from wandering off course. Instead, various sized tunnels led in different directions and chasms gaped, waiting to swallow someone up if they stepped too close.

A shudder passed through Sera as she contemplated the creation of the trail. What sort of creatures had worn such a course? Were there many, or was it a repetitive loop trudged by a few? Her skin tingled as she imagined what might lurk just beyond the light—watching them, unseen. This was precisely why she hated haunted houses.

An incessant drip, drip, drip of condensation splashing into puddles followed them as they walked. The puddles kept Sera's shoes and socks wet and squishy, a feeling she loathed. The dampness also contributed to the constant smell of must and mold.

After what felt like another hour of grumbling about the current state of things in her mind, Sera became aware that the nearly impenetrable dark was gradually becoming less pervasive. The rocks and puddles began to shine with a new light.

They stepped into a cavernous hall filled with stalagmites and stalactites reaching toward each other in ominous formations. Some even stretched up with clawed fingers as if trying to escape this hell. Water continued to drip from the rocks above into murky pools of water beside the path.

The source of the light, which was a blueish green in hue, came from something glowing across the ceiling and down parts of the walls. Sera couldn't tell if it was a fungus or an insect of some sort, but the image was almost pretty considering the location of where it chose to grow.

Be careful, Bacchus warned, settling onto his feet as he glanced around warily. His chaise fizzled away. *Something doesn't feel right here. Don't stray from the path.*

His unease was her unease, and goosebumps prickled across her skin like a fast-moving flood with his words. A crisp breeze rushed through the cave, rustling her hair and clothes. Odd. Where had that wind even come from? Were they closer to the surface than she thought?

"Bacchus said to…" her voice trailed off as a figure moved in the shadows.

Her grip tightened on the handle of her gun. Maybe she could test out its ability to work in the underworld with whatever approached. She really should have put the dagger from Hel in a more easily accessed location than her backpack. Such a dumb move.

Something about the figure seemed familiar, but she couldn't place it from a distance.

"Hey, don't come any closer," Sera called out. "Who are you?"

Renee gave her a perplexed look then turned to squint at the shadows. "Who are you talking to?"

"Someone's approaching," Sera said, not taking her gaze off the person. It was clear now it was a human. Or at least human-shaped.

Danae snickered. "I think you're seeing things. Have you finally cracked?"

The figure stepped into the light, his familiar brown hair and olive complexion warming Sera's heart. Her breath caught in her throat. But the vision couldn't be real. How was he here? Was he going to help them, or did they need to help him?

"Hiro?" Sera asked tentatively when she could breathe again, removing her hand from the gun.

Holy shit.

Guilt flooded her thoughts. Not once had she considered seeing Hiro in the underworld. With his kind soul, generosity, and desire to help others, she had been sure he'd be in a much better place than here. But what did she even know about where the dead went before now. She still didn't really know much despite visiting the damn underworld.

"Sera, there's no one there," Renee said gently, putting a hand out to stop her.

But Sera didn't listen as she brushed past her friend, intent on finding out what had happened to Hiro after he died. If Renee couldn't see him, than Sera's Gift must be showing her Hiro's soul.

She reached out a hand toward Hiro and stepped off

the path. A chill sank deep into her skin, a frigid cold that no heat would ever be able to penetrate. But she didn't care. Hiro smiled at her and raised a hand to take hers. His flesh was solid. He was real.

"Sera," Hiro said lovingly. "You came for me. I knew you would."

He pulled her closer and wrapped his arms around her. She breathed in his scent, one she would recognize forever, her heart feeling like it was about to burst from her chest. She couldn't believe this was happening.

Voices called her name from somewhere far away, but she wasn't ready to face them just yet. She needed more time with him. She needed to explain everything that had happened and how sorry she was that her selfish choices had led to his death.

"Hiro, I'm so sorry for what happened to you," she said, her eyes filling with tears as she held him tight.

"Shh, it wasn't your fault," he murmured against her hair. "I know that now."

"How are you here?" she asked, pulling away to look at his face. "Why aren't you somewhere better?"

He adjusted his glasses which had fallen askew when they hugged. So very Hiro.

"The vampire cursed me when she killed me," he said. "I was sent to you by some creature here. It told me we only had a short amount of time to get out and told me how. Quick. We have to go before it comes back."

He grabbed her hand and pulled her deeper into the shadows. A memory tugged at the back of her mind. Had she come here for Hiro? She must have. But where exactly was 'here' again? Her thoughts were too fuzzy to focus on.

"I thought I had someone to find…" she said.

"And you found him," Hiro said, smiling back at her

His face shifted for a second, displaying an impish grin that wasn't usual for him. Then it was back to Hiro's smile.

Despite the lingering feeling that something wasn't right, that she was forgetting something, something important, she followed him deeper into the dark. This man deserved to be alive, more than most people did. She would bring him back, even if her heart had moved on.

Colors bleached into a deep black, the chill seeping into her very bones, slowing her movements.

So cold, she thought, her teeth chattering as she trudged along with him.

A loud chant echoed around her, and a moment later she flew backward from Hiro, crying out as she lost her grip on his hand. Hiro—or whatever had been pretending to be him—screeched, the fake human skin sliding off of the creature beneath like an ill-fitting jacket. The demon, for there was no other word for this *thing*, stood awkwardly on two legs, its claws reaching for Sera.

But the most terrifying and disgusting part was its lack of flesh. As if the demon had been flayed alive, bones, muscles, and tendons were revealed as it glared at the light shining behind Sera.

She scrambled back as another command rang through the darkness, and the creature's head exploded.

CHAPTER 19

Solomon

The market in Helheim turned out to be as loud and lively as any other real-world market, only this one was devoid of smells and colors. Greys, blacks, and all shades in between filled the entire landscape. Dull didn't even begin to describe the place. Everything lacked the vividness and realness of the world above.

Solomon stuck out like a sore thumb.

Heads and gazes turned to follow him as he passed, seeking out the woman Ragna. But when he approached individuals one-on-one to ask for directions, they turned away and pretended like they couldn't hear him. Their behavior was infuriating because he knew they heard and understood him—their shoulders would stiffen when he said the woman's name. But it also angered him because his

Immortal *influence* did nothing here.

He knew because he tried.

After five such incidents, Solomon was ready to start decapitating the uncooperative souls. He let out a heavy sigh as the next person attended to something that didn't require the man's attention.

"Psst!" a small voice caught his attention.

Peeking out from behind a clothing stall, a little girl with mischievous eyes and bright blonde hair crooked her finger at him before turning and running around the corner. She couldn't have been more than six or seven years old.

"Hey, wait," Solomon called out as he picked up his pace to follow.

Finally, *someone* had acknowledged him, and she wasn't nearly as colorless as the rest. He knew better than to take someone's age or appearance at face value, especially in the underworld.

But when he turned the corner, the little girl was gone.

Instead, he found himself in the middle of the market square, facing a well-built stone well. A washerwoman with grey hair held tight in a bun on the top of her head sat on the edge. She pulled bucket after bucket from within its depths, handing them off to a line of customers who would place an item or two in a box at her feet as payment. A bartering system of sorts. No money in the afterlife.

As he approached, the woman met his gaze with tired eyes the same lackluster color as her hair. "Hel sent you, I suppose."

Her blunt statement caught him off guard, but it shouldn't have. Perhaps the lack of colors and scents affected him more than he had realized.

"You are Ragna?"

She chuckled, prickly hairs on her chin quivering. "In the flesh. Tell me what you need."

"Mortality," he said.

"Hm. Unusual request, most folks visiting want the opposite. But no matter. It can be done." She passed off the last bucket to a waiting soul and placed a hand on her knee before pushing herself to her feet with a grunt. She was a small woman, made smaller still by slumping over in her older age.

The line of souls waiting for water grumbled and threw glares in Solomon's direction as they turned away.

"Oh, quit your bellyaching," Ragna said to them with a swat in the air with her hand. "Never letting me take a break," she grumbled as she waddled away. "And they wonder why they're still here."

They followed a sloped cobblestone road leading down whatever hill or mountainside on which the city rested, taking a few turns as buildings blocked the way straight. The always present mist in the air slowly turned into a thicker fog the farther down they went.

When Solomon could scarcely see more than a few feet in front of him, Ragna stopped and rang a bell attached to a wooden post that hadn't been there a moment ago. The fog parted as a small skiff sailed in, manned by a standing robed figure holding a staff with one end in the water. They had reached a river.

Ragna jerked her thumb at the boat. "This guy will take you across."

"Who is it?" Solomon asked, trying to see a face under the long grey hood.

She shrugged. "He doesn't speak, and he's from the other side."

She began to waddle away.

"Wait," Solomon reached out a hand to stop her. "What's on the other side? What should I do once there?"

"Across this river lies the realm of Hades. Nyssa will take it from there." She waved to him as she moved away and disappeared into the fog.

After turning back around, Solomon eyed the man with the staff, not entirely trusting someone who didn't—or wouldn't—speak or show his face, and stepped into the boat. Not like he had any other options.

As Ragna had said, the figure guiding the boat across the river never spoke a word. But in all fairness, Solomon didn't either. The two stood in silence as the hooded figure pushed the pole against the ground beneath the murky water, a dense fog cloaking their journey. It was impossible to tell how deep the river was as the other end of the pole never appeared. Solomon could have waded across the river for all he knew.

Only he didn't want to face any monsters that lurked beneath the surface.

A few minutes later, the figure stopped pushing. The boat slowed and bumped into something, which turned out to be another dock as the mists around them cleared. A striking woman with hair the color of a fiery sunset and wearing a white dress that looked a bit like a folded toga stood to wait for him.

"Nyssa?" Solomon asked as he stepped off the boat onto the wooden planks of the dock.

"Welcome to Hades, Solomon," Nyssa said, her striking

blue eyes meeting his. "I pray you find what you seek here, though I advise against the attempt."

She took his hand in hers to lead him away from the shore.

When he turned back to thank the man on the boat, both were gone. The fog had already swallowed him and his vessel up again. So much for etiquette.

"Why do you advise against it?" Solomon asked, returning his attention to his current path and the woman guiding him.

"It will be a demanding road to travel, and a more challenging life to live should you return," Nyssa said. The silk fabric of her gown whispered against her legs as they walked.

Her words unsettled him a little, but Solomon was used to difficult roads. His entire life had been one.

Back on land, the farther they walked, the more the fog dissipated. Soon, snow-capped mountains appeared in the far distance, across rolling green fields stretching toward the horizon. From time to time, a breeze would sweep through, rustling the grasses and Nyssa's hair.

This must be the heaven many dreamed about. What was it called in Greek mythology? The Elysian Fields? He would have to confirm his guess when he returned to the land of the living.

Ever since his Immortal transformation, Solomon hadn't put much thought into the afterlife, until now. He could see how this peacefulness could be appealing. Someday, he would have to put more thought into it, just not yet.

"Where are we going?" he asked.

He was a tolerably patient man, but he also wanted to get back to Nora with good news. He ran a hand over his closely cropped hair as he realized he finally may have some good news to share.

"To regain your mortality, you must face and say goodbye to your past," Nyssa explained. "You will drink the water from each of the five rivers of Hades, and each will challenge you in a new way. Should you succeed with all five, you will have what you seek."

The explanation was said casually, but Solomon had a feeling it would be much more intense than it sounded. He clenched his jaw with determination.

Whatever it took.

As they crested a hill, an enormous tree somehow stood before them. Its diameter had to stretch at least fifty feet or more, dwarfing the largest known tree on Earth. Solomon should have seen the giant long before then, but things didn't seem to work logically in the underworld.

Far above him, green leaves filled the tree's branches, which stayed close to its trunk as if hugging it. Beneath those limbs, water bubbled up from the soil, quite possibly from the tree itself. The water flowed out in the form of streams, which flowed into the distant fields, growing broader in size as they wound away from the tree.

"The rivers of Hades," Nyssa said, holding out an arm like an introduction.

She led Solomon to the closest stream and settled herself on a bumpy root perfectly suited as a seat. Beside her, a goblet made of golden glass shimmered into being.

"Shall we begin?" she asked as she raised her gaze to meet Solomon's.

He nodded and took a seat opposite her on the same oversized root. Looking down at the water flowing beside them, two separate streams quickly merged into one. The bubbling flow drowned out any other sounds of life that might exist in the branches far above them. If there was any.

Nyssa dipped the goblet into the water and handed it to him. "First will be Acheron and Cocytus. The two go hand in hand and naturally flow into one another."

Not knowing what to expect but willing to do anything, Solomon drank without hesitation. The water was clear and crisp and pleasantly refreshing. And then he felt himself falling back into oblivion.

***

SOLOMON STUMBLED TO HIS feet in pure darkness. Not even his hands were visible when held in front of his face. He was certain he hadn't actually gone anywhere, that the sense of travel occurred solely in his mind. But then this was the underworld. Its magic could have transported him anywhere, he supposed.

Patience was a virtue, they say, and Solomon had a couple of centuries to hone his. He waited in the dark, an experience he was sure was meant to make him worry or feel lost or something. But Solomon felt peace settle over him in the quiet, wondering what was to come first. Whatever it was, he would prove himself worthy. He had to. The most beautiful woman in the world waited for him.

A pinprick of light in the distance caught his eye. As the light floated closer, Solomon saw it was a person. A white man he knew well because it was the first person Solomon ever killed.

The man gazed at Solomon with sorrow in his eyes while blood seeped from two deep puncture wounds on his neck. Wounds Solomon had made after Lorenzo gifted him with his Immortality. Draining this man had completed the transformation.

Only he could see now what he couldn't see before in his mortal life. Back then all he could see was hate. Hate for the men and women who had enslaved his kind. His own *mother*. Taken her from him. But now, black circles under the man's eyes and wrinkles in his leathery skin, skin that was far too old for the man's age, spoke of a more hardened life than Solomon had realized at the time.

The severe slump to the man's shoulders seemed to drag him toward the ground. His clothes hung from his frame as if he hadn't eaten a good meal in weeks. Maybe longer. His shoes and pants had holes in them, and dirt-stained skin showed through. When was the last time the man had bathed?

A deep sadness penetrated Solomon's core.

He had killed a man—a stranger—in exchange for Immortality. But it was more straightforward than that. Solomon would have killed him regardless because he was white. But this man wasn't a slaver. He wasn't responsible for Solomon's horrific upbringing. Not directly, anyway. But what had he done to stop the atrocities?

Nothing.

Then a little girl, no more than four or five, stepped out from behind the man and took his hand. They looked at each other with love and adoration before the man faded away into the darkness. The stricken little girl was left holding air.

She put her hands to her face and cried, wailed, at her

loss. Her tear-streaked face looked at Solomon. "Why?" Her voice broke as she spoke through her sobs. "Why did you take my daddy away?"

Solomon's heart dropped into the pit of his stomach. He had done this to her, taken her father away from her. He hadn't considered what taking the man's life would mean to those left behind. He had never even wondered. They had taken so much from him, why would he have cared?

But now, Solomon wondered. What kind of father would he be with his past haunting him? Did he deserve to be a father after what he had done?

A young woman with a heavily pregnant belly appeared next to the girl and took her hand. Together they walked past Solomon, a single bag on the woman's back. Solomon turned as they passed, seeing the early greys in the woman's otherwise brown hair.

A rowhouse appeared in the misty darkness as the woman and child approached. She knocked three times on the door, then looked down at her daughter with such sadness it was going to break Solomon in two.

The door opened, and a well-dressed woman let them in. Her upper lip curled in disgust at the sight and smell of the two newcomers. Before the door closed, Solomon spied businessmen and soldiers lounging in a parlor, being waited upon and teased by scantily dressed women. A whorehouse.

Solomon had killed the woman's husband, the child's father, and their only source of living. She'd had to find a new way to earn a living, and Solomon had driven her to whore herself, even while with child. Sure, there were worse fates in life, but had she been able to shield her daughter from that life?

He knew better than to be that naive.

And so the cycle continued. Face after familiar face materialized out of the darkness to show Solomon what he had taken from them. Hundreds of people would need to appear if he was to see them all.

He was.

CHAPTER 20

Serafina

Out of instinct, Sera raised an arm to block the barrage of blood and guts raining down on her as the demonic creature's head exploded. Hands, real human hands this time, grabbed her arms and hauled her back onto the path and into the light.

"What the hell just happened?" Sera asked as she scrambled back to her feet and tried to wipe the sticky, steaming gore from her clothes. But she ended up just making more of a mess.

"Something found you to be easy prey," Danae said without looking up, kneeling and washing off her hands in a pool of water on the path.

"You scared me to death," Renee said and helped pick chunky black bits of guts off Sera, sticky tendrils clinging like they didn't want to let go. "No pun intended."

You scared me, too, Bacchus said quietly beside her, his wine glass nowhere in sight. He must have been terrified.

"Did you just save my life?" Sera blinked at Danae, not quite sure she was processing everything correctly yet.

"Whatever that was…" The Eternal glanced into the darkness and narrowed her eyes. "Just trust me, you're better off with the Ordog."

"I thought you'd welcome any outcome for me as long as it didn't involve winning."

"There are some outcomes I would not wish upon my worst enemies." Danae met her eyes as she stood. "Including you."

Sera's mouth hung wide open as Danae turned and started down the path again. Now what the hell was she supposed to do? The creature that had ruined her life several times over had just saved it.

One act of kindness doesn't a saint make, Bacchus said by her side, watching Danae with a soft expression. *But she wasn't always a monster.*

Before following the girl, Sera opened her backpack and withdrew the dagger and a length of rope, which she tied around her waist, then around the handle of the blade. A makeshift holster that would just have to do. She shrugged at Renee's comically quizzical look before slinging her pack back over her shoulders.

What happened to her? she asked Bacchus.

Ask her. His floating chaise reappeared, and he settled onto it before drifting back behind her. His hint that he was done answering questions.

Sera fell into step beside Danae. "Why do you hate

mortals so much?"

The girl glanced at her with a smirk. "Are you actually curious or did Bacchus tell you to ask me where I came from?"

"Of course he did," Sera said, "but I still want to know why you hate us. Well, them now, I guess."

The girl turned her attention back to the path ahead. "What do you know about ancient Crete and the Minoans?"

"Just a high-level overview. Thriving civilization until some kind of catastrophe occurred."

"A volcano," Danae said. "Across the Mediterranean. The resulting tsunamis devastated our coastal towns and ships, our way of communicating and trading with the outside world. The ash and soot clouds lasted for months, altering our very climate, and ruined our crops. We were dying.

"Back then, we believed that the gods controlled everything. The priest-kings convinced everyone that we had done something to incur divine wrath to end our way of life. So, they sacrificed what was most precious to them."

Danae's fists curled into balls at her sides. "Their children. All of them."

Sera remained quiet as she processed just how old Danae actually was—at least three and a half *thousand* years, if she actually lived during Minoan times. It was hard to comprehend living for so long, particularly because this one looked and acted so young. Sera had heard similar theories about the fall of the Minoans but never had it confirmed by a source who had actually witnessed it. Because until a few months ago, a primary source hadn't been a legitimate possibility for Sera.

Her thirst for this girl's historical knowledge made her mouth salivate.

"I tried to stop them," Danae continued. "I was an orphan, but not young enough to be considered a worthy sacrifice. They had me whipped close to death as my punishment. The street ran red with my blood until someone stopped them. My savior. When I woke up, I was in the temple of Bacchus and given a new choice in life. I took it, of course, and here I am."

"You blame all of humanity for the acts of something that occurred thousands of years ago?" Sera asked, only partially incredulous. The girl didn't exactly come across as entirely sane.

"Oh, Serafina, you really are naive," Danae said with a laugh. "You think the atrocities ended there? If you had witnessed what I have over the millennia, you wouldn't be questioning my motives."

"You murder people like Hiro, the real Hiro, who was good and kind and making the world a better place," Sera said, a flush of anger rising in her cheeks. "You slit his throat without any hesitation. You're no better than the humans you blame."

"Tell me that after you've seen babies and innocent children murdered senselessly as an offering to gods who couldn't be bothered to care less." Her top lip pulled up into a sneer. "Ask Bacchus how much the gods care. Ask him why none of them ever stepped in to stop the suffering. Ask why children are still starving, still massacred, still abused."

The sacrifices broke her, Bacchus said, his chaise drifting close once again. *One of the kids was her baby brother, who she raised like her own child. Her only family.*

A battle raged inside Sera's mind and body. This woman, this *girl*, had condemned Sera's mother to an eternal life with the devil, had murdered the man she loved, and tried to destroy the entire mortal world. In addition to trying to kill Sera. But that very same mortal world had created this monster.

Did they deserve the treatment Danae wanted to give them? Were they, was *Sera*, even worth saving?

Granted, technically Bacchus had created the *immortal* monster Danae became, but humans had destroyed her mind first. A twinge of sympathy tugged at Sera's heart. She couldn't even imagine witnessing what Danae had and losing what she had. She had felt destroyed after losing Hiro, even knowing he wasn't "the one." He was one of the best *humans* she had ever known.

Losing her mother had been awful, especially the older she got. She missed all the moments they should have had together. At least she'd still had her father, even with his years of not being fully present. His grief ran deep.

But Danae had no one else. What would it have been like losing the only family she had known and as a teenager, one of the most volatile ages in life? Sera was all about forgiving people who deserved it. Did Danae deserve forgiveness? Not yet.

But maybe she could get there.

Sera swallowed hard, getting ready to say she was sorry for all that had happened to the girl, but Danae pushed ahead of her. "I vowed to see you safely to the Ordog. I'm done talking."

Ugh. Well, thank the gods she hadn't apologized. She had fallen for the Eternal's bullshit completely. After all that thinking that maybe Danae deserved a little sympathy, and in reality, the girl was just doing it for herself.

Only part of it was for herself, Bacchus said, his gaze focused on the back of Danae's head.

If you think that, then you're too gullible. Sera bit the inside of her cheek, hating that she took her anger out on him. He knew how she really felt, but it didn't make her feel any better.

Not gullible, he said. *Hopeful.*

* * *

WE'RE HERE, BACCHUS said quietly, now walking beside her. His wine glass was nowhere in sight. After the encounter with the fake Hiro, his missing wine almost terrified Sera more than the cavern they entered.

The domed cavern they entered was beyond vast, with at least a dozen dark tunnels leading out in all directions. Like the previous widening in the caves, a blueish-green luminescence covered the ceiling high above them, as well as the walls, trailing down to the floor. The substance lit up the cavern enough that Sera extinguished her own magical orb. This time she could tell it was a fungus and not an insect of some sort, not that it mattered much down here. Either one could be deadly.

Her breath puffed out in front of her as the temperature dropped significantly in the open air. Renee pulled her scarf tighter around her neck with a shaking hand.

So much for hell being an inferno, Sera thought.

Columns of thick black rock had formed from stalagmites and stalactites finally meeting. They stood alongside the main path that continued inside this hall-like room, as if someone had created them that way on purpose. They towered high, the top of the cave at least a few stories up, if not more.

As she approached the closest column, Sera squinted at the design. Images had been carved into the rock. In one, a demonic creature grinned as he held up an arm torn from a screaming body.

Shuddering at the savagery, though not entirely unlike Bacchus's favorite fighting style, Sera turned her attention back to the path ahead of her.

A raised throne made of towering glossy black stalagmites that looked like hands with sharp claws reaching for the ceiling loomed before them, menacing any who approached. Sera glanced around warily and drew her gun, sensing an overwhelming ugliness about the place. Out of the corner of Sera's eye, Renee withdrew a handful of crystals she had packed, and Danae grew still.

The throne became hazy as if she stared at a mirage, and a seated figure appeared from within the haze, one leg crossed over the other.

The Ordog.

He was grotesque. Massive understatement, but Sera didn't have any other words to describe the real-life monster that sat before them. He vaguely resembled a satyr—half man and half goat. But that's where the similarities ended.

While far from human, his top half was more humanoid, covered in dusky greyish-brown skin, and his rotund bare belly glistened in the heat of the room. He reached one of his hands up to scratch at his stomach with long, yellowing claws. Something dark—dirt, or blood most likely—caked the undersides of those wicked claws.

His head was part human, part goat, and part demon. Blackened horns protruded from his forehead, twisting upward and outward like ram's horns.

His lower animal half was covered in pitch-black wool, ending in scorched cloven hooves. A long tail, more rat-like than anything but ending in a razor-sharp blade, lazily flicked by his legs. The creature uncrossed his legs, and Sera caught a glance of his oversized genitals rising between them.

Her stomach lurched, sending bitter acid to coat the back of her throat. She swallowed it down, wincing as it burned in both directions.

Four-legged creatures, just like the ones who attacked them outside of Helheim's city walls, melted out of the shadowy tunnels, their eyes glowing green as they prowled among the rocks. A black tarry substance dripped from their bodies and out of canine-shaped mouths, sizzling on the ground beneath them. Not quite enough of them to surround Sera's small group, but enough to make the devil's strength known to them.

As one creature stepped a bit too close for Sera's comfort, she tossed a glare in its direction, the golden light in her eyes flaring to life with the god's power. It yowled as if burnt and stepped back, hissing at her and revealing rows of sharp teeth. Maybe they were more like cats than dogs. It was hard to tell.

"What a delightful treat you've brought me, Danae," the Ordog said in a deep voice, more like bleating.

Sera grimaced as the sound ground against her already frayed nerves. If there was ever a time she missed Theo and Solomon—hell, even Lasirenn—it was now.

"As promised," Danae said, a smirk on her lips.

A creeping sensation skittered across Sera's skin at Danae's words. She knew the witch had been working with the Ordog, and she had made no secret of wanting to accompany them to the underworld. But Sera was the one who abducted Danae and planned this whole trip… wasn't she?

Had they unwittingly just walked into a trap?

CHAPTER 21

Serafina

"Whatever deal you think you have with Danae, it's not happening," Sera said, lifting her chin in defiance. "I'm here for my mother and the other witches, whose lives you stole unjustly."

The Ordog's smile made her stomach curdle. The teeth that showed briefly in his mouth were jagged and nearly all black with decay.

"Ah, yes," he bleated. "Rachel Finch. Such a spirited young filly. She was difficult to break, but they all do in the end."

A hand pulled back on Sera's arm as she stepped forward. Rage threatened to rip her apart, but she clenched her teeth to keep it in check as she turned toward Renee.

Somehow her friend's energy calmed her enough to keep from making a mistake, for now. But she couldn't stop the shaking as she held in her magic. She wanted to incinerate everything in front of her.

Some of the Ordog's minions tittered and scampered away, probably sensing her fury about to burst.

"I do not simply give away my toys to anyone who asks," the Ordog said.

"I'm not asking." She glared back at him. "I *will* be leaving here with the witches. All nine of them."

The Ordog leaned back against his throne and considered her, scratching his engorged genitals in the process. While she refused to let him get the upper hand by making her look away, she still had to swallow down the burning acid rising in her throat again. A bitter aftertaste coated her tongue.

"I would like to see if Danae told the truth about you," he said and snapped his fingers.

Before Sera could open her mouth to question his meaning, the blueish-green fungus illuminating the cavern erupted into flames all around them. Even from where she stood, the heat was like the midday sun bearing down in the middle of summer. The demons closest to the fire yelped and skittered away. One was not so lucky, and the fire engulfed its entire body. The creature emitted blood-curdling shrieks before disintegrating completely.

The remaining beasts lunged at Sera.

Without hesitation, she let the divine side of her genetic code take over. Bacchus's shimmering image beside her faded away, and they became one moving unit. They raised their gun and fired, not even bothering to aim as a human would. The bullets found their marks, earning yelps and shrieks but not stopping the demons as they had hoped. When their ammunition ran out, they flipped the gun up to catch it by the barrel and used the grip to bash against a demon's skull instead.

Hey, whatever worked.

Burning pain seared through their leg. Another of the creatures had ripped through their calf and was biting through their skin with its razor-sharp teeth. The same damn leg as on the wall.

Sera and Bacchus's blood pounded in their ears as rage rose within them, and they let out a guttural roar so fierce it caused the demon to let go and glance up warily. They took that moment to pull out a golden thread of magic. The strand slithered down their arm, past their hand, and wrapped itself around the handle of the gun. There, it stretched out the barrel into the form of a blade. A divine sword of fury.

Now *that* was much better.

As the demon who had bitten them lunged for their leg again, they thrust downward and through its head. Black ooze bubbled out of the hole. They kicked the body at the next nearest creature, sending the two tumbling into the waiting flames. The demon still alive shrieked in pain before fleeing down a darkened tunnel, flames licking at its heels.

A quick glance over their shoulder showed Danae and Renee on their feet and unharmed but somehow immobilized. The Eternal stood as still as a statue while Renee glared at the Ordog, wriggling against her invisible bonds. At least she was okay, and Sera and Bacchus could focus on the fight.

Holding the grip of the gun-turned-sword with both hands, they sliced at the seven remaining hell beasts. The creatures circled them on four legs, looking for a weakness. As one, the demons leaped toward them.

Using the blade to deflect their teeth and claws, they parried the attacks. When they saw an opening, they lunged, and the sword found its way through a beast's chest to puncture its heart. If it even had a heart. Whatever the creature had inside, the sword did its job.

They continued to fend off the beasts' attacks while bringing them down one by one. Slicing and thrusting became a monotonous movement, their muscles moving in a dance only a god could perform. When the last beast fell, they wiped inky black tar from their eyes.

A pile of body parts lay between two columns, black blood pooling out beneath them.

Bacchus stepped out of Sera's body to stand at her side once again, though he made a point of giving her a wide berth. As she panted, the creatures' tar-like blood dripped off of her body and down the blade of her makeshift sword.

Behind her, Renee let out an exasperated huff and stepped closer, no longer restrained by the Ordog's magic. She eyed Sera up and down, her open mouth and wide eyes a mix of awe and concern, before giving Sera a questioning look.

"I'm fine," she said to her friend, although she may have been lying. Her muscles quivered as she tried to process what had just happened. She was a little in awe of herself, even if it had been Bacchus's chaotic nature in control.

How very contradictory.

"You are a beautiful killing machine," the Ordog said,

drawing Sera's attention back to him. "Let us make a deal."

"What deal?" She took a deep breath to calm her panting.

A slick sensation made her glance down at her arm where a chunk of… something from one of the creatures slid down her sweat. A black smear followed behind it.

Sera shook the piece off, grimacing. She was going to need an hour-long shower after this was all over. Maybe two.

"It's simple," he said. "You give me something that I want, and I give you the witches."

She snorted. Simple. Right. Whatever he wanted, she couldn't possibly give to him. It was a devil's trick, but two could play at that game.

"How do I know you still have them?" she asked, pushing back strands of wet hair from her face. She didn't want to know if it was damp from sweat or demon blood. Some things were better off a mystery.

He spread his arms wide. "Where else would they be?"

"I want to see them for myself," she said firmly. "Bring them here, and then we can talk."

He considered her again before flicking his hand toward one of his remaining demonic creatures. The beast turned and scurried from the cavern down one of the smaller tunnels untouched by the fire that continued to rage around them. As it disappeared into the dark, more creatures slunk into the cavern to replace the dead.

Just how many of these demons did he have at his beck and call?

"Let's wrap up our deal, shall we?" Danae said.

"Patience is not your virtue," the Ordog replied.

Danae seethed up at him. "I have waited *millennia* for

this. Do not try my patience."

Hairs stood on end all along Sera's body. Whatever Danae had bargained with the devil for, Sera most definitely did not want to find out. The goal was to get out first, Danae in tow and back in custody once again. Or dead. That would be okay, too.

A repetitive clanking sound followed by scraping echoed through the cavern from one of the tunnels, distracting them from any further speech. The canine servant appeared, this time standing on just two legs like a dancing dog while pulling on a heavy iron chain with one of its front paws. Sera's eyes widened, not realizing they could stand that way.

With its other paw, the hound cracked a whip toward something still hidden in the tunnel, grinning at the echoing groans it created. A line of manacled humans stumbled into the cavern, squinting against the light of the roaring flames, a few shying away from the heat.

They were beyond filthy, with dirt and blood clinging to their tattered clothing and skin. Seven figures emerged from the tunnel, and it was the last that Sera recognized, even looking past all the grime. She could paint that face in her sleep. The face she had studied in pictures for the past twenty years as her memories faded.

Her breath caught in her throat, her chest constricting with happiness and grief. So many moments together lost, yet so many more to come once they got home.

"Mom," Sera's voice cracked as she spoke.

She took a few steps forward before the creature holding the chain hissed at her, steaming spit spluttering to the ground.

Her mother looked up, meeting her gaze. Confusion turned to recognition a moment later and her mouth dropped open.

"S-Sera…?" her mother's voice was halting and faint, scratchy as if she hadn't used it in a very long time.

"A beautiful family reunion," the Ordog interrupted before either woman could say more.

Rage like she had never known built within Sera, and she had to bite the inside of her cheek to keep it from exploding as she turned to glare at the devil. Copper coated the back of her throat as she swallowed hard. The magical blade of her sword hummed in response to her anger.

This creature had stolen a life from both Sera and her mother, lives neither one of them could get back. Not fully. And here he was, ruining what should have been a joyous moment. She balled her fist at her side, feeling Bacchus's fury burning bright and hot within and beside her.

A sudden realization pulled her gaze to the line of witches, counting them again. Seven. She hadn't miscounted. "Where are the other two?"

"One was too weak to survive, and I needed to make an example of one to keep the others in line." His eyes wandered over each witch, a grin spreading across his face as they flinched and dropped their gaze to the ground. Only Rachel kept her eyes locked on Sera.

"So, you see they are alive," he continued, "Now, for what *I* want."

"What is it you want?" she asked between clenched teeth.

Her entire body shook with fury, her blood pumping like fiery ice. It had taken her twenty years to discover the truth, and in that time, they had lost two of their own.

"You."

Sera blinked at the beast on the throne, sure she had misheard since she had been lost in her thoughts. "Say what?"

"A Gifted witch merged with a god of chaos would make a far more powerful queen to rule by my side than this creature." He gestured loosely at Danae as if she wasn't a concern to him anymore.

"Sera, no," her mother cried out, trying to step forward.

The chains connecting her to the other witches held her back, as well as a sharp jab to her stomach from one of the creatures. Her breath whooshed out, and she doubled over.

"Stop!" Sera's magic flared out from within as she raised her free hand, a blast of golden energy hitting the hound square in its chest.

Its skin sizzled and popped as it fell backward, screeching in what she hoped was pain. Intense pain.

The Ordog smiled, his eyes gleaming. "Such untapped power."

Danae bared her extended fangs, her eyes blazing red as if from an inner inferno. "We had a deal of our own."

"Yes, and we've fulfilled both sides of our bargain," he said, his gaze not straying from Sera's. "You brought me the girl, and I gave you dark magic."

Danae let out a sharp laugh. "As if that would have been a fair trade. You promised to make me a queen."

He turned his demonic eyes on her then. "And I did make you a queen, just not *my* queen. It's not my fault you lost your throne, despite the shield I placed over your compound."

"I will be Queen of the Underworld," Danae retorted, crimson lines creeping outward beneath the surface of the skin around her eyes. "Or you will lose *your* throne."

He sneered at her and uttered a command in a language Bacchus didn't know. Hell beasts surged out of the tunnels, avoiding the flames to surround Danae. They snapped their powerful jaws as they closed in on her.

Despite the threat, Danae didn't flinch or even look away from the Ordog. She continued to simmer in her fury at being deceived.

Sera almost felt bad for the girl. Her "friend" had just turned on her. Who was the naive one now?

The devil returned his gaze to Sera and held out a hand. "Come, my queen. Come, and claim your throne."

The Ordog continued to reach his cracked and stained claws toward Sera as her mind raced, considering all the angles. She had expected to fight the Ordog, not make a decision to become his queen in return for the witches' freedom. What exactly did becoming the devil's queen entail anyway? Did that also mean his bride, like, in the bedroom?

Not going there, Sera thought with a shudder. She would definitely lose whatever food and acid were left in her stomach if she did.

Bacchus remained quiet beside her. His inner thoughts had made it clear that the Ordog would be able to hear anything he said directly to Sera.

The devil's realm, the devil's rules.

No other options presented themselves in her mind, but her mother and the others captured with her had suffered for long enough. There was no way she would let them stay, especially after giving them this glimmer of hope for freedom. And maybe, just maybe, she could find Hiro's soul as well, his *real* soul. If nothing else, she wanted to hug him one more time and tell him how very sorry she was. No one deserved to live more than he did.

Sera would accept the devil's deal, for the witches and for Hiro, and she and Bacchus would escape. Neither of them knew how yet, but Bacchus seemed to think he had been in worse predicaments. That, or he was trying to make her feel better while hiding the truth. He had been known to do such a thing before.

And yet…

If they couldn't escape somehow, then she would be giving up Theo as well. Her lungs constricted as if the air had been sucked from the cavern. They hadn't even had a chance to see what they could be, if anything, because she had been so focused on getting *here*. And now she was here and regretting not taking advantage of the time they had together.

What the fuck was wrong with her?

Maybe it was better this way if she was never going to return. Nothing for him—for either of them—to lose. She took a deep, shuddering breath.

"If I accept," Sera said, "you need to also allow this human witch, Renee, to return with the others."

The Ordog gave a casual nod, though his fingers gripped the arms of his throne. "Anything my queen wishes."

Renee put a hand on her arm again. Quietly, she said, "No, Sera, we will figure out another way."

Anything she wished? There had to be a catch. Bacchus's memories filtered through to her present thoughts, reminding her of Danae.

"Considering your loophole with Danae, how do I know you will uphold your end of the bargain?" Sera asked, placing a hand over Renee's.

"I upheld my end of the bargain with the Bacchae witch."

Danae opened her mouth to retort, but Sera held up a hand. By some miracle, the girl obeyed.

"How do I know you'll do as you say?" Sera asked again.

"You have my word," the Ordog said.

She laughed. Trust the devil's word. Yeah, right. But it would be a life for a life. It would be enough. It had to be.

The Ordog regarded her, rapping his ghastly nails on the arm of his throne. She tried not to think about those nails being anywhere near her once this deal was complete. Was she making the biggest mistake of her life? Her *eternal* life?

A warm, firm hand slipped into hers, and she looked over at Bacchus. He squeezed her hand and smiled, though it didn't quite reach his eyes.

Sera glanced at the line of witches. Each of them had become still and quiet during the conversation, chains no longer clinking together. Only their eyes darted back and forth between Sera and the Ordog. Avoiding her mother's gaze so as not to lose her nerve, Sera could only assume they were waiting with bated breath for their new sentencing.

"I would also like a few minutes with my mom before they go back to the land of the living," Sera said.

"It shall be done," the devil said, licking his lips as he leaned forward. His eyes narrowed with anticipation, and the fire filling the cavern grew even hotter and brighter.

Sweat slid down Sera's face and dripped off of her eyebrows.

"Then I acc—"

"I don't think so," Danae interrupted.

She held out her palm, now covered with blood, toward the witches and chanted a word. Crimson dripped from her fangs and down her chin.

Before Sera could react to protect them from whatever spell the girl had cast, the chains binding the seven witches glowed brightly then dropped from their limbs.

They were free.

CHAPTER 22

Nora

Calliope, Clio, Erato, Euterpe, Melpomene, Polyhymnia, Terpsichore, Thalia, and Urania. Not only could Nora recite the names by heart and in any order, but she could also tell you all sorts of historical—and sometimes boring—information about each of them. She had spent the last few weeks on the internet, in the library, and talking to other professors about the nine Muses.

Anything to keep her mind off the fact that the others still weren't back from the underworld, and her best source of information, the Roman god who caused all these problems, had gone with them. She even tried tracking down additional ancestors online, but that turned out to be a nonstarter. She wasn't technologically savvy enough—nor did she have the patience—for a detailed search.

So, she did the next logical thing—she sent a vial of her spit to one of those companies who would do it all for her. The cost would be worth every penny if she found others like her.

Nora glanced out the diner window with a deep sigh. Snow fell to the ground, blanketing the District's streets and sidewalks in white. It had been snowing nonstop this winter. Probably less than it felt like, but after the storms in France and now February flakes in the District, it was getting old fast. They could still see winter weather for the next two months, but Nora needed the sunshine to lift her mood.

Oi. February meant it was almost Sera's birthday. Nora and Sera hadn't missed celebrating each other's birthdays since they met as kids and certainly hadn't planned to with this excursion to hell. But almost two weeks had passed without a peep from below.

Nora should have just forgotten classes and gone with everyone. Sera had been the smarter of the two, no real surprise there, to take a leave of absence this semester. They could have just celebrated her birthday with candles lit by the fires of hell.

Nora had no idea if they were even still alive—

They are, darling, Freyja chimed in.

—or if they were finding any success. She wanted to summon Hel on several occasions, but Freyja had warned against the attempt without Renee's assistance. Too many things could go wrong.

Nora took in a deep, shuddering breath as she thought about the woman who was like an aunt to her. Renee had been in her life as long as she could remember, and now there was a chance she was never coming back. They hadn't even had a chance to say goodbye.

Biting her lip to keep it from quivering, Nora forced her mind back to Hel. Freyja had also mentioned it wouldn't be wise to interfere with the others' plans below. If Nora summoned Hel while the others were trying to talk to her, well, that could cause some major problems.

If you're finished with your little pity party, the Norse goddess said, *Theodore has arrived.*

Nora looked up from the over-medium egg she had been stabbing with a fork rather than eating. Watching the yolk ooze out had been oddly soothing. The bell above the door to The Morning Grind diner jingled as the detective walked in. As did Lasirenn.

Ugh. Always with the water spirit. Maybe she'd focus on getting *that* one to head home.

The Morning Grind had become Nora's second home over the last few years, and the servers, cooks, and even the dishwashers had become like family. The diner had been a staple in the more corporate-like neighborhood that had grown up around it over the last few decades. Despite multiple offers to buy back the space, the owners had refused to budge.

Nora would do her part to keep it in business by eating there every single day if she had to. But that serpent of a woman didn't even eat to begin with—she just took up valuable table space.

Wait a second, what's happening? Nora thought, raising an eyebrow as the other two spoke in heated tones by the door.

Lasirenn shot a glare in Nora's direction before shaking her head at Theo. She pushed open the door and left. Theo stood for a moment, clenching his fists before his shoulders slumped forward. Defeated. Whatever had just happened, he must have figured it was futile to fight it.

Nora couldn't tell if she was more excited or scared about what they had just argued over. Beneath the table, she crossed her fingers that the woman finally went home. For good.

Theo removed his coat and scarf, hanging them on the rack by the door, then made his way over to Nora's usual booth against the window. He slid into the bench opposite her, and the red vinyl fabric creaked beneath him.

"What was that about?" Nora asked. No time to waste time with pleasantries. She wanted the details, good or bad.

He sighed. "She's upset that I didn't instantly fall back in love with her after we… completed our bargain."

Don't say anything, don't say anything, Nora repeated in her head, keeping her lips pressed tight together.

Theo must have noticed because he rolled his eyes. "If Sera wants to know, I'll be honest with her. A deal's a deal. But I'm also not going to rub it in her face."

"Is Lasirenn coming back?" she asked.

"Not today."

A minor victory, but it was a start.

Cheryl made her way over with a fresh cup of tea for Nora because the matronly woman was obviously a saint or a guardian angel. The woman had done up her many braids in an elaborate bun on top of her head, and the dark brown of her hair blended almost seamlessly into the skin around her face.

Not a wrinkle in sight despite her age. Nora loved the woman almost as much as her own mother, but she would also kill to have skin like that as she grew older.

Cheryl placed her hands on her voluptuous hips. "Mornin', officer. Where's your lady today?"

Theo coughed after Cheryl's insinuation while Nora quirked an eyebrow up. So it wasn't just her own perception in defense of her best friend. The two *had* been coming into the diner a lot lately and usually sat together. Nora would make correcting that a priority going forward.

The Muses could wait.

"She has business to see to," Theo said with an attempted smile.

"They're not together," Nora added.

The woman chuckled, her smile saying she didn't believe Nora. "Mhm. Well, anythin' to eat? Drink?"

"I'm good," he said.

After Cheryl left to help a new table, Nora gave a heaving sigh. "Freyja says time moves differently in the underworld but doesn't have much of an idea of how much longer it'll take."

"I know this is difficult, for all of us." Theo ran a hand through his hair, his eyes holding a worry his words didn't match. "Lasirenn has been reminding me to trust that they will be successful."

Anger sparked within Nora like a lit match. Just how close were those two getting while Sera and Sol risked their lives? She opened her mouth to ask just as a low, deep rumble met her ears, making her pause. Then the water in their glasses began to shake, and all the dishware clattered against each other as the entire earth seized.

Am I causing an earthquake? she asked Freyja, her pulse racing with excitement more than fear.

She didn't like the idea of Lasirenn and Theo

connecting, but Nora didn't think she had been all *that* mad about it. Then again, she had Muse in her blood. Maybe she could move mountains with her thoughts.

Freyja let out a musical laugh. *No, darling.*

A loud crash made Nora jump and turn to see what had caused it. A picture frame next to the kitchen had fallen to the tile, the glass shattering.

The rumble settled a moment later, and Nora breathed a sigh in relief that it hadn't been more disruptive. The last major quake in the District had cracked the Washington Monument. She held a hand over her chest as her breathing finally slowed.

"In other news," Theo continued, seemingly unperturbed by the disturbance, "I've been hearing from friends that some of the Bacchae are getting restless."

"How many is some?" she asked, righting the napkin holder which had tipped over. Well, this could be a better distraction than dealing with the water spirit.

"I don't have exact numbers, but a dozen here, a handful there," he said. "The main issue is the lack of control. The newly created are acting out in highly urban areas."

"Acting out?" Nora asked, her skin prickling with unease and a touch of excitement.

"The Bacchae nature is to be a predator," Theo explained. "Those who go to the underground and hidden blood bars keep their instincts at bay, but those who aren't are feeling the pull. And their prey is everywhere, just waiting to be eaten."

Nora stared at him, her mouth agape.

"From their point of view, I mean," he said.

"Why don't they all go to the damn blood bars then?" Nora asked as she pushed her plate of eggs away. Her hunger had fled with his words. "Wasn't that the whole point of opening them?"

"Having your food handed to you on a silver platter only denies the predator inside," he said. "The beast within them craves the hunt."

"What about the Eternals?" Nora asked, trying to hide the shiver his words caused. "Aren't they able to use the hive mind thingamajig?"

"They are, but mind control is only effective while they're using it. It's not as efficient as ruling with an iron fist, and that's off the table now that they're in custody."

Theo scratched at the scruff on his chin as his gaze turned thoughtful. "I'm also getting the sense that there's one among them who might be going behind the others' backs."

"Eratosthenes?" Nora asked.

She remembered the guy had been against the Eternals standing down, even if it meant immunity. He must have been Danae's favorite. Her lip curled at the idea.

"He's the one," Theo said. "I'm going to set up a meeting with Liviana about the recent activity. See what we can do to help."

This was just the kind of distraction she needed.

"Count me in," Nora said.

CHAPTER 23

Serafina

Stunned wasn't even close to describing how Sera felt at that moment, her jaw just about dropping to the cavern floor. Danae had freed the witches. And if she hadn't known better, Sera wouldn't have believed the seven witches had been enslaved for so long.

Twenty years of torture and rage unleashed themselves on the Ordog and his minions without hesitation. Almost like they knew their moment was coming.

Black blood and blobs of guts splattered against the cavern's walls and floor as the demonic creatures were hit with magical attacks, unable to react fast enough to the witches' speed.

Sera's eyes opened wide as she watched the carnage. She had no idea how they were using magic without preparation, except by intention alone. Their willpower must be strong, and *angry*.

The Ordog roared with fury and rose from his throne, bringing his full height to well over seven or eight feet. His tail lashed out behind him, sending rocks flying as the blade at the end of it slashed across the walls. As he stepped down from the dais, the cave trembled beneath his hooves, shaking loose pebbles down around them all.

"You would betray *me*?" his voice boomed as he glowered down at Danae.

Sera had to give the girl some credit—she didn't even flinch the way Sera would have, and Danae didn't have a god on her side. Either she was more psychotic than Sera thought, or the girl had more extensive powers than any of them knew. Neither option sounded like a good one to Sera in the current situation.

"Such a hypocrite," Danae snapped back at him, earning herself another roar. "Take back your offer to the human."

"Demons, to me!" the Ordog yelled, his voice booming and echoing in the confines of the cavern and shaking the very Earth.

As Sera raised her arms to keep her balance against the rumbling cave floor, one of the smaller tunnels collapsed beneath the falling rocks and flames. Dust and ash billowed out across the cavern.

While the group of freed witches continued to defend themselves, more of the Ordog's four-legged creatures swarmed into the area like ants after sugar crumbs. They were moving too fast to count, but Sera guessed there had been a dozen to start, and now they continued to pour in from the tunnels. A demonic horde ready to serve their master.

Sera gripped her sword in two hands again and swung the blade at the closest demons, their brains exploding or limbs collapsing in pain. Her goal wasn't necessarily death, just total mayhem.

Bacchus was starting to rub off on her.

A shield of rippling magic appeared all around her like a bubble as Renee appeared at her side.

"I sure didn't see *that* coming," Renee said, wiping off sweat dripping down her forehead with the back of a hand, leaving a streak of black ash across her skin. Her other hand clenched around a humming crystal.

Sera couldn't help the quick smile that sprang to her lips at the familiar line. If they could still crack jokes, maybe they could win this thing. But then her stomach twisted in on itself with a new realization. If Sera escaped, then Renee would be trapped, or vice versa. A life for a life was the only way.

"We need to get to the others," the silver-haired witch said.

Shaking herself free of the miserable train of thought plaguing her, Sera nodded and took Renee's free hand. They would figure it out. They had to. She led the other woman across the cavern and sliced at any minions getting too close.

Some of the witches had cast similar defensive spells, only to see them pop as the demons raked their claws across the barriers. She still didn't know how they were using magic. Sheer will and good intentions only did so much. Renee's shield seemed to be more durable by far, probably due to the crystal and not being enslaved for the past two decades.

The majority of the hounds aimed for Danae, who they must have seen as the real threat. Evidently using her blood as a catalyst, the girl's defensive shield wrapped around her like a whirlwind, dark and ominous. Lightning burst from within its depths to strike at any target close enough, electrocuting some and melting others.

It was an awe-inspiring, yet totally gruesome, display of power.

The Ordog didn't know who he had made a deal with. Neither had Sera, apparently.

Sucks to be him, she thought before turning her attention to the escape. Never in a million years would she have thought Danae would be the distraction they needed.

As they neared the group of witches, Sera saw they had lost another member to the beasts. She lunged at the creatures feasting on the man's maimed body. It may have been too late, but that didn't mean she would allow them to desecrate him.

Cries of pain came from her left, and Sera whipped around to see one of the creatures latched on to a witch's forearm. Sera raised her blade and swung, slicing off one of its forelegs. When the hound released the witch, squealing in pain, Sera grabbed the beast by one of its remaining legs, spun in a circle, and launched the creature against the closest wall. It hit with a sickening thud before sliding down the wall unmoving, leaving a streak of black blood in its wake.

Sera looked back at the witch to grin before moving on, but her breath caught in her throat.

"Sera? Is it really you?" Rachel asked, her hand pressed to the oozing bite wound on her other arm, her mouth agape.

Shock ran like ice through Sera's veins. Seeing her mother up close and in the flesh was an indescribable feeling. For twenty years, she had longed for this moment, for this woman. Maybe not quite this way, but wishing and hoping that her mother would come back to her. And here she was.

No time for that now, Bacchus whispered in her ear.

As she remembered where she was, fear slithered its way through her body to constrict around her lungs. She gasped and took a step back.

"I'll explain later, but for now, we need to go while they're distracted," Sera said, casting a quick glance at the Ordog and Danae.

Somehow, the girl was holding her own against the god and his devil dogs, although he was definitely gaining ground. Sera would have bet the Ordog regretted his decision to fuel the girl with his death magic.

"We know a way out," Rachel said, pulling Sera and Renee back over to the group of witches still fighting off the demonic creatures.

Renee reached out a hand to the closest witch, and her defensive shield merged with the others to blanket the entire group. As the hounds attacked the barrier, electric bolts shot out to zap them away. Their yelps made it clear it hurt, but it didn't stop them. The witches' will and magic were fading. They would need to move quickly.

"It's time," Rachel said to one of the male witches who towered above the rest. Introductions would have to come later.

The tall man she addressed nodded and ducked his head to lead the group down a side tunnel, while Sera hung back to guard their retreat. She glanced back one last time before following, guilt gripping her heart as she watched Danae fight the devil.

Even though that girl had gotten them all into this mess, she had also saved Sera's life. And then freed all the witches. A woman scorned and all, but still.

Maybe she really was redeemable.

As Sera started to turn back toward the tunnel, the Ordog roared and leaped at Danae, grasping the girl's body in a gigantic hand. Her magical shield burst like it was little more than flimsy drywall. Wrestling against her as she continued to fight him, he pulled her closer to him, her body turning as she wriggled until her back was pressed against his chest.

He let out a chuckle that sent shivers of revulsion down Sera's spine before sinking his sharpened teeth into Danae's shoulder, his claws piercing through the girl's stomach and limbs. Blood spurted out and oozed down her body, coating her in red.

The scream that ripped out of Danae's throat chilled Sera down to the bone.

When she met the Eternal's gaze, Sera was surprised to see the pleading in the girl's, through the pain. Crimson froth sputtered out of her mouth. Sera couldn't watch anyone suffer like that and not do anything. Not after Hiro, and Bacchus better not try to stop her.

I'm with you, the god said beside her, his glass raised in a toast. *To the end we go.*

Turning to the others calling her name in the escape tunnel, she met her mother's gaze.

"Go," Sera said with a smile.

She sent her magic out as a rush of wind, golden

sparkles of dust flying through the air and forcing the witches farther into the caves, out of sight. Then she threw a ball of energy at the rocks above the entrance, collapsing the tunnel.

A life for a life. Sera would give hers so that Renee, and the others, could be free.

Removing the dagger given to her by Hel from its rope holster, Sera held it by the grip in her free hand. With the golden sword still in her other hand, she approached the Ordog and Danae. The girl was still alive, but barely, and the devil didn't seem to notice Sera closing in.

"Let her go," Sera called out, slicing downward with the sword at a demon who lunged at her. Its head rolled away from its collapsing body.

The Ordog looked up, his bloody lips pulling up into a grin. She raised the dagger, turning it so that the runes caught in the light of the flames and grinned back when his smile faltered. Danae's limp form fell from his hands, and he stepped over her toward Sera.

"Where did you get that?" he hissed.

Was that fear she sensed in his words?

"I've got friends in high places." Sera paused and tilted her head. "Well, deep places. Hel doesn't seem to like your whole take-over-the-world plan."

The Ordog growled, sending terror slithering through Sera. Despite her merge, she still faced the devil with the intent of killing him or being killed.

One of them was going down.

"She should learn to mind her own business," he snarled, crimson frothing along his lips.

"Are you really this dumb?" Sera scoffed at him. "You

made it her business. Your plan threatens her realm."

A new warmth, internal, filled her essence as Bacchus stepped closer before disappearing altogether. They were one, and they were very, very angry.

The Ordog roared and lunged at them. They parried his outstretched claws with the sword and thrust upward with the dagger. The black blade sunk into his forearm, igniting the runes. The devil bellowed, in pain or fury or both.

The blade pulled free as he stumbled back, his hooves scrabbling on the rocky floor while he clutched the wound on his arm. When was the last time he had felt pain? Never?

Not waiting for him to recover, Sera and Bacchus pressed forward, slashing at him with both the sword and dagger. Their arms moved, one after the other, not letting up the barrage of attacks. It wasn't pretty, but they didn't need much skill for this job.

Both blades cut through his skin, but the openings made by the runed dagger didn't heal. His black blood splattered against the columns and rocks as they pressed him farther back into the cavern.

"Attack, you idiots!" the Ordog roared at his devil dogs, who had stopped to watch as their master bled.

Sera and Bacchus hadn't even noticed when they stopped. Nor did they care. Their only concern was the massive beast in front of them.

As the hounds shook off their awe or fear or whatever it was that had held them back, they snarled and crept forward, eyeing the whirling blades with caution. Before they could strike, the ground rumbled beneath their feet. A low chanting caught Sera and Bacchus's attention, and they turned toward Danae who was now on her knees.

The Eternal had both palms on the ground, blood pooling beneath them. Her eyes bled red and blazed with her fury, which she focused on the Ordog as she chanted. Rocks shook loose from the walls and ceiling, and the trembling of the very earth caused more tunnels to collapse.

One of the biggest boulders rolled toward Danae, stopping beside her. A cracking sound echoed through the cavern just before the boulder burst outward.

Sera and Bacchus quickly flung up a shield of magic to stop the debris from hitting them.

When the dust settled, a guardian formed from the rock stood in front of Danae, swinging massive stone arms at the Ordog.

Holy fuck, they thought together.

They didn't wait to see what happened. Running forward, they plunged the dagger into the Ordog's side, pushing upward to where his heart should be. The devil let out another bellow that shook rocks loose from the ceiling and sent flaming fungus tumbling. Sera and Bacchus threw themselves to the side, just barely escaping his swiping arms.

They had missed.

The rock guardian grabbed the Ordog's arms with its stone hands as he tried to reach for the dagger. Taking advantage of the moment, Sera and Bacchus ducked beneath the Ordog's barbed tail and reached for the handle. He roared again as they tugged the blade loose, his hand swooping down to smack them sideways into the nearest wall. The handle slipped from their grasp and went flying across the hall.

Flames singed their skin and hair as they hit the stones and slid down to the floor. Disoriented, they shook their head before rising, searching for the dagger. Dread churned within their stomach when they spotted it.

Danae bent to pick the iron blade up, where it had landed at her feet. Her smile turned into a grin that turned into a laugh.

"You fool," the Eternal said as she circled the Ordog, brandishing the dagger. "Thinking an all-but-dead god would be more powerful than I am."

The Ordog growled and lunged toward the girl, his remaining hounds doing the same.

As much as they wanted to stay and find out who would win, Sera and Bacchus took that as their cue to exit stage left while everyone and everything was distracted. Swiping at any hell beasts who came too close on their way to assist their master, Sera and Bacchus ran for the nearest open tunnel and plunged into the darkness. Their blade sent black blood splattering against the floor.

Their eyes didn't need any additional light, but they pulled embers from within, flinging the magic behind them to collapse the opening. Just in case. Shudders continued to rock the earth as the two monstrous forces dueled to the death. Hopefully for both of them.

Bacchus had never been to the Ordog's realm before, but his divine consciousness knew which way to go. Left then right then right again, then Sera lost track of which directions they turned. It all seemed random to her, but the god's confidence never wavered.

Only a few moments into their escape, a scream rent through the very walls, reverberating off the rocks, followed by an equally loud bellow. With any luck, they had killed each other in the battle.

At last they stumbled into another expansive domed cavern, only this one seemed brighter than it should have been. The group of witches stood beneath a hole a few arm widths in diameter in the ceiling, which let in light. But from where?

"This tunnel leads up and out." Standing a head taller than anyone else, the man who had led the group pointed at the hole a few dozen feet above them. "The Ordog has forbidden his hounds from using it, but that command will be lifted once he realizes we're gone."

Sera and Bacchus couldn't believe their luck. They had made it. They were getting out.

CHAPTER 24

Nora

The earthquakes didn't stop. For the last three days, the Earth had rumbled and rolled, wreaking havoc on city infrastructure and causing widespread panic. Because it wasn't happening in just the District—it was happening *everywhere*.

The quakes weren't huge and disastrous by any means, but the frequency and widespread nature of them freaked everyone out. Nora included. Conspiracy theorists jumped out of their closets like ghosts bit them on their asses, claiming government involvement, global warming on crack, or even the Bacchae.

How the government or the Bacchae could cause earthquakes was beyond Nora, but at least global warming was close. Unfortunately, the truth was far worse.

Nora sighed, the sound snatched away by the fast pace of the clunky Metro train car and the whooshing of the tunnel walls whizzing by. No sound-dampening on these bad boys. She did her best to ignore the stranger's elbow jabbing into her side whenever the car jerked to the right. That was just Metro life.

Freyja and Xolotl had confirmed the seismic activity was caused by something happening in the underworld, a battle, most likely. The information did little to make Nora feel any better. Her best friend—her goddamn soulmate—and her future husband were down there fighting for their lives. She hoped that a fight meant they had found both the Ordog and the witches. Now they just needed to get out.

How much more time would pass aboveground before that happened, and what else would happen to the mortal world?

Nora pursed her lips. Just when the world was adjusting to the idea of the Bacchae, now they had inexplicable earthquakes to deal with. Fabulous.

The Metro train's brakes squealed as it reached its stop at the Pentagon. As the doors whooshed open, Nora let go of the hand strap she had been hanging on to—the train had been much too crowded to find a seat—and followed Theo through the crush of people.

Despite the urgency, a meeting with Liviana had to wait until her return to the District—something about quelling a rebellion in the Florida Panhandle. The last thing they all needed was some Bacchae uprising leaked to the news while the earthquakes were still happening. At least the Eternal knew firsthand what they were coming to talk about.

Security was quick and stress-free at the Pentagon.

Neither she nor Theo needed to carry weapons, and no one besides a handful of top officers knew about the gods. Which also meant Lasirenn had declined to come with, for what was probably the first time ever. Her existence was still a secret, and she didn't want to have to explain who or what she was.

Oh, darn.

After stepping through the metal detector and getting the all-clear from a guard, Nora gave him an award-winning smile. The award may have been bestowed upon her by her childhood dentist, but she would take it. She pulled her knee-length pink coat back on over her dress then reattached Freyja's torc around her neck.

As usual, she had dressed to the nines for their excursion, from her fake tortoiseshell glasses right down to the white tips of her French manicure. One never knew when a photographer might be present, after all.

They followed an assistant through the building to the designated meeting room. Liviana stood with a smile when they entered. The girl may have been turned as a teen like Danae, but she was far more regal than that witch would ever be. Her navy-blue pantsuit, cream-colored silk blouse, and matching floral-patterned scarf had Nora drooling. Not to mention the sleek high ponytail to hold her brown hair back.

Ugh, she's too young to be this chic, Nora thought to Freyja, whose laugh rang in response.

"It's a pleasure to see you both again," the Eternal said.

She waved to two chairs across from her at the conference table as if she were truly a government official and not a captive. The girl may have enjoyed immunity, but freedom was a thing of the past.

Two guards remained inside with them, silver handcuffs and silver-plated batons at the ready. Nora was sure their guns had been loaded with silver bullets, too. She couldn't really blame them, especially if Eratosthenes was behind the rebellions. The whole human world had been *rocked* when the Bacchae came out.

"Thank you for meeting with us, Liviana," Theo said as he sat in one of the offered chairs. "We need to speak with you about—"

Liviana held up a finger and shook her head. A moment later, the door opened and one of their CIA contacts walked in, a laptop and several folders held beneath one of his arms. Nora was terrible with names, but at least his face was familiar. He nodded his head at the two guards who stepped outside.

Theo stood and shook hands with the newcomer. "Mr. Dawson, thank you for meeting with us."

Ah, that was it. Kevin Dawson. Handsome guy. Short blond hair, brown eyes, chiseled jawline. His suit jacket did little to hide the muscles beneath. Just the kind of guy Nora used to date when she was single. She had definitely upgraded with Sol. Nora reached out a hand to shake his from her seat. She was a classy broad, after all.

He's delightful to look at, Freyja sighed in her mind, although they both agreed Solomon was far more handsome.

"Mr. Pratt, Ms. Eisler," Kevin said with a nod for each before setting down his things and taking a seat next to Liviana. "I presume you're here about Florida."

Ms. Eisler. Nora tried not to scoff. The name sounded

so old. Like her mother.

"Not just there, I'm afraid," Theo said. "There has been a bit more activity."

Kevin shot a glance at Liviana who hesitated a moment before nodding.

"Why didn't you inform me?" he asked the Eternal, his cheeks turning a soft pink in anger, or maybe embarrassment. Either way, it was cute.

"I had hoped we'd have it under control without needing to cause any alarm," Liviana said. "Control has become more… difficult lately."

"Eratosthenes, you mean," Nora said with a quirk of an eyebrow.

The Eternal's sharp gaze turned on her. "Yes."

Kevin groaned and leaned back in his seat. "He hasn't exactly hidden his stance on the situation, but I didn't realize it was that bad."

"Eratosthenes has always been one of Danae's biggest supporters," Liviana explained. "He's doing what toddlers do best and testing our boundaries."

"We need to cage him," Kevin said.

"We need to lead him by our own example." Liviana shook her head. "He needs to learn a better way."

Theo cleared his throat. "With all due respect, Eratosthenes is not a toddler. He's had over a millennium to learn a better way."

"I disagree," Liviana said. "He's had a very long time to learn a bad way. We need to give him more time to shed those bad habits."

"That's not something we can afford to do," Kevin said. "And this is way worse than just 'bad habits.' Lives are at stake."

"Some of the Bacchae will not be happy hearing he has been put in a cell," the Eternal said.

"Too bad for them," Kevin said with a shake of his head. "Besides, that's what you and the others are for."

Liviana bristled, her lips pressing together in a thin line. Clearly she didn't like the insinuation that she was being used just for the hive mind control, even if it was the truth.

Toddlers were finicky people, and Nora's much younger brother had been a prime specimen. Punishment only went so far, and setting a good example took time the government wasn't willing to give.

But toddlers also loved to feel autonomous, independent, and they didn't necessarily have the brainpower yet to understand they were being led to one particular choice. The description suited what she knew of Eratosthenes.

"What about giving him a choice?" Nora asked.

Kevin furrowed his brows. "What choice?"

"Instead of deciding his fate for him, let him pick: encourage the Bacchae to cease and desist, or spend the remainder of his long life in a silver cage just like Danae's."

"Isn't that just an ultimatum?" Theo asked, though his expression was one of calculation.

Nora waved a hand dismissively. "You say tomayto, I say tomahto."

* * *

WHEN THEY HAD FINISHED discussing Liviana's plan of action to bring the other Eternal back in line, Nora replaced her scarf around her neck, getting ready to leave.

"We'd like to discuss one more thing with you," Kevin

said, staying in his seat as Theo stood.

"What's that?" Theo asked, zipping up his jacket.

"With Ms. Eisler."

Nora stopped adjusting her scarf to look at the agent. "What did I do?"

Liviana laughed and reached over the table to place a hand on Nora's.

"Absolutely nothing," the Eternal said, a twinkle in her eye. "Nothing wrong, anyway. We'd like to offer you a job."

Both of Nora's eyebrows shot toward the ceiling. "A job? For me? With the CIA?"

"We'd like you to lead a support group here in the District for those who have lost loved ones during the Bacchic Uprising," Kevin explained.

Nora glanced between the two of them. "While I appreciate your votes of confidence, I have no background or training in therapy or grief counseling."

"No, but you have something most counselors don't have," Liviana said. "A uniquely charismatic personality and a close relationship with one of the reformed."

Before Nora could protest again, Kevin passed her a file.

"We would provide all the necessary training as well as full benefits and a competitive salary," he said. "We'll work around your school and teaching schedule. Most of the sessions will be after a typical workday, anyway."

Nora opened the file and skimmed the offer letter.

The salary was…

"Holy shit," she said. "Is this a typo?"

Kevin chuckled as he stood. "You start Monday."

CHAPTER 25

Solomon

"You have seen Sorrow and Lament," a woman said, though her voice sounded muffled. "Do you wish to continue?"

Solomon opened his eyes, which he hadn't remembered closing, and looked up at Nyssa, who simply waited. He was on his knees beside the enormous tree and the streams again, his hands cupped over his ears. Lowering his arms, he stood on shaky legs.

"Yes."

"Come." The woman led him farther around the tree, stepping lightly through the grass and wildflowers, to another river flowing from its knotted roots. She knelt on a patch of spotty green moss next to the water and filled the goblet.

When she stood and offered him the cup, Solomon held out a shaking hand. The skin along his jaw tightened as he clenched his teeth together, annoyed at his body's display of weakness.

"Next is Phlegethon," Nyssa said.

He downed the liquid in a single gulp. If he could face his demons and live through the pain of the past as he had just done, he could handle anything else.

Anything.

And then he burst into flames. His body, his mind, his very being burned and smoldered, from within as well as out. Solomon fell to the ground, roars of agony tearing from his throat. He rolled instinctively to snuff it out, but the inferno persisted. His insides bubbled and boiled, becoming pools of molten lava as his body incinerated.

As he burned, his Immortal flesh repaired and healed, and then he ignited and smoldered once again. A never-ending cycle of devastation. At least until the fire won. His body would give in eventually as it ran out of fuel. The question was, how long would this torture last? How long would his sanity last?

He could feel his mind begin to shatter through the panic. The absolute pain and torment were too much to bear. But he had to hold on. He had to hold on… for… for what? He gritted his teeth as he tried to remember anything through the pain. His entire being felt like it was leaking to the ground as it melted. It actually was oozing—his skin loosened its hold on his body and slid toward the ground.

A curly blonde head bobbed through his memory.

Nora.

He had to hold on for Nora. Yelling against the fire and

ice that burned his being, he rolled onto his knees and struggled to push himself up on bones beginning to liquefy once again. His vision blurred as his eyelids drooped, melting.

He cried out in triumph as he stood, the smoke from his burning flesh making his eyes water.

And just like that, the fire went out. Solomon was whole again, the pain vanished. He marveled at the sight of his brown skin, not a single mark displaying the torture he had just gone through.

"You have risen from the Fire," Nyssa said, her blue eyes almost sad.

Why would she be sad he had succeeded?

"Do you wish to continue?" she asked.

"I do," he said.

Exhaustion pulled at this body, urging him to lay down and rest. Except he didn't have time for that. His love for Nora would see him through to the end. He knew that now, as sure as he knew his name was Solomon.

Once again, he followed the red-haired woman around the tree, over moss-covered roots sticking out of the fertile soil. They stopped beside another body of water flowing from beneath the giant trunk.

Nyssa dipped the goblet into the flowing stream and handed him the cup. "Styx."

"Dare I ask what it means?" he asked as he took the cup.

"Hate."

His muscles quivered with fatigue as he raised the golden goblet to his lips. Before he could drink, a boom rolled through the area, shaking the ground they stood on.

Leaves and small twigs fell from the tree above. Both he and Nyssa staggered to remain upright, and the water sloshed in the glass.

"What the hell was that?"

"A battle has commenced," Nyssa said, her gaze unfocused and distant. "Your friends fight for their lives."

He needed to finish this ordeal and get back to them as fast as he could. Raising the cup to his lips again, he paused before drinking. Get back to them as a mortal. Would he even be able to help them without his Immortal strength and speed? Renee was mortal as well, but she had magic to fight with. What did he have? His bare hands?

If he didn't continue drinking, then his chance at mortality would be gone. This was it. The only salvation after weeks of searching. Failing meant losing Nora. But failing to save her best friend?

He stared at his wavering reflection in the cup as he weighed his options. Shaking his head, he drank. He had already come this far, he would have to figure it all out later.

When he lowered the goblet, the sight before him was enough to break a man. A woman whose face he knew well despite the many years, his *mother*, knelt before a wooden pole, her hands bound to it, her back exposed to the air. Tears streamed down her face.

A white man wearing riding boots without a single mark or scratch on them and shining spurs stood behind her with a whip, which he raised, again and again, a grin on his face. The man enjoyed whipping Solomon's mother. The cracking of the whip made Solomon flinch as he remembered his own whippings.

Rage filled Solomon as his mother cried out, and he

took a step forward. Only the image shimmered and changed before him. Now a tree held a young man with skin the same dark color as Solomon's, swaying by a noose around his neck. A lynching. The angry mob at his feet full of white men and women, cheering on the execution.

You wish to return to this life? a voice whispered through the air.

"The world isn't like this anymore," he replied, though he clenched his fists tight as he witnessed the brutal murder. No one stepped forward to stop it.

No?

In response, image after image flashed before Solomon's eyes, visions of modern-day atrocities. Black men walking down the street shot down by white cops, black children starving across the world while white men laughed through five-course meals. The hate grew and grew until he could taste blood in his mouth, his fangs piercing his tongue. Was this the world he wanted to bring his children into?

You can make them pay, the voice whispered. *Pay for what they've done to your kind.*

As an Immortal he could. He could rally the others, and they could become vigilantes. Go after the guiltiest. Who was he kidding, they were all guilty. He would kill them all, every last one of them for what they had done to his brothers and sisters.

Lorenzo, his Italian maker, strode toward him, a sneer on his lips. Solomon's lungs seized as he faced the man who had enslaved him when he had been most vulnerable, before he understood the actual terms of an Immortal lifetime. Another fucking white man.

It was all enough to break a man.

But Solomon was still more than a man, and he had Nora waiting for him. Beautiful, kind, fierce Nora. A woman who loved him for everything he was. A woman who made him want to be *more* than he was, whose skin color didn't matter.

He couldn't save his mother, it was far too late for that, but he would never let Nora down. Somehow, he would protect their children. Struggling back to his feet, he panted at the exertion.

Nyssa regarded him without emotion as he rose, then led him to the next river. He barely noticed his surroundings anymore, the whole world was blurry. She handed him the final water-filled goblet. At least he hoped it was the final one. How many cups had he drunk?

"Last will be the river Lethe, if you wish to continue."

"What does the name mean?" The water sloshed in his quivering hand.

"To forget," she said quietly.

"Forget what?"

"Everything."

"What do you mean, everything?" he asked, meeting her steady gaze.

"To reclaim your mortality, you must forget your past life."

"Even Nora?"

"Yes."

Anger filled him once again and steadied his feet. "What was the point of all this if I'm just going to forget the reason I'm doing it?"

Nyssa tilted her head to the side. "You fell in love with her once. Are you afraid you won't do so again?"

He glanced at the liquid inside the goblet. It wasn't that he feared his own reaction—he would love Nora in any life. But he feared he wouldn't be the same man for Nora to love. Who would he be without his memories to guide him? Would he even be a good person, or was he innately evil? He had no idea. His entire life had been shaped by the men who ruled it.

Until she came into it.

Letting out a sigh, he raised the glass cup in a toast and downed the contents. He had to believe in Nora. He had to trust in their love for each other.

A moment later, he blinked. Nothing happened. He still remembered everything.

"It didn't work," he said to Nyssa.

"It will." Her smile, her entire expression, was sad. Another rumble echoed around them, shaking leaves loose. "Go. Help your friends."

"But what about what I came for? How do I make it work?" He couldn't leave, not yet. He had come so far. How could he leave without an answer?

"When the time comes, you'll know."

Solomon muttered under his breath at the vague response but knew better than to try to get more of an answer. He followed the woman a final time around the tree, back to where they had started.

Only now the tree displayed a door carved into the trunk. Scenes of horror had been etched into the wood—men, women, and children caught in demonic claws and pulled down into a fiery pit. Despite the brutality, the carvings were masterfully created.

Nyssa turned the knob and opened the door before

moving back, sweeping her arm toward the awaiting darkness. Her hand on his arm stopped him as he stepped over the threshold.

"You'll know."

* * *

Nora

"I'LL SEE YOU ALL AGAIN next week," Nora said with as warm a smile as she could muster.

The group of people she met with that evening thanked her as they filed out of the conference room. At least a few looked a little more hopeful than when they had first walked in.

Kevin's idea of training included a fifteen-minute briefing before her very first session on Monday. Oh, and a checklist of questions to ask her meeting attendees just in case she forgot what he had said. She couldn't have rolled her eyes any harder if she tried.

Honestly, though, what these people needed the most was someone to listen and a shoulder to cry on, and Nora happened to be pretty good at both. They weren't ready to hear about any "reformed" Bacchae just yet or what Nora thought of it all. That would come in time.

At least the meetings would be much needed distractions to get her through until the others returned. Nora had gotten the fantastic news just that morning that Lasirenn had officially returned to Haiti. The water spirit claimed it was to check in with Manny, but her stiff demeanor and refusal to look Theo in the eye had suggested otherwise.

When the last attendee had left, Liviana entered the room and leaned on the back of a chair, the end of her blue scarf grazing the plastic. "You're a natural."

A one-way window on the wall had allowed Liviana and Kevin to observe Nora, while also looking out for any verbal or, more importantly, nonverbal cues of a potential human threat. As much as Nora would have liked to believe the government truly cared about its citizens' mental health by providing necessary counseling, she knew the truth the moment she saw the window. She just wasn't sure how she felt about it yet.

"Yeah, well, Freyja tells me I'm descended from one of the Muses," Nora said as she stood and pulled on her knee-length coat.

Darling, are you sure it's wise to tell people before we know more? Freyja asked as Liviana's mouth parted in surprise.

Liviana may be one of the best people to tell, Nora replied.

"Talk about a rare ancestry," the Eternal said with a smile. "It's been a few centuries since I last met a Museborn."

See? She didn't necessarily want to rub it in the goddess's face, but she had been right.

I will trust your instincts, Freyja said with a light laugh.

"Museborn? So you have met others?" Nora asked eagerly.

"Only a few, but it certainly helps explain your magnetizing personality," Liviana said. "Shall we discuss it over a drink?"

Nora raised an eyebrow. "They let you out to go to bars?"

The Eternal chuckled. "Alas, no. But they do let me keep a bottle of whiskey in my office."

Snatching up her scarf, Nora hurried after Liviana. She couldn't wait to tell Sera and Sol what she learned.

CHAPTER 26

Solomon

Solomon stumbled through the dark, his body weary and dragging. He wanted to lie down and rest for a while, but he had something important to do. People to help. He just couldn't quite remember who, or why.

Rocks shook loose from the ceiling and walls as the earth rumbled again. He was in the underworld, right?

Yes. A fight. He was on his way to help his friends fight the Ordog. Friends? He let out a sharp laugh. Like he and Serafina would ever be friends. Regardless, Serafina and Renee needed him. They would all escape hell and return to the District. That was right. There was someone there he wanted to see.

Memories were sifting through his thoughts, some harder to cling to, dancing out of his mind's eye before he could grasp them.

Lorenzo wouldn't be waiting for him, that much he knew. Would anyone? Solomon shook his head and caught himself before falling. The movement had made him dizzy.

Where was he going again?

* * *

Serafina

RENEE TURNED TO ADDRESS one of the witches and caught sight of Sera, her mouth dropping open. "You made it!"

After dropping the empty gun on the ground, the magical blade dissipating into the air, Sera closed the distance in a few strides. Bacchus shimmered back into being beside her. She enveloped the other woman in a quick squeeze before pulling back to locate her mother.

And there she was. Tears streamed down her mother's face as she held a hand to her mouth.

Unable to speak, Sera ran to her mother and hugged her tightly, never wanting to let her go, relishing the feeling of her mother returning the squeeze. She honestly couldn't remember the last time she had held or even touched her mother, and the thought made her sad and happy at the same time. Now she wouldn't have to forget this feeling, ever again.

A hand stroked Sera's hair as her mother whispered, "Sera, oh my sweet Serafina."

Emotions Sera had thought long since buried rose to the surface, and a sob escaped her lips. Shudders shook her shoulders. Every other sound fell away as she held onto the woman she had needed her entire life.

A moment later and much too soon, Rachel pulled away, looking at Sera and holding her face in her hands. Her grey eyes roved over Sera's face, down her body and back up again, her disbelief evident.

"Whatever new form of torture this is, I'll take it," Rachel whispered, fresh tears creating smeared stripes through the dirt caking her otherwise pale face. Without the grime covering them, a smattering of freckles would dance their way across her nose.

Sera reached up to squeeze her mom's hands against her cheeks. "This is real. I'm real. I can't believe *you're* real."

Howls echoed down the tunnels.

"We have to go," one of the witches said, her eyes wild with fright. "They're coming."

That could mean only one thing—Danae was gone, and the Ordog had won. It wasn't the death nor the afterlife she had envisioned for the Eternal. Still, Sera would gain some consolation knowing the Ordog had avenged Hiro, and Sera's savior had escaped a life worse than death, too.

Standing beneath the vertical tunnel leading out of hell, Sera couldn't see anything but a distant pinprick of light, which she hoped was the actual sky. The hole in the ceiling itself had to have been at least two stories above her head. She took off her backpack and opened it up, pulling out the rope and grappling hook.

"Time to climb." Also time to see if she was better than—or at least as good as—Solomon with the swing.

Snarling and growling echoed closer down the side tunnels around them, setting her pulse racing. The minions had found a way through. No time for a rope swinging competition yet. They'd need to hurry if they wanted to make it out in one piece.

Chewing on her lip, Sera stood under the circular hole, unable to see the sky, but able to sense the difference in the air, cleanliness she hadn't realized she'd missed. She swung the rope around a few times to get a feel for it before releasing it upwards with a magical boost.

Unlike Solomon at the wall outside Helheim, she couldn't rely on just luck or skill right now. Maybe they could have a competition once they escaped. She tried not to get her hopes up, but they were so close to getting out.

The hook flew up and out of view until it snagged something and stuck. Giving the rope a few hard god-assisted tugs, Sera determined it was safe, or at least as safe as it could be without more time. She could only hope it had reached the top or close enough to it.

Sera grabbed the hand of the witch closest to her. "You go first and help each of them out."

The dark-haired woman nodded, the weariness in her face and drooping limbs speaking volumes. Reaching for the golden orb of magic living within her, Sera withdrew a strand and shaped it into a ball of energy with a whisper. She placed the ball into the witch's hands, where it absorbed into her skin and made her glow.

The woman grabbed the rope and climbed hand over hand, wrapping her feet around the end to assist. It would be a struggle for all of them, even with the magic ebbing through them.

Before each of the other witches started their ascent, Sera withdrew some of her magical energy and imbued them with it. She gave them just enough to assist with their climb and still leave her with some to fight off any creatures that made it through.

The magical well within her continued to refill but not as fast as she spent it, especially not after that fight. She hoped she'd have enough left for whatever else they'd need to face. Unless they got lucky and made it out without another fight.

The scrambling and snapping of the approaching demons grew louder as each of the witches thanked her before climbing. Sera did her best to meet each gaze and memorize the features of their faces through the dirt and grime. It might be the last time she had the chance.

First, a woman a few inches shorter than Sera with tired, toffee-colored eyes. Then a man with a scruffy beard that was covered in soot but still sprouting auburn patches, followed by another woman with silvery strands and crow's feet beside her eyes, reminding Sera of Renee. She etched each face into her memories.

Beside her, Bacchus guzzled down wine. She tried not to think about why he was drinking so much so quickly, knowing their time to figure out an escape was coming to an end. Instead she sped up her pace, urging the others to do the same as they climbed.

"They're here." The man who led the witches out pointed at a collapsed tunnel where the rocks shifted. It was just him, Sera, her mother, and Renee left.

Right on cue, the demons burst through the rocks and into the cavern. Their claws dug into the floor and sent up showers of dust and pebbles in their haste, sizzling saliva dripping from their open mouths.

Rachel cast fireballs at the closest while Renee sprayed the last of the dragon fire from her flask, sending the creatures flying or skittering back with a hiss or growl. The other witch climbed up the rope. Sera launched herself at a group of the hounds, kicking and grabbing limbs to use bodies against the other creatures.

Another roar came from down a tunnel on their right. Sera's heart sank, and her mouth ran dry. They would be outnumbered too soon. This was it.

"Mom, go!" Sera yelled behind her.

She had already given her mother and Renee the energy they'd need to make it to the top. She would protect their ascent or die trying.

"I'm not leaving you," Rachel said, blasting the next demon closing in with fire.

Sera groaned at her mother's stubbornness just as a new creature burst out of the tunnel on her right. Only this was a creature she knew well. One of the Bacchae. And not just any Bacchae—Solomon.

Wait, why is he still one of the Bacchae? she thought.

No time to stop and ask questions, Bacchus urged her on.

Solomon tore the demons within reach limb from limb, sinking his fangs into tar-like flesh and ripping throats free. Black ooze dripped down his chin, his skin sizzling and smoking from the contact with the acidic liquid.

With the creatures distracted by the new threat, Sera ran back to Rachel. "He's with us. Go!"

She didn't wait for any more protest from her mother before practically throwing her toward the rope.

Turning toward Renee to say her goodbyes before helping her up the rope, the woman grabbed her hands. Sera opened her mouth to say she would stay to guard their escape.

"Don't even think about it, kiddo," Renee cut her off with a sad smile. "Go. Live. *Love.*"

"No." Tears blurred Sera's vision. "I can't leave you here."

"You won't be," Renee said. "I'll return to Helheim and—"

A demon grabbed her arm before she could say more and pulled her away. Another hound fell on her as she tumbled to the ground, tearing through her side with one bite. Her scream shook Sera to her core.

"No!" Fury rippled through Sera like molten lava, and she grabbed the leg of the creature closest to her

Tearing its leg free from its body with a god-enhanced pull, Sera used the limb like a bat against the other demon, sending it flying. She stomped on the head of the one missing its leg, smashing its skull into the rocks, and tossed the leg away.

Falling to her knees beside her friend, Sera took her hand. This wasn't how it was supposed to end. She couldn't lose another person she loved. Not like this. Tears fell down her cheeks as Renee gave her a pained, bloody smile. Someone knelt beside Sera, wrapping a warm arm around her shoulders. Her stubborn mother.

"Go," Renee coughed out through a froth of red foam.

Bacchus knelt down on Sera's other side, then disappeared as he took control of their body. Together, they looked at their friend with love. "Do you trust me?"

By the way Renee blinked her eyes, they knew the witch understood it was the god speaking, and, hopefully, what he implied. Her head nodded a fraction of an inch.

They sliced one of their wrists open with a sharp rock, and Rachel let out a cry of surprise. As blood flowed from the wound, the god pushed the opening and warm liquid to Renee's mouth. Too wounded to revolt against it, the woman drank.

Renee's eyes closed, and she let out a rattling breath before her body stilled. They had been too late. A half-sob escaped their lips, and they closed their eyes against the anguish threatening to rip them asunder. Rachel hugged them, crying quietly.

A hand grasped theirs, and they glanced down to see Renee staring back through wide eyes. The gaping hole that had been her side shimmered in gold before stitching itself together, the gore pulling back inside where it belonged.

Within a few heartbeats, Renee was whole again. She had become one of the Bacchae.

They helped her sit up, too cautious to hug her.

"You'll need to feed soon to complete the transformation," Bacchus said through Sera's mouth. "But for now, we need to go."

"Wait," Rachel said. She leaned forward, pulling her hair away from her neck, exposing her pulsing artery. "Quick."

Without hesitation, Renee bit, her new fangs extending mid-strike. She sucked eagerly at the lifeforce seeping from Rachel's neck. Bacchus reached Sera's hands up to pull them apart only a few seconds later.

"No time for more," they said.

As Sera and Bacchus rose to their feet, a hand touched their shoulder. They whirled to face Solomon. Without a second thought, they threw their arms around him and hugged him. At least Sera did. Solomon hesitated before returning the gesture.

Then Sera remembered she was supposed to hate him, and they let him go, but with a smile on their lips. Maybe it was time to let go of her hate as well.

The walls shook as a rage-filled bellow echoed down one of the tunnels.

He's coming, Bacchus said, no longer controlling their movements as he shimmered back into being beside her. The god's fear filled her with dread, her bones turning to ice.

"Let's go," she said to the others.

After helping her mother and Renee up first, Sera grabbed the rope and started to climb.

CHAPTER 27

Serafina

The rope beneath Sera's feet went taut as Solomon started up behind her while Bacchus floated on ahead. She climbed as quickly as she could, her breath coming out in short bursts, knowing that their lives depended on their speed. Possibly the entire world. No pressure or anything. She would have rolled her eyes if it had been any other situation.

Far above her, small dark shapes moved against the outline of the sky. Bacchus and the other two women. Garbled shouts echoed down the vertical tunnel.

Snarling followed by Solomon's shout alerted her to the fact that they had company. She looked down and saw green-eyed hounds climbing the rope behind them. After the wall incident outside Hel, she didn't think they could stand, let alone climb. Her skin prickled as hair rose all along her body.

Oh, how wrong she had been on both counts.

Gritting her teeth, she focused her attention and energy on up and out. They would deal with the beasts on level ground. They reached the ceiling of the cavern and into the tunnel itself, and the rocks closed in around her as the tunnel narrowed the higher they climbed. It would be a tight squeeze at the top.

Solomon let out a grunt, causing Sera to look down. The closest demon had sunk its talons deep into his leg. Blood dripped down beneath him into the waiting darkness. She couldn't see the floor anymore, or even how many creatures swarmed and climbed below them.

"I'm going to cut the rope," she yelled down to him.

She pulled out one of the small knives she had sheathed and hacked at the rope above her head, doing her best to hurry as Solomon fought with one of the creatures. She didn't want to give the demons any chance to grab onto the rope if she cut lower. Hopefully she wouldn't be wrong about their inability to cling to the rocks.

"Grab the rocks!"

As the last thread snapped beneath the blade, she leaped for the nearest rock jutting out of the cliffside like a small ledge, using her feet to steady her. She looked down and threw the knife at the creature shredding Solomon's arm, his other hand gripping a rock like she did, and his jaw clenched tight.

As the blade sank into one of the creature's green eyes, it howled and released Solomon, falling back into the cavern.

She reached down toward Solomon. "Grab my hand,

I'll pull you up."

As they clasped hands, she almost lost her grip on the ledge from the additional weight. Three demons attached to various parts of Solomon's body, two on his legs and one wrapped around his waist.

Fuck! She bit into her lip until she tasted warm copper, not knowing how much longer she could hold on. Even with her new strength, these demons were fucking *heavy*.

"I'm not going to condemn us both," Solomon said, his amber-colored eyes meeting hers.

"Don't you dare let go," Sera said through clenched teeth as she hung on to the ledge.

Think, think, think.

She looked back up as her fingers started to slip, and she could hear the sounds of the demons still clawing at Solomon's flesh as they tried to climb up. She reached for the magic within her core, only to find the well too low to draw out. It fizzled in her attempt.

"Tell Nora that I love her," Solomon said. "And that we'll meet again."

Sera glanced down and saw the determined look on his face. "Sol, no!"

But he released her hand and fell back toward the hole leading down to hell. He smiled at her as the creatures swarmed over his body, screeching as they ripped into his flesh. A moment later, they disappeared as the darkness swallowed them whole.

A sob tore through her as she realized he was gone. Why did he let go? Did he see it in her eyes? Did he know she had nothing left? He must have, and then he had sacrificed himself to save them, to save all of them. Her vision turned blurry with her tears, and she kept climbing, numb.

Hand over hand she climbed, her palms rubbing raw and leaving red stains on the rope. The physical pain meant nothing compared to the deep emptiness she felt inside. Arms reached down to pull her up to safety. Voices chanted, and the ground rumbled. Rocks fell into the hole, sealing it off once again. The gateway to hell was gone.

Solomon was gone.

Sera collapsed onto the dirt, panting and sobbing on her side, letting the tears fall to the earth beneath her. They had done it, they had gone to hell and escaped with the trapped witches. But at what cost? Two lives before they had arrived, another lost to the demons in the fight. How would Renee even feel about becoming one of the Bacchae?

And Solomon.

Sera gasped for air, not caring that a rock dug sharply into her cheek. She had known for a while she'd judged the man wrong. He had proved himself worthy of her trust more than once. Now, she would have to tell Nora he had died to stop the demons from taking him and Sera both. He was a goddamn hero.

"Serafina," her mother's voice sounded like music to her ears just as warm arms wrapped themselves around her. Her mom rocked Sera in her arms as they both cried.

"My angel."

CHAPTER 28

Serafina

Their group had resurfaced bloody but mostly in one piece in the middle of rocky forest, not unlike the area they had left behind in Georgia. Although they may have been back above-ground in the land of the living, fear continued to plague them all. What if the Ordog managed to follow them?

They didn't want to wait to find out.

A short jaunt through the countryside led them into a city Sera knew—Budapest. Of course they would end up in the Hungarian country whose culture had spawned the Ordog.

The entire group was tired and weak, their feet dragging as they walked. Everyone was drained physically and emotionally, displaying cuts and bruises too numerous to count. A few more widespread stains on clothes hinted at deeper wounds and broken bones as well.

Sera hardly even noticed the stares they received as they walked, though she imagined they made for an interesting sight with their blood- and dirt-splattered clothes and skin. She was sure bits of demon guts stuck to her as well. The smell probably didn't help.

An hour's walk through the heart of the city led them to the front gate of the American embassy. Holding her mother's hand the entire way, as if she might disappear if Sera didn't, she gave it a squeeze before pushing the buzzer outside the embassy. It was quite likely they'd be separated as soon as they got inside.

"*Segíthetek?*" a female voice asked through the intercom.

Sera cleared her throat. "Um, hi. My name is Serafina Finch. I'm an American, and I'm seeking asylum along with..." she closed her eyes as she remembered their losses, "seven other Americans."

It should have been eleven.

"One moment please," the voice replied.

Sera and Theo had gotten to know a few of the embassy officials and their staff when they had visited the first time, before the library had burned down. Hopefully they still remembered her name because she was sure it would be hard for anyone to recognize her as she existed now.

A shiver ran down her spine as if being watched.

Sera turned to glance over her shoulder, not all that surprised to see they had been quickly and silently surrounded by members of the military. American military. Despite the fact that guns pointed in their direction, she breathed a sigh of relief.

They had made it.

At first, there was a lot of confusion over what to do with everyone. The officials didn't know whether to arrest or celebrate Sera and Renee on the rescue of the seven refugees, considering they'd had to abduct and lose a supernatural terrorist to do it. It didn't help the confusion any that all seven new faces had been declared dead two decades ago.

After a phone call to Sera's contact at the CIA, the officials went with the latter. They weren't quite off the hook, but they weren't going to be immediately thrown in prison either. Their decision may have been different had they known about Renee's recent immortal metamorphosis.

Sera had gotten the weirdest look when she asked a clerk for the date, but the answer proved a month had passed since they had entered the underworld. A month above, two days below. Of all the things Sera had learned about the *real* world, the one most people didn't know existed until recently, the time-lapse perplexed her the most.

At least she hadn't been separated from her mother. Humanity had survived.

* * *

LATER THAT EVENING, Sera sat on a full-sized bed in one of the embassy's guest rooms, her eyes closed as she relished the feeling of her mother brushing her damp hair. A hot shower, or two in some cases, and a warm meal had done wonders for everyone's spirits.

One of the witches, Roseann, took the death of the other witch during the battle especially hard. His name had been Jonathan, Sera learned. They would have a burial for all of those lost as soon as they returned to the States.

Renee finally shared what Hel had said to her before they left Helheim and why she had thought to return there before she gained her immortality ticket out. Apparently, the goddess of death wanted Renee to come back, offering the witch a job to help her find something. What that something was, either Hel hadn't said, or Renee wasn't able to.

Sera wouldn't push, but reassurance filled her heart, knowing she wouldn't have doomed her friend to an eternity of torture had she not made it out.

Thankfully, they hadn't had to make that decision.

"How did you know it was me in the cave?" Sera broke the silence at last.

Her mother gave a quick laugh as she continued to brush Sera's hair. "Part of a mother's magic, I guess. I would know you anywhere, no matter what age or amount of time passed."

They fell back into a comfortable quiet.

"I still can't get over how long it's been," Rachel said behind her a few minutes later, accompanied by a sigh. "I've lost so many moments with you."

Sera turned to look at her mother. Again. She wasn't sure she'd ever get used to the sight, and she was okay with that.

Now that it had been washed, vibrant auburn hair fell in wispy waves around her mother's shoulders, pulled back in a clip to keep it out of her eyes. Eyes the exact same steel-grey color as Sera's. The dark circles beneath them, too. Her cheekbones and jawline were much too defined to be healthy. Near-starvation had a tendency to do that, but in

Sera's eyes, the woman would always be stunning.

And the weirdest part of it all—she hadn't seemed to age a day. Sera hadn't noticed it at first below ground. Besides the darkness, she had just been so excited to see her mother again, and there was the small issue of a battle raging around them, keeping them distracted.

Plus, all the witches had years' worth of dirt and blood covering their bodies. It had been hard to tell what *any* of the witches really looked like.

After some deliberation, it was determined the witches had only aged two years, give or take a few weeks. Sera wasn't sure she felt entirely relieved that her mother and the other witches had been tortured for "only" two years of their lives, but she'd cling to whatever good news she could at this point.

The world had changed significantly in twenty years and yet was still remarkably the same. Technological advancements would take the rescued witches some getting used to, and they'd probably receive some odd looks for their ignorance, but at least they were out of hell. They were free.

Rachel lowered the hairbrush and her gaze, biting her lip as Sera often did. The similarity made Sera smile.

"What is it?" she asked her mother.

"How's your dad?"

Ah. Sera had been wondering when they'd need to discuss him. She really wasn't sure how her mother would take the news that he was dating again, and only recently. Her mother was almost a stranger to her still. A familiar, warm, comforting stranger. It was a weird blend.

"He's… good," Sera began. "He took your presumed

death really hard for a long time."

Rachel nodded as she picked at the bandage on her arm, feigning nonchalance. "And is he remarried now?"

Sera laughed. When her mother looked up startled, she placed a reassuring hand on her mother's arm, careful to avoid the wounded part. The bite from the demon had pierced through to the bone and wasn't responding well to standard treatments.

"I'm sorry to laugh," Sera said, "but no. Definitely not. He just started dating for the first time right after Thanksgiving." She hesitated for a moment but felt like her mother deserved the truth. "This is the first time I think he's been happy."

To Sera's bewilderment, her mother let out a sigh of relief.

"That's good," Rachel said.

"It is?"

"I'm not the same woman he married," she said, meeting Sera's gaze. "Two years in the Ordog's lair changes a person. I will love your dad forever, but I'm happy he's moved on."

Sera was actually grateful herself. Her father had been really excited about dating Susan.

"When do you want to see him?" she asked.

"I don't." Rachel stood and placed the brush on the room's small dresser, observing herself in the small mirror hanging on the wall.

"Wait, what?" Sera asked, swinging her legs off the bed.

Her mother turned to face her again. "Honey, seeing me again would be very difficult for your dad. It may have been years since I've seen him, but I still know the man I married, and he doesn't change. He'd feel obligated to have me come home no matter how hard and long I argued against it."

"But… doesn't he deserve to know you're alive?" Sera asked.

"Doesn't he deserve to be happy?" Rachel asked quietly.

Sera just stared at her mother who stared right back. Able to understand both sides, she had no idea which was the right answer. She could feel her brain sinking into a state of analysis paralysis trying to figure it out.

Don't hurt yourself thinking too hard, Bacchus chuckled from his place on the other empty bed.

Rachel sat back down next to her and took her hands. "Nothing needs to be decided right away. Let's just get to know each other for a little bit. Didn't you say you were dating someone as well?"

Sera's cheeks grew warm as she thought about Theo. "I mean, dating might be too strong of a word for what we are, but I hope to call it that someday soon."

And then her heart sank as she remembered she had been gone a month and Lasirenn had been with him. "If he's still available anyway."

"Uh oh," Rachel said. "Tell me all about this situation."

Confiding in her mother felt as natural to Sera as breathing, and she filled Rachel in on all she had missed long into the night. They cried together over Hiro's death, laughed at some of Nora's more theatrical antics, and shared an equal hatred for Chad, may he rest in misery.

At some point, talk had turned to Bacchus. Sera and the god had taken turns catching Rachel up on a world that now included awareness of the Bacchae—a world which Renee would get to know intimately. More than once, Bacchus apologized for causing her and the others such a fate. Well, for pretty much everything.

The Bacchae were his creation after all.

In turn, Rachel explained the witches' discovery in the underworld—they could tap into the fiery currents of magic running through the place using nothing but their will. Unlike above ground, the magic below practically leaked into the air. Over time, they had been able to store massive amounts of that magic inside of them much like Sera's own reservoir of divine energy.

Using Rachel's telepathic Gift to communicate after their rescuers arrived, the witches' unanimous goal had been to get Sera and Renee to safety as soon as an opportunity arose. They were all prepared to give their lives to see it happen. When Danae released them, they had seized their moment, not even sure if their stolen magic would be enough to inflict real damage. Their success had been as much of a surprise to them as Sera. Add in the help of a god and another witch, and it had all but assured victory.

They had used the devil's own power against him, and they had won.

Her mother must have said she was proud of Sera at least a dozen times, and it was one of the best feelings Sera could ever hope for. A feeling she had longed for her entire life.

* * *

THE NEXT MORNING, Sera chewed on her bottom lip in anticipation as she waited in the foyer of the embassy. Her heart must have been beating double time, and every part of her felt sticky with sweat even though it was still basically freezing outside.

Theo and Nora would be arriving any minute now, and her emotions were going through the wringer. Excited beyond words to see Theo, but also nervous that he had moved on with Lasirenn. Scared—make that terrified—of telling Nora about Solomon, even though Freyja would be with her to see her through the pain. Sera had refused to talk to anyone on the phone, knowing she wouldn't be able to lie to her best friend.

The sound of car doors shutting rang like claps of thunder in Sera's ears. A warm hand slipped into her own and squeezed. Her mother's. Sera leaned her head on Rachel's shoulder, her heart lightening at being able to do so.

When the door opened, a flurry of blonde curls raced through and straight into Sera. The squeal that accompanied her best friend's sudden appearance nearly deafened her.

"You did it!" Nora's face was streaked with tears, but her smile stretched from ear to ear. She let go of Sera and glanced around. "Where's Sol?"

Taking Nora's hands in her own, Sera forced her friend to look back at her. "I'm so sorry, Nor."

"Sorry for what?"

"Solomon sacrificed himself to save me," Sera explained. "To save all of us."

"Sacrificed how?" Nora asked, her smile faltering though her expression told Sera she hadn't processed the words yet.

Freyja stepped up beside her friend, placing a shimmering hand on the girl's shoulder. A pink aura enveloped them both.

"He's gone, Nor."

Nora shook her head, her blonde curls hitting her chin with the movement. When she spoke, her voice came out in a whisper, "I don't believe you. I can't."

Sera's lungs felt like they were being squeezed, leaving her at a loss for words. She was ripping her soulmate's heart out of her chest with this news, and Sera understood the pain all too well. Her own heart broke once again.

Rachel stepped forward. "Hi, Eleanor."

Nora turned her tear-streaked face toward Rachel. "Hi, Mrs. Finch." Her expression turned puzzled, but her eyes remained dazed from the earlier news. In shock. "Why do you look the same?"

Renee approached as well, and the two women led Nora away to a side room. When Nora finally digested the news, Sera knew she would want privacy. They had set up a space ahead of time for her to grieve in.

As Sera watched them walk away, another hand slipped into hers. This one was calloused and rough, but equally warm and familiar. Biting her lip, she turned to look up at Theo, not quite sure what expression to expect.

His other hand reached up behind her neck and pulled her close before he rested his forehead against hers, his lightning-streaked eyes searching hers. "I missed you."

Her heart fluttered in response. Maybe he hadn't moved on after all. "I missed you, too."

His thumb came forward to stroke her chin, and with that move, she threw all hesitancy out the window. She threw her arms around his neck and pressed her lips firmly to his. Heat radiated from her mouth down to her toes. As he returned her kiss, fiercely and with intense hunger, her body pulsed with desire.

A woman coughed behind Theo.

Lasirenn. Leave it to the water spirit to ruin the moment. As usual.

Oh for the love of Venus, Bacchus grumbled.

Sera pulled away, flushed and breathless. She grinned at Theo as he brushed a few strands of stray hairs back behind her ear. Then she faced the water spirit.

Only it wasn't Lasirenn.

"Look what the demons dragged back up," Hareni said with a grin, twirling loose strands of her long black hair around a finger.

Sera wouldn't say the light-hearted woman was the last person she expected to see, but she was pretty darn close. Hareni worked alongside Durga, the actively worshipped Hindu goddess. Because she still had so many worshippers, Durga had no need of a relic or merging with a human, but she chose favored mortals to be her voice when she wasn't nearby. Hareni was one such human.

It was this woman's bold move to join the fight against Danae on her own that finally convinced the Indian goddess to help as well. Without Durga, they most likely would have failed to bring the Eternal down.

After a quick, tight hug, Sera asked, "What in the gods' names are you doing here? And where's Lasirenn?"

In typical Hareni fashion when not in Durga's temple, she wore leggings and a long, chunky deep blue sweater that complemented her darker skin tone. Boots with fluffy socks sticking out the tops completed the look.

"Lasirenn went back to gaining worshippers, I guess,"

Hareni said with a shrug. "And Durga wanted me to come and thank you for saving the world. Again. She totally would've come herself, but some of the Bacchae are giving her trouble."

Sera held back her sigh of relief at no longer having to deal with the water spirit's presence, but she pulled her eyebrows together at the mention of the Bacchae. "Trouble how?"

"We'll catch you up on everything later," Theo said as he wrapped an arm around her shoulder. "Let's just say this past month has been anything but boring."

* * *

A HAND CARESSED THE side of her cheek. Theo must have thought she was asleep in the bed they spooned in after she had gone silent, exhausted beyond belief. Rachel had quietly moved her own things over to Renee's room earlier in the day, giving Sera and Theo some privacy to catch up. It had been another long night of talking, though this night included cuddles and soft kisses.

Turning her head towards him, she rolled onto her back. His eyes glowed a soft gold in the dark, and he looked at her with questioning desire. Lifting her lips to his, she kissed him. Scorching heat raced through her body at the touch, igniting every nerve.

As he returned her kiss, their mouths opening and searching each other's, her need to be touched, to be explored, to be wanted, intensified. Running her hands through his thick hair and tangling her fingers in it, Sera allowed herself to give in this time, to feel something other than grief and anger and guilt as she had over the last few months.

She felt *happy*.

His mouth moved down her face to her chin, then her neck, kissing every inch of her skin as he went. Everywhere his lips touched, an electric pulse reverberated inward through her body, creating an intense heat between her legs. When he reached the sensitive area of her collarbone, a moan escaped her lips.

At the sound of her pleasure, he sat up, pulling her with him and onto his lap as he continued to explore her mouth with his own, only breaking apart to remove her sweater. His strong, calloused hands wrapped around her waist and ran up her back to unhook her bra. He flung it to the side and returned to his passionate investigation of her body, laying her back on the bed when he reached her breasts.

She lifted her hips to help him remove her leggings before he pulled off his own shirt. When he lay on top of her, the tattooed conch shell on his chest felt hot. His lips found hers once again, and his hands caressed the sides of her face.

He pulled back, hesitating, but she reached up and drew his mouth to hers again, sucking in and biting his bottom lip. She let him know with her lips that he wanted what she wanted.

CHAPTER 29

Nora

Two months later

A cool breeze swept over Nora's exposed skin, causing the hairs on her arms to rise with goosebumps. It had been a long time since she had gone on a run, and she had missed it. The exhilarating feeling when she covered ground faster than she did when she walked, and the warmth of the sun on her skin, never got old.

Today's run to the Lincoln Memorial had been a good one, allowing her mind to clear, although the place was crazy packed. The cherry blossoms had made their appearance late this year, nearly midway through April, thanks to the bitterly cold winter. The number of annoying tourists had only increased since then.

Sure, tourists were great for the city. They kept all the businesses running and made it an enticing place for prospective college students. Of course, the changing dynamics also meant even more gentrification and more multi-generational families getting pushed out. The unchanging history was one thing Solomon had loved about New Orleans and they both wished for the District.

Her heart seemed to skip a beat, and her breaths grew shallow.

Oh, Solomon.

He had loved the Lincoln Memorial—not because of the man, revered as only those who hadn't encountered him personally could, Solomon had said—but for the view. He had loved looking back over the waters of the reflecting pool, the symmetry of the World War II memorial, and finally, the stately beauty of the Washington Monument.

It was Washington he had admired, and the city he had come to love. She loved Solomon even more knowing he had given his life to keep demons from escaping hell and potentially destroying historical monuments like these.

Nora sat on the top step of the Memorial, ignoring the crush of people around her, as she remembered their best moments together. He would be with her forever in this city.

I've been meaning to talk to you, darling, Freyja's musical voice broke through her melancholy thoughts.

I'm always here, Nora thought back with a small smile. It was all she could muster.

I was going to wait until after... well, until later, Freyja continued, *and that later is now. There's a little bit more to your being a descendant of a Muse.*

Oh?

Your ancestry also means you would be more powerful, nearly unstoppable, with my help, the goddess said. *Merged.*

Nora's breath caught in her throat. Unlike Sera, Nora loved the idea of being immortal. But not if it meant not having Solomon's babies. But now? Now he was gone. The future she had built in her mind was gone. Sure, she would find love again. Not the same kind of love, but she could be happy.

Her new job as a counselor had been challenging, to say the least, since losing Sol, but Freyja had seen her through, giving her strength when she thought she had none left. Keeping her afloat when she thought she would drown. But the people she helped needed her optimism and reassurance. They needed hope. How much more effective would she be merged with a goddess of love *and* war?

Nearly unstoppable… Now that was an enticing thought.

* * *

Serafina

LIFE WAS WEIRD. NEVER in a million years did Sera think she would become a contracted agent with the CIA, handling special cases involving the Bacchae and witches. Just like she never would have imagined Bacchus and other ancient gods were real, let alone vampires, witches, and shapeshifters.

Yet here she was at The Morning Grind, her favorite diner, reading a case file over the last of her blueberry pancakes across from Theo. Her partner. At work and at home. At least Lasirenn was no longer around to rile Sera up.

Stranger still for studious Sera—finishing her degree was on indefinite hold while she helped keep the Bacchae in line. Oh, and Bacchus was hanging out at the jukebox, having fun pissing people off when the wrong song came on.

Just… weird.

"Hey, Cher, can I get the check?" Sera called out to her favorite server. She swallowed the last bite of the pancakes.

Cheryl waved her hand in acknowledgment before waddling back toward the kitchen.

"You know eating isn't required as an immortal," Theo said, nodding his head at the empty plate.

"Some habits should never die," she said as she wiped off a smudge of syrup on her cheek with her napkin.

Theo chuckled. "Jiao got back to me. He's on board to help with this case."

"He's the one merged with a dragon god, right?" Sera asked.

"That's the one. Merged with Tianlong. He'll fly out here tomorrow."

"When does his flight land?"

Theo grinned at her, his dimples showing. "He's not taking a plane."

She blinked at him, though she really shouldn't have been surprised by now. Of course a dragon wouldn't need to take an airplane. How silly of her to think otherwise.

Before she could reply, Cheryl arrived with the check. They paid then bundled up to leave. It may have been almost May, but it was still chilly in the District. Spring had come late this year.

"At least we're headed somewhere warm," Sera said, the bell chiming over the door as she opened it.

The wind blew against her face, and she winced out of habit. She could do without that habit. She didn't really feel the cold anymore, not with Bacchus's DNA forever a part of her. One of the major perks to merging with a god, along with the missing klutziness. They had bundled up solely to avoid drawing any attention to themselves.

Theo chuckled and took her hand in his as they walked toward his Jeep. Her cheeks warmed at the gesture.

"The thought of you in a bikini is all the warmth I need," Theo said, squeezing her hand.

She laughed and nudged him with her elbow as he opened the door of the SUV for her.

EPILOGUE

Waves lapped against the snow-covered rocks, pushing shells and sand farther up the abandoned coastline. As seagulls flew overhead, they dove into the frigid ocean before rising with their wriggling meals. The round orb of the sun sank toward the horizon, spreading golden rays across the endless water.

It was peaceful.

Appearing on the side of one remarkably large rock, a crack spread across the rough surface like breaking ice. Tiny greenish-brown fingers with jagged talons for nails pushed their way through the fracture as if coming out from inside the stone itself. The crack widened, tearing the very fabric of reality.

Folding as if it were made from little more than cloth, the rock split open, allowing the being to haul itself through and collapse onto the shore. Behind the creature, the tear sagged, but remained open, like a piece of rock-colored fabric flapping in the cool breeze.

It had escaped.

The creature blinked its green beady eyes at its surroundings, its rat-like tail swishing behind it. It lifted its nose into the air and sniffed. An unusual scent caught its attention, and it crept forward on four deer-like legs toward the thing creating the smell.

What the thing was, the creature didn't know, so it sniffed up and down the length of the thing, coming to a stop near the head. It was definitely a head. There were eyes, a nose, a mouth. Just like the creature.

But it was much larger than the creature, with straight limbs and some ugly fur sprouting from the top of the head.

Now it remembered. This was a *man*. The creature hadn't seen one in the flesh before, only the souls of the man-things as they fought their endless torture. It didn't like to torture souls, but one didn't argue against Master. The creature shuddered.

Never see Master again, it thought. *Escaped.*

The creature reached out its hand and poked the man's dark brown face with a talon.

The man groaned as he moved his arms up to push himself off the sandy rocks. After opening his eyes, he squinted against the fading light and rubbed at a scar running through his eyebrow. The man caught sight of the creature and blinked at it.

The creature blinked back.

"Where am I?" the man asked, brushing sand off his body as he stood. "*Who* am I?"

Thanks for reading!

Please consider adding a short review on Amazon and Goodreads to let other readers know what you thought.

I love to get to know my readers. You can reach me on Facebook, Instagram, or Twitter **@stephaniemirro**. Sign up for my mailing list to get new release information, special deals, giveaways, become a part of my ARC team, and more. I look forward to hearing from you!

www.stephaniemirro.com

GLOSSARY

Gods, Mortals, & Others

Bacchae (Bock-eye) – the vampire-like creations of Bacchus

Bacchus (Bock-uhs) – Roman god of wine, chaos, festivities, and frenzies

Berenice (Bare-a-nees)– Bacchae; one of the Eternals on the High Council

Cassandra – friend of Theo's living in Haiti; has the Gift of Sight like Renee

Charles "Chad" Lambert – professor and world-renowned archaeologist; *deceased*

Danae (Duh-nigh) – Bacchae; one of the Eternals on the High Council; possibly the oldest Bacchae among those still living

Durga (doo-r-gah)– Hindu warrior and protective mother

goddess

Eleanor "Nora" Eisler – Serafina's best friend; chosen by Freyja

Eratosthenes (Air-uh-toss-the-nees)– Bacchae; one of the Eternals on the High Council

Eshu (Eh-shoo) – Yoruba messenger and trickster god

Eternal – an original Bacchae, one created directly from Bacchus's blood before they could create new Bacchae from their own blood

Freyja (Fray-uh) – Norse goddess associated with war, death, love, sex, beauty, fertility, and gold

Gabriel – French intelligence contact at the American embassy in Paris

Hareni (Har-en-ee) – Durga's human apprentice

Hiro Saito (Hee-ro Sigh-tow) – Serafina's boyfriend; *deceased*

Imhotep (Im-hoe-tep)– Bacchae; one of the Eternals on the High Council

Immortal – a name the Bacchae have given themselves

Jiao (Gee-ow) – Chinese operative; merged with the dragon Tianlong

Jonathan – witch; enslaved by the Ordog

Kevin Dawson – CIA agent

Lasirenn (La-seer-en) – African water spirit; also known as Mami Wata

Leif Karlsson – witch; previously a member of Renee's coven

Liviana – Bacchae; one of the Eternals on the High Council

Lorenzo Vicari – Bacchae; created by Danae; Solomon's maker

Manny – human teenager chosen by Eshu; now living in Haiti with Cassandra

Nestor – Bacchae; one of the Eternals on the High Council; *deceased*

Others – generic term given to witches, Bacchae, gods, etc.

Rachel Finch – Serafina's mother

Renee Colette – witch; Serafina's mentor

Roseanne – witch; enslaved by the Ordog

Roseline (Rose-a-leen) – Cassandra's daughter

Serafina "Sera" Finch – archaeology student chosen by Bacchus

Solomon Jones – Bacchae; created by Lorenzo

Susan – Serafina's father's new girlfriend

Theodore "Theo" Pratt – DCPD detective; merged with the god Xolotl

Tianlong (Tee-ann-long) – flying dragon of Chinese mythology

Xolotl (Sho-low-till)– Aztec god of lightning and death

Yumiko (You-mi-co) – Bacchae; created by Danae; closest bodyguard to the queen

Sera's story continues in…

RISE

OF THE

DEMONS

IMMORTAL RELICS BOOK FOUR

Coming late 2021

ACKNOWLEDGEMENTS

Trust me when I say that writing the acknowledgements of a book is more difficult than writing the damn book. How do I put into words the gratitude I feel toward each and every person who has not only helped me with this book, but supported me in my life while doing so? It's next to impossible. I'll do my best…

To my parents, who taught me to live my dream, *thank you*. To my husband Tim, who has discovered a new level of patience while I spent all the money learning better ways to work in this industry, *thank you*. To my kids, who make all of this craziness worthwhile, *thank you*.

To my editor, Margo Bond Collins; my critique partners, authors Savannah J. Goins and V.M. Darkangelo; to my beta readers: Thomas Mirro, Martin Wilsey, Leilani Lopez, Erica Rue, Devon Lawson, Lauren Harr, Kimmie Stack, Jessica Rodrigues, Stephanie Gautreaux, Riley Tune, Shelley Shearer, Michelle Court, Alisha Hudson, Rachel Green, Elizabeth Frenette, Jeremy Holloway, and Mike

Holmes, *thank you.*

To Christian Bentulan, who created the stunning cover of Serafina that caught your eye, *thank you.*

To all my family and friends, who showed their support in so many ways—asking how writing was going, becoming Patrons on Patreon, and following me on all things social media—*thank you.*

To you, my dear reader, for picking up this book and making it through to the end, *thank you.*

I think we're stuck with each other now.

ABOUT THE AUTHOR

Stephanie Mirro's lifetime love of ancient mythology led to her majoring in the Classics in college, which wasn't quite as much fun as writing her own mythology stories as she did growing up. But that education, combined with an overactive imagination, being an active fantasy reader, and having a vampire obsession, resulted in the *Immortal Relics* series.

Born and raised in Southern Arizona, Stephanie now resides in Northern Virginia with her husband, two kids, and two furbabies. This thing called "seasons" is still magical.